LIKE LIGHT THROUGH WATER

LIKE LIGHT THROUGH WATER

Book One of the Sun Shower Series

Erin Whitford

RESOURCE *Publications* · Eugene, Oregon

LIKE LIGHT THROUGH WATER
Book One of the Sun Shower Series

Resource Publications
An Imprint of Wipf and Stock Publishers
199 W. 8th Ave., Suite 3
Eugene, OR 97401

www.wipfandstock.com

PAPERBACK ISBN: 979-8-3852-7565-6
HARDCOVER ISBN: 979-8-3852-7566-3
EBOOK ISBN: 979-8-3852-7567-0
VERSION NUMBER 03/23/26

Copy Editing by English Proper Editing Services

To those waiting for the sun

ACKNOWLEDGEMENTS

I ACTUALLY LOVE READING the acknowledgements in books, gaining insight into all the real-life characters who played a part in an author's dream being realized. It feels very surreal that I get to have one of my own, a gift for which I am eternally grateful.

A forever-thank you to my husband, Brandon, for all the nights on the back porch listening to me ramble on about a new world and for reading a million iterations of the early stages of Tabrass. And thank you, particularly, for the homework that helped me fix a fight scene. You help me dream bigger dreams all while helping me live a real one with you.

To our kids, Judah, Elijah, Micah, and Rory, thank you for being the best hype crew and greatest joys of my life.

Mom, Dad, and Travis: thank you all for always celebrating and encouraging and championing no matter what it is. It's not lost on me that the support I've always had is pretty singular, and y'all make me believe that something working out is always on the horizon.

To the OG beta readers (Sadie, KJ, Mom, and Meg) whose comments and voice memos made me laugh, cry, and squeal. Thank you for giving me the confidence that these characters, this world, and this story could resonate with others too.

Thank you to Salima Alikhan for your instrumental help in the developmental editing stages and to English Proper Editing Services for your editing prowess.

And thank you to Wipf and Stock Publishers and Resource Publications for giving this world, that started off as a scribbled idea on a post it note, a place in reality.

Lastly, for those who have made it this far, this isn't the end for Iridienne and company. Book Two awaits!

CHAPTER 1

No one in Tabrass had seen a natural sunbeam in a generation.

Long after the manufactured sun stopped backlighting the dirty clouds on the eve of Sun Shower, the drones and workers prepped the open fields. The hums, zips, and mechanical whirrs laid background noise late into the night.

A barren contrast to the thick green crops ready for harvest, the adjacent ground was prepared to receive the blood offering just hours later. The DNA sequencing units looked foreign, presiding ceremoniously over the entry of each row in the unplanted fields.

Once the work was finished, the machines held vigil over the tilled dirt. All sharp angles and sterile steel, they looked alien against the rural dust. Even the steel was stained bronze in the dusty light as the morning glow began predictably on the horizon again.

In the interior of the residential sector, the chimes of Iridienne's alarm met her in her dreams before her hand found the button to silence the digital prodding for a bit longer. The cacophony of the field preparations the night before were regular interruptions to an already punctuated pursuit of sleep. Now, of course, that sleep clung heavily to her lids as she brushed her long, loose waves from her face. On nights like that, especially before Sun Shower, she would dream fitfully of skies and clouds she'd never seen.

In the muted morning haze, she absently thumbed the scars on her palm as she waited for the kettle to whistle, her blue eyes distant as she chased questions like fog curling down a path. The gurgling note that the water was ready snapped Iridienne back to the realization that Rhomy was waiting for her to walk together to Sun Shower, the ceremony the late-night preparations had been for. Iridienne poured a messy cup of water and tossed in some teabags as she slung her tan tote across her simple clothes and rushed through the door.

Rhomy would be waiting for her in her usual spot on the bench at the corner of where the brick apartment buildings splayed out from the city center, each building group shaped like a windmill blade, with the widest cluster of buildings at the back. While the brick was worn and the paint was dingy, they kept the streets and thresholds tidy. The living setups were humble, but they were theirs.

Iridienne moved through the streets past the quarters that were situated on the east side of Tabrass. She glanced past familiar businesses, crop suppliers, and the schoolhouse mirrored on the west portion, her reflection in the windows following along fluidly like water over berms in a river. Tabrass was clean but worn; the buildings and structures wore weary scars of mending and limited supplies.

She paused at an intersection long enough to test the hot water to her mouth. Tilting the cup upward, her eyes met with the Taxalis building that sat at the head of the region like a commanding shadow. The slick metal and glass of the structure stood polished and pristine, while the rest of the region bore the quiet grit of survival. The Taxalis was responsible for testing, sequencing, and sustaining life in Tabrass as well as identifying the terraforming needs for life on Iterum, where plans were underway in preparing the relatively close planet as humanity's next home. Iridienne's eyes traced the arcs and lines of the building, home to the governing sectors that buzzed with precision, efficiency, and relentless scientific efforts, an ever-present reminder of where the power lived.

In the rest of Tabrass, the brick on the sides of the building still displayed worn-down paint, pictures, and signs from a life before the sky disappeared behind what Tabrassians called the Shroud. There were even a few remaining old farmhouses in the distance towards the fields and outskirts of the city, though no one lived in them anymore.

Tabrass was all Iridienne had ever known. They taught about what life was like before the sky disappeared, but it was just memories and warnings. She knew nothing aside from the shifting colors of sand and dirt.

Sipping carefully, Iridienne kept moving, the ideations of the Taxalis halls keeping her company. The droning from the monitoring screens grew louder and quieter again as she passed through an intersection. Those screens and accompanying cameras were the liaisons between Tabrass and the Taxalis. The weather-proofed screens perched high on poles every few intersections, angled downward for a better view. Used primarily as scrollers for information or passing reminders, the prompters provided visual noise in an otherwise muted landscape.

Where the screens provided information, the cameras, on the other hand, gathered it.

On a constant feedback loop for consistent monitoring, they were the Taxalis's eyes of protection for the citizens. Today, one of the more famous faces in Tabrass, Lumi, one of the Immune identified five or six years before, smiled warmly down from the screens and spoke to no one in particular about the festivities of the day. Not that anyone needed reminding. The scrollers had been at it for weeks, cycling familiar faces of the Epitopes—the identified Immune—plucked from the very fields and shops and corners everyone else frequented.

"*It could be you. . .*" Lumi's voice trailed off as Iridienne kept on.

Iridienne rounded the corner, now sipping freely on her cooled tea, and smiled as she saw Rhomy's thick, inky curls fluffed around her shoulders as her gentle fingers skimmed through a book, the cinnamon-colored dust skating around the sidewalk. Just about everything was covered in it now.

Since she and Rhomy sat side by side in school learning about life before the existence in the present day, and then the hope of moving off planet, she had a flip book of images in her mind of Rhomy waiting at their meeting place through the years, a halfway point from their homes. Even though they had long moved into their own apartments, the chipped concrete bench remained a constant checkpoint.

Iridienne whistled a high punctuated string of notes. Rhomy's ears perked, and she looked up with a grin, creasing the corners of her eyes as Iridienne closed the distance.

"Morning, sunshine." Rhomy was always early and never in a hurry.

Iridienne smirked and grunted in reply. Rhomy hopped up, securing her spot in her book with a worn-out ribbon pulled from a branch of a past Sun Shower celebration. They started to the fields in lockstep, the same strides down the same roads since they were kids.

This would be their twenty-sixth Sun Shower. Although attendance was compulsory for every citizen in Tabrass, the nostalgia and almost mysticism of the ceremony conjured people from their homes without protest. The hope and pride of being discovered for such an honor was kinetic, reminding the Tabrassians of what could be. The crowds were growing as they filed down the wide dirt road that cut through the sections of fields straight down the middle. They were set into four quadrants but offered a stark contrast as the wheat and sorghum crops ready for harvest whispered on the west side of the road while the east side lay tilled but bare, waiting for the secondary portion of the ceremony. Looking out over the swaying fields, some of the plant tops sat a head above the rest of the shifting waves, unable to hide. Like targets.

Iridienne and Rhomy's gaits slowed to a shuffle to accommodate the number of people, eventually coming to their stationary place in the crowd. They all stood expectant, ready for the day. Buzzing conversation, hopeful murmurs, and memories of laughter hung in the air like low-lying clouds. While the strict environmental regulation allowed for year-round planting and harvesting without concern for seasons or droughts, Sun Shower was reserved for once a year.

Every now and then a jagged or rattling cough would break up the otherwise happy vibrancy of sounds, causing those close by to give pitying glances and shift uncomfortably until the excited swell covered the concern again.

After a muffled cough peaked from a few people back, Iridienne flinched subconsciously and touched her watch, the one her mom wore as far back as she could remember. At least before her mother died from the coughs. Iridienne was just a girl then. She lost her dad a few years later to a deep grief that took up residence after her mom was gone. No one was exempt from the sting of death at this point in Tabrass. The coughs were indiscriminate, but so was immunity. Iridienne never spoke of it out loud, but she secretly dreamed of what it would be like to hear her name called, to be Immune.

She shook the idea loose again. Hope deferred is a slow-healing wound, but maybe this year the layer of scars on her hand would be worth it.

Rhomy leaned over to Iridienne and said, "I've heard after last year's Epitopes, they're getting closer to finding a viable treatment for the coughs."

"Mmm?" Iridienne replied, half listening.

A girl in the crowd next to them, not quite a teenager, leaned over and whispered, "Are they really getting closer?"

Rhomy whispered, "That's what I heard."

It was movement enough to bring Iridienne back to the present, who winked at the girl after Rhomy's response. The girl smiled sheepishly and shuffled back into place.

A haggard-looking man shot a sharp glance at Rhomy and snorted. "Been waiting a good while for that, ain't we? What makes this year's batch special?" He spit at the ground, barely missing the person's heel in front of him. He didn't seem fazed either way.

The friends glanced at each other and rolled their eyes. "Did you really hear that? About a treatment?" Iridienne asked quietly from the corner of her mouth. Rhomy just shrugged.

Iridienne continued to survey the familiar landscape, a camouflage of tans, browns, and sepias broken up only by the green of the fields. While her eyes roamed across the scene, she felt the familiar slip of an arm across her shoulder as Cyrus settled in next to her.

"Hey, Rids." His wide smile spread and creased his eyes as her hand instinctively went up to his fingers draped around her neck.

"Hey, Cy." She grinned and turned into him, her blue eyes meeting his brown like the ground kissing the sky.

Cyrus looked over Iridienne's head, shooting a nod and friendly grin at Rhomy. "Rhomy."

"Morning, friend," she said, patting his arm.

He turned his full attention back to Iridienne. "I'm being called into loading, but I wanted to see you before our next flight."

Iridienne's expression dropped. "Oh, that's different that they're sending you during the Shower. See you soon then? When you get back?" Iridienne looked back up at him; his wild brown waves stirred a bit in the breeze, face shaved smooth.

"Like light through water, Rids," he murmured the familiar Tabrassian farewell into her hair, kissing her head. She squeezed his rough hand. Then he moved off into the crowd; his broad shoulders cut through people as he smiled and nodded to others, a quiet confidence and kindness that she loved, as he headed to the pilot platforms past the fields.

Then, the giant speakers flared into Tabrass's anthem:

Through dimmed skies
And hazy air
We toil the same
The burden shared
Our blood and soil
Mixed in one
Show the way
For the days to come

The music died away. The angular and strong-jawed, disembodied head with black hair streaked white like lightning flickered on the screen as Astor Jettica, Governor of Tabrass, looked out over the growing crowds, waiting for the ceremonial openings to begin. His voice echoed like a stone skipping across water, as the speakers reverberated his words to the collected crowd.

"Citizens of Tabrass. The seventy-seventh Sun Shower has begun, a tradition that is as much a symbol of our resilience as it is of our collective spirit.

"Nearly a century ago, the Tabrass region was born out of necessity. For many years, scientists worked tirelessly to adapt, to find a way to make life possible in the face of what we had lost from our deteriorating climate. While we discovered new avenues to sustain our life here through geoengineering, there was one discovery we hadn't predicted or expected: the genetic immunity to the atmospheric pollution that certain individuals began to present. It became clear that the most precious resource wasn't something we could engineer. It was something inherent in the people themselves."

"Light, that man loves to hear his own voice. Telling us mess like we ain't living it. . ." the same gruff man as before grumbled to himself but loud enough to catch a few turns and snorts.

Astor continued, ". . . *And so, Sun Shower began, both as an experiment and as a way to preserve our culture. Every year, we line up to undergo the testing of our blood. An act that has come to symbolize both our survival and our collective responsibility. As we will see, the crops provide the answer of who is immune from the Cloud Coughs caused by the Shroud through the offering of blood into the ground, then topped with seed and soil. The Epitopes, the Immune, are then identified by the noticeable health of their plant that grows above the rest; this ceremony ultimately ensures that each of us plays a vital part in the ongoing preservation and growth of our community.*

"This is no longer a question of whether Earth's climate can be restored. It cannot. Through the effects of generations of cloud seeding, weather modification, and overconsumption, we have learned the painful truth: Earth's climate, as we once knew it, is irreparably damaged. But instead of allowing that truth to defeat us, we have embraced it."

"This is so exciting!" the girl whispered to her mom next to her. "What if you get picked this year?"

"Well then, that'd be something, hm?" Her mom looked down with a kind smile, barely masking the tired undercurrent of her voice.

"The Sun Shower is no longer just a test of survival. It is a testament to who we are, to the strength we draw from each other, and to the ways in which we continue to adapt, evolve, and thrive together."

Astor paused.

The side screens flanking the Governor's image changed to a scrolling montage of vignettes, field workers, military formations, scientists working in labs, and then flashing to the familiar sphere of the distant planet and the text: "Iterum, for better days to come."

"It will help us enter into a new world equipped with the knowledge of this immunity as the terraforming of Iterum is nearly complete.

"Today, as we gather for this year's Sun Shower ceremony, let us remember that while the challenges we face are great, they are not insurmountable. It is not the world we once had that defines us. It is the strength, ingenuity, and unity we share that will see us through to a brighter future.

"Our blood and soil, mixed as one. . ."

Astor paused, waiting for the echo.

"Show the way for days to come," the crowd finished.

As the final words faded, the drones descended, scanning the fields for the Toppers, the ready plants that grew notably taller than the rest. With one precise laser and one clawed arm catching the decapitated plant, the drones collected what would be the names of this year's harvest of Immune.

Iridienne and Rhomy's eyes tracked the crew of drones as they flew their prizes to the head scientists of the Taxalis.

"Looks like there's five this year," Rhomy said quietly.

"That's more than the last few years," Iridienne replied. "Last couple of years there were just two, right?"

"Mmhmm. Maybe that's a good sign. . .immunity is increasing?" Rhomy said, ever the optimist.

The drones hovered over the sequencers, depositing the five sorghum tops, and the scientists stood attentively as whirs of code unfolded across the screens, each line bringing them closer to the name of the next Epitope. The eagerness and shifting began among the waiting people. There were never many Epitopes in any ceremony, and the opportunities that came after being identified, not to mention the potential of helping decipher the secrets of immunity and even a cure for the coughs, made the hope intoxicating even all these years later.

"You think they'd be able to get an immediate answer at this point," Iridienne whispered to Rhomy. She picked at the scars on her palms, antsy.

"Right? I know it only takes a few seconds, but I think they like the tension of it all," Rhomy quipped.

Polite dings alerted the attendees that the answers were ready, and Astor stepped forward again. His face flashed on the screens for the masses to see. A sea of wide eyes and expectant faces waited for the announcement.

"Citizens of Tabrass. We have the names of the Immune. This is a special designation, but also a burden of humanity. This is no ordinary honor; it is a profound responsibility.

"To those whose names will be called, you are the vanguard of hope. Your immunity makes you not only survivors but also stewards of humanity's future. This is not a privilege to be celebrated lightly, but a burden to be borne with courage, humility, and purpose. You will stand where others cannot, confront challenges few can endure, and help guide us all toward a better tomorrow.

"Know this: you do not carry this burden alone. We, your fellow citizens of Tabrass, stand behind you. And now, the moment has come. Let us honor those who will shoulder this extraordinary task. Here are the names:

Elio Roth

Adad Abras

Donar Merrick

Iridienne Voht

and Azileh Roche."

Astor was finishing up the niceties of his speech, but Iridienne had frozen; the sounds around her became muddled and distant, and her eyes were glued open, her chest beginning an exaggerated rise and fall. "*This is real. They called you. It's real.*" Iridienne's thoughts were breaking through the guarded hope in her head.

"Rids, they called you. It's you! You have to go forward. Go, Rids!" Rhomy was rubbing her arm, nudging her forward.

Iridienne nodded and mumbled, "Thank you," offering half-smiles and escaped laughs to the people who patted her back, cheered, and clapped as she walked towards the front. Like drips of water running down a window, the other four were pulled onward. They were five moving streams through a stationary crowd, being poured into a larger, unfamiliar vessel.

Iridienne fumbled with her watch, thinking of her mom, her dad, this new future that was rocketing toward her. She suddenly felt very exposed, unsure. "*What do I have to offer? Maybe this was a misread, a mistake. No, the genetic readers don't make mistakes. It's code. What if Rhomy is right? What if they are closer to a treatment. . .Maybe I really could help. . .*" Her thoughts were swallowed by the cheers as she kept cutting through the whole of Tabrass standing together.

Before she made it to the platform, she locked eyes with Cyrus, who was standing off to the side with his squadron. A contrast to the celebratory responses, Cyrus's face looked worried, eyebrows furrowed in concern. The corner of his mouth turned up slightly as he winked when he saw her.

Iridienne was still too shocked, her body regulating the cocktail of excitement and uncertainty, to fully process Cyrus's response, but the troubled expression made a temporary home in her mind, a conversation for later.

All five convened at the base of the stairs to the platform, having finished their trek through their fellow citizens who still clamored and clapped, an attendee gestured the group upwards, and they climbed the steps.

Astor smiled proudly at the dusty, earth-toned group, announcing, "Tabrassians, I present to you the Sun Shower Epitopes. Now, let the second part of the ceremony begin."

CHAPTER 2

Up on the platform, Iridienne was sandwiched between Azileh, a statuesque woman in her mid-thirties with rust-colored hair and ruddy skin, and Donar, a dark-headed, fair-skinned man probably in his early twenties with a mean scowl and prowling eyes.

"Never thought I'd see The Letting from here," Azileh mentioned half to Iridienne, half to herself.

Iridienne hummed a noise in agreement and nodded, thumb tracing the map of scars on her palm again. Donar huffed through his nose. "I just want off this platform."

She didn't disagree. It was display-like up there, like the separation had already started. When they cut the Toppers, they severed something for the Epitopes too.

The dusty shuffle of feet scratched on as the people moved towards the churned earth of the tilled fields. The DNA-sequencing machines at the beginning of the rows waited to receive them.

From this new vantage point, Iridienne could see the faces of her friends and the loved ones of others glancing over, trying to catch the Epitopes' attention as the masses moved in droves toward the fields. Hands would come up in waves or claps or the Tabrassian gesture, where the ring finger would reach to meet the thumb and tap a couple of times, the other three fingers pointing up, a quiet gesture made for approval or celebrations.

Finally, the last stragglers were accounted for in the lines at the sequencing machines. Each citizen stuck their hand in the machine, palm up, and it would make a quick incision, enough to break the skin, past years of scars for some, to draw enough blood to pool into the cupped and cut hand. Some had been through enough Sun Showers to have mounding scars on both palms. They would continue to the end of each row, person after person filing behind, until each citizen stood like statues frozen in a pose of offering before the prepared ground.

Astor's voice echoed again over the speakers, but he was close enough for the new Epitopes to hear it directly. He now addressed the group of five on the platform.

"The newest members of our Immune. While your blood is not required for the ground, we ask for one final offering for your community."

Astor stood in front of the five with a hand-held version of the cutters that towered over the rows of the fields. Each of the Epitopes held their palm out in benefaction as the laser cut through the scars one final time. Blood began to pool a deep red in the bowls of their hands.

"Now, turn towards your people. Give the blessing to continue."

Iridienne had seen this year after year, skin prickling with pride as she saw the previous Immune clench their bloody fists and raise them to the sky, crooked paths of blood running down their forearms, facing the crowded fields. Now, it was her blood traveling down her arm.

Next to the stage down below, a selected group of Epitopes from previous years stood facing the newest additions. Lumi, the face from the screens, was among them, stoic and proud. Their fists were already raised in salute to the new group. The Epitopes' faces ranged in age and reaction; some were distant or even bored. Some were smug, important. But a handful wore an expression of guilt.

Her own fist raised, Iridienne faced her people and the fields she bled in only just a year before, and The Letting began.

"We are as much part of the soil as it is of us. Back to the ground from which you came and where you will, in time, return." Astor finished the benediction and signaled for the release.

Palm after palm squeezed and let the blood drip into the ground on the seeds in the earth. The next cycle had begun.

As she watched the ceremony unfold, Iridienne skipped back through all the past memories of Sun Showers as far back as she could recall. Even though The Letting is only required for adults, they let children follow their parents down the rows to watch, no doubt creating early bonds for the traditions of Tabrass.

"Now, to seal the ground and our hope for the next year, you may cover the christened earth." Astor stood proudly, surveying masses as backs hunched, legs crouched, parents pointed and explained as the blanket of dirt covered the latest batch of hope in Tabrass. Even through the noise of bodies and dirt moving, the sounds of coughs popping up like plumes over the fields left the nagging feeling, like waking up from a dream you can't quite recall.

Suddenly, an ache caught in Iridienne's throat as she remembered the image of her mother's hands covered in dirt and blood. Hands worn from years of work yet still comforting in their touch. Iridienne's smaller hands, fresh and soft, scooped a small pile of dirt onto her mom's. That was the year her mom's hands had started to turn a grayish blue, a direct contrast from the neutral tones that surrounded them. That year was her mom's last Sun Shower before the coughs claimed her.

Her mother's cough had started the same way they all did: a rasp, dry and nagging. She tried to brush it off, acting like she had a tickle in her throat. From there, though, they eventually turned wet, metallic, the sound thick enough to feel in your own chest when you heard it. The doctors blamed the air; years of cloud seeding and sky engineering turning on them, lungs and blood poisoned with what once promised regulation.

Iridienne remembered her mom asking the doctors in hushed tones after she was diagnosed, "My daughter. . .just because I have it doesn't mean she'll get it?" Iridienne had stood very still just outside the doorway, straining to hear. The doctors confirmed it wasn't hereditary. And that Taxalis-sanctioned treatments were nonexistent.

The binding connection was that there still weren't answers to why certain people were affected by either extreme: sick, not yet, or immune. The members of the military, and particularly the agricultural sectors, were the most affected.

Once the coughs started, it was the end creeping in, like how the blue started under her mom's nails.

Iridienne shook her head, looking up, loosening the raw grip of grief for a moment. Instead, she forced herself to imagine her mom out in the sea of people, but only her mom's face was looking towards her, hands clasped under her chin, smiling, proud.

"*For you, Mom, and for others to have a chance*," Iridienne promised under her breath.

The crackle from the speakers jarred her back to the present. "And now, may the rain seal the ground and refresh our hope."

Synthetic light flared through the thick atmosphere, as close to real sunlight as anyone had seen. Then, as the gentle rain started, like clockwork, thanks to the predictability of weather regulation, the air seemed to pulse with warmth. Droplets beaded on people's arms and hair. A gentle washing. Even though it was man-made, the Sun Shower still felt miraculous.

Faces in the crowd turned, eyes closed, to the sky. The end of the Sun Shower ceremony provided enough rain to water the freshly planted fields, and once the moment was sufficiently held, the droplets began to wane. Iridienne wondered if it was as simple as a lever or as complicated as atmospheric coding. Maybe that answer, among others, lay in her future.

"Almost as good as the real thing," Donar mumbled.

Iridienne glanced over. "Mhmm. Can you imagine the real thing?" she replied, the sincerity clear on the edges of her words.

"What if there never was the *real thing*?" Donar grumbled under his breath.

Iridienne raised an eyebrow. Donar was a different one. Something about him, though, made her linger just a bit. He was smart, no doubt, but the undercurrent was something else. Her eyes tracked his face for nuances in his expression, looked for shifts in his stance. *Why was he so angry?*

Astor's voice swelled with pride. "I dare say our Taxalis scientists have outdone themselves yet again. The most beautiful Sun Shower yet. And now, that concludes this year's ceremony. You may move towards The Compass for the banquet and celebrations. Like light through water, Tabrassians."

Astor then turned abruptly to the group of five. "And so it begins. See you all soon." Without another word, he strode away.

Donar wasted no time heading across the platform and down the stairs, into the crowd. The other four smiled politely, and maybe a bit awkwardly, at one another and slowly moved in the same direction.

Her feet carried her toward the crowd by habit, but every face she passed felt a degree removed, like glass between her and the world. It seemed impossible to just go back to life as it was before. She longed for the familiarity, and yet everything felt irreparably different. Cyrus's expression popped back into her mind. She still couldn't quite place why he reacted that way, but she wished she could talk to him now. It would be at least two days before he returned home with the rest of his flight crew, Rafferty, Torrey, and Rays among them.

In the midst of feeling the disorienting sensation, like being just born into a world she didn't know, she glanced out and saw Rhomy, now with Cirrus and Cirro, waiting for her out of the flow of the crowd. Their excitement seemed electric even from afar.

She half-waved, but before Iridienne headed down the stairs to her friends, an attendant gave her a card that read: *Report to the Taxalis tomorrow at 9:00 AM. Don't be late.*

Less than twenty-four hours.

CHAPTER 3

With as many faces that filled this space just minutes before, the citizens of Tabrass had all dispersed towards the central courtyard, The Compass, for the remaining festivities of the day. Sun Shower also meant a day off from work, once-a-year type fares covering the tables, and lights, ribbons, and bells strung through the implanted trees.

The ground was covered in memories of the people's footprints, easily erased as Iridienne kicked up the dust and dirt, adding more tinge to the air. Iridienne closed the distance to her friends, to Rhomy, who was already hopping up and down, and Cirro and Cirrus, the twins, whose bright smiles beamed against their dark skin.

"Rids! You've been hiding this secret this whole time," Cirrus laughed, looking down at her as he squeezed her shoulder.

Cirro, identical to his twin, grinned and raised an eyebrow in agreement.

"I'm just as surprised as you," Iridienne answered honestly. It still felt unreal. A swirl of anticipation, hope, and the unknown. "They're not wasting any time either. I'm supposed to be at the Taxalis in the morning."

"Oh, wow, yeah that *is* fast," Cirro agreed. He paused, then said, "You know, they keep close ties on the 'Munnies once they're picked."

Iridienne snorted a laugh at the nickname Tabrassians had for the Immune and nudged him with her shoulder. "You can't get rid of me that easy. I'll be around." Although, Iridienne didn't know how true that would be. Epitopes were rarely seen out around Tabrass. The very select were even housed in the Taxalis and only saw their family and friends a handful of times a year.

"Who knows. . .Maybe they'll realize their machines messed up, and I'll be back in the fields by tomorrow night," Iridienne offered.

"Oh, stop! They don't make mistakes! Rids, this is such an honor!" Rhomy couldn't contain her excitement, tears brimming in her dark lashes, and her hair bobbing on the off beat of her hoppy jumps.

The brothers chuckled at Rhomy's bubbly reaction. Cirro turned as the laugh morphed into a cough, catching in his throat. Iridienne and Rhomy both kept the worried questions sequestered in their minds. Catching their expressions, Cirrus leaned in a bit, trying to divert attention. "Ah well, we got you covered. You know we found that route around the new cameras anyway, so we can sneak you out to the Pit for the next meet up, if nothing else," he said.

That made Iridienne grin, and creases fanned around her eyes. She reached out and squeezed his arm. "Alright then, if that's a promise?"

"Always, Ms. 'Munnie," Cirro added with a bow.

With that, Iridienne let out a half shout, half sigh of relief, "Ah! I can't believe this!" and joined Rhomy in a hug, jumping in a circle.

"We have to celebrate! To The Compass!" Rhomy squealed.

She and Iridienne linked arms as the twins paced easily beside them towards the courtyard. Rhomy was chattering away, but Iridienne's eyes were distant, lost to the realization that this might be her last time to celebrate like this with her friends. She took mental snapshots of their faces, the timbre of their voices, and even the crunch of the path under their feet, leading them closer to the center of Tabrass.

The sound of laughter and music met them long before Iridienne, Rhomy, Cirro, and Cirrus rounded the corner towards The Compass. There were some other stragglers headed to the party behind them, but from the sounds of it, their group were some of the last arriving.

Melding of conversations, swells of laughter, and strums of instruments all added to the feel of nostalgia and simple joy. At least for a day.

The four friends crested the entry of The Compass, and the cheers erupted. They weaved through the rows of faces to an empty spot at a table as person after person turned to offer cheers, congratulations, and clasps on Iridienne's arms. She offered little waves and sheepish smiles, not comfortable or accustomed to the attention. As she glanced around the rows of tables, she caught eyes with the other Epitopes; Azileh was the first, surrounded by her kids who all shared the same rusty hair, and she gave a wink. Elio raised a glass, and Adad gave a nod. Donar just stared, eyes locked with Iridienne, following her as she made her way to the empty space on the table bench. Even in a sea of faces, somehow, she could already find the other four.

Sliding into the remaining seats at the table, the family-style food splayed generously, and those sitting around Iridienne and her friends gladly handed dishes that smelled of costly herbs and colorful vegetables. While they knew the greenhouses were past the neighborhoods and on the other side of the Taxalis buildings, only the horticulturalists, botanists, and other Taxalis scientists were privy to the details of the stores. The inner workings of the Taxalis were known only to those chosen to bear its secrets.

At this point, Iridienne realized how hungry she was and didn't care to think about the origins or details of the rosemary and carrots and eggplants, just their final destination. She loaded her plate to the brim as Rhomy, Cirrus, and Cirro did the same, passing slices of bread and butter and platters and plates back and forth.

The best anyone in Tabrass would eat all year, Cirro was all but asleep with his head on the table, fork still in hand, when they all finished.

The hustle and clamor of dinner had subsided, and now the musicians ebbed and flowed between songs for dancing, storytelling, and remembering. The light was fading into a sunset; even though the sun wasn't directly visible, they still called it that. The glowing clouds dimmed, the sky melting from deep brown overhead to an amber closest to the horizon. The lights gave everything a hazy, soft glow, and the wind whispered through the bells, ribbons, and fabric tied in the trees. Though devoid of many other colors, the smells of savory plates, sounds of harmonies, sways of dancing limbs, and tinkling of bells painted a rich enough picture to last Iridienne a lifetime.

"I won't eat until next year," Cirrus groaned. Though he had stashed some more food in his handkerchief he pulled from his back pocket earlier.

Rhomy's eyes were shut, and she smiled at Cirrus's dramatics as she reclined back, listening to the lilt of the instruments and voices.

Iridienne tilted her face toward the glow of the lights, memorizing the warmth against her skin, trying to trap it somewhere she could keep, settling it beside the gratitude and honor she felt from the day. She wished she could stay in this moment. Where nothing would change. She'd see these same faces, walk the same paths she always had. She'd sit with the people she loved, hum the harmonies of old songs under the dusky haze of the Sun Shower evening. It was an honor to be chosen, to serve her community, but the taste was bittersweet at best.

Iridienne caught Rhomy peeking at her from one open eye. Iridienne snorted and looked down, knowing Rhomy could read her face.

"Where you at, Rids?" Rhomy asked. She smirked and gave Iridienne a teasing look before resting her eyes again, just enough for Iridienne to know she'd been caught in her own thoughts as she often was.

"Oh, nowhere. Just right here. And glad to be," Iridienne answered as honestly as she could.

The wind picked up slightly, jostling the bells in the limbs even louder, and she couldn't help but notice the heaviness of the air. Then in the distance, a flash of lightning ripped the sky, demanding attention like a slap.

"Did you see that?" Iridienne sat up, eyebrows creased at the sky. Several others around her were sitting erect, chins turned upward, alert.

"No, I wasn't looking. What?" Rhomy was up now too, both eyes open. The wind continued to press closer.

"It was lightning. But they didn't have a storm planned, right? Not on the night of the Sun Shower. It's getting more humid, too," Iridienne said, looking around.

"Maybe it's just left over from the Sun Shower?" Cirrus offered. But it had been a few hours, and the regulations meant there weren't lingering weather effects. There were clear starts and stops and schedules.

Now, the music had died down, along with side conversations, and most faces were quiet with concern, facing the sky. Weather systems were always planned and always announced. This was not.

Lightning flashed again, and a gust of wind rattled some of the lighter plates, tossing napkins into the air, spinning frantically. Thunder followed quickly after, roaring in deep baritones through the region. Then the rain came. Fat, heavy raindrops slapped skin and ground alike, coming stronger and faster than the crowds could find cover.

"This doesn't make any sense. This feels off. We need to leave, at least find our way inside somewhere." Iridienne's skin prickled with the chill of rain and wind coupled with the unusual humid heat that lay low on the atmosphere.

At this point, people were moving with fear and direction, either heading to their own homes or grouping with others in closer places.

Another bright swipe cracked across the sky, backlighting what every Tabrassian thought had been eradicated from the weather-modifying decades before: a funnel cloud.

"Was that. . .?" Cirro trailed off.

Rhomy stared, mouth open in disbelief at what they were all seeing. "It's headed southeast. . .toward the fields."

As they stood staring at the swirling sky, two Taxalis analysts ran by, one with a datapad in hand. Iridienne overheard one saying, "The weather regulators aren't responding. The system's been hijacked."

"Not responding? Hijacked?" Iridienne's questions were drowned out by the noise.

"Our place is closest. Come on!" Cirrus boomed over the rising noise in the air. Iridienne grabbed Rhomy, pulling her into step with Cirro and Cirrus, who were reaching back to grab their friends' hands. The wind was spraying dirt and sand against the brick buildings, and it stung their skin as they ran while trying to shield their eyes from the grit. The four ran in a huddle towards the brick buildings that fanned out east. The twins' apartment was at the beginning of the neighborhood closest to The Compass.

They still taught about weather formations in school, what the environment was like before, and the potential damage that could be inflicted. Iridienne's mind scrambled for the lessons they'd memorized in school: pressure systems, wind rotation, words that felt useless now that the thing was real.

Then the region's screens began to flash warnings, and the speaker system crackled through the deafening winds and swirling clouds: "Tabrassians, this is an attack. Take cover immediately."

CHAPTER 4

THE FRIENDS SKIDDED IN the door, shut the shutters, and huddled in the bathroom as the lights began to flicker.

Backs against the wall, the four were shoulder to shoulder with their knees tucked to their chests, hands covering their ears as the storm raged outside. The lights shuddered and fixtures rattled as the foreign sounds outside mixed with the storm sirens wailed in the distance.

"It's too loud!" shouted Rhomy with her forehead pressed into her knees.

Cirrus groaned through his teeth as Cirro shifted closer to his brother.

Iridienne silently pleaded that Cyrus's flight team was out past the storm before it started. "*They should be off planet by now, taking supplies to the storage station between here and Iterum. He had to be fine. He had to be safe.*"

She caught herself before she spiraled, noting the rapid intake of breaths. She retreated inward, brows furrowed, focusing on steadying her breathing. *Inhale. Hold. Exhale longer. Inhale. Hold. Exhale longer.* Over and over until her focus narrowed to the rhythm of her lungs expanding.

On her last exhale, the roars outside the apartment began to wane, the volume eventually lessening until the eerie silence was almost more unbearable than the noise. The sirens had stopped, too. "*Were they damaged?*" Her mind flashed back to the videos of destruction from these types of storms. A pit formed in her stomach at the thought of what was beyond the front door.

The friends rose slowly from the floor, legs unfolding skeptically, eyes wide, ears alert. Her ears rang in the quiet, each breath too loud. The silence felt wrong. The sensory overload, mixed with the swirling questions of how this even happened, hung heavy in the room.

They made their way to the front door, unsure of what to expect past the turn of the doorknob.

"What if it made it to the fields? The west crops won't be harvested until tomorrow. The seeds that were planted today. . ." Rhomy trailed off. The implications were too much.

"We have to go see," Iridienne half-whispered as she cracked open the door. A mound of rusty dirt lay piled at the door, and more hung in the air, suspended, waiting for the atmosphere to settle. It was well into nighttime; the sky was the same color as the soil, and the streetlights shone a warm glare in patches, fuzzy with dirt, around the neighborhood streets lined with the four-story apartments.

A handful of doors opened, and faces popped in windows as Cirro, Cirrus, Rhomy, and Iridienne made their way back down the main road toward the fields to see what was left. Others were already on the road headed that direction, looking tentatively at the deepened sky. A few followed from their homes. Cirrus pointed to some of the cameras that were damaged. The announcement screens flickered; some were black. Others sat eerily frozen with the warning "Take cover immediately" glowing in the dusty haze.

It was hard to breathe between the humidity, fear, and dust. Cirro coughed into his sleeve as he and his brother walked in twos behind Iridienne and Rhomy, everyone's heads turning and eyes glancing in different directions. The alert, "This is an attack. . ." kept cycling through Iridienne's thoughts. "*Attack? But who?*"

Iridienne checked her watch; it was after 10:00 PM now. Just that same day, they walked this same road on the way to Sun Shower. It might as well have been a lifetime.

The closer they got to the fields, the more green shrapnel of ruined plants littered the road.

"All these years working out here, I've never seen the crops torn and tattered like this. . ." Iridienne trailed off. She picked up one of the ragged plants, holding it gently in her hands. Severing the Toppers or harvesting crops was expected. This felt personal. She laid the broken frond back on the ground.

Iridienne caught Rhomy watching her and she shrugged. "A small dignity. . ."

They could see the flare of lights over the fields while the platform sat dark, free of the pomp and circumstance from earlier, as the small crowd filtered into the field area. Just as many Taxalis workers and scientists, and an equal amount of military personnel, swarmed the area, too. Sweat beaded on people's foreheads as they scurried and fumbled about in the crudely lit dark.

From what they could see, the fields were intact for the most part. But as Iridienne and her friends caught up to the others who were ahead of them, the military personnel had already created a barrier keeping the other citizens from going much further, explaining that the situation was still being assessed. Beyond them, Iridienne caught a glimpse of Astor, who was dressed unusually casual, obviously pulled from whatever private life he maintained to manage this anomaly. He was gesturing to some who would hurry off and then turning to read digital input from datapads from others.

Iridienne was locked in, trying to catch some idea of what was going on, when she heard Astor mention to a group of technicalists, ". . . destroyed the most southern thousand square feet of both the eastern and western sides. . ."

"The most southern. . ." she calculated. For the western fields, that meant ruined crops that would have been harvested not even six hours from now. For the eastern, newly planted fields, though, the attack was just shy of the middle portion of the plot where The Letting happened early that day. The storm just missed it. She breathed a sigh of relief.

Iridienne turned to Rhomy and whispered out the side of her mouth, "Did you hear that? It missed The Letting section. It got some of the western crops, but not the new ones." Iridienne caught the brothers' eyes, who nodded, turning in relief back towards the hurried actions beyond the soldiers and workers in front of them.

Rhomy shifted from foot to foot, half whispering to herself, "But the storm. . .How did. . .?"

Around them, people spoke in fragments, questions without verbs, prayers without names. The word *attack* still hung in the air, whispered in rasping gossip. Iridienne remembered learning in school that after geoengineering, cloud seeding, and ecological coding wrecked the atmosphere in Tabrass, the Taxalis reverse-engineered and adapted the science and technologies to control the weather patterns. They had yet to restore the sky from its captivity beyond the shroud of clouds, however. Now, though, the weather was always predictable, and that meant no seasons but also no extremes or unpredictability. Until this.

One question collided with another. "*Was the weather adapting? Was the science behind the regulations not working? Were they running out of time to terraform Iterum? But, still, they called it 'an attack.' From who?*" Each one gave way to another before Iridienne could grab hold.

Again, she was jolted back as her subconscious registered her name being called.

"Iridienne! Let her by. Come here!" Astor was staring straight at her with intent, impatiently gesturing for her to come to where he was standing with half a dozen Taxalis scientists.

Shocked, she pointed at herself, and when Astor shouted, "Now, Iridienne!" she shouldered through the others around her, shooting a confused glance at Rhomy as she went. She covered the distance quickly. As she came over, she heard Astor rumble a quick, mostly unintelligible comment to the closest scientist, but Iridienne did catch, "location . . . intentional. . ."

She masked her concern, hoping for a neutral expression, not wanting to be caught eavesdropping as Astor turned his focus to her again.

Her pulse jumped to a gallop in her throat. "Yes, Governor, how can I help?"

"Were you at The Compass when the attack hit?"

"Yes, sir."

"Explain what you saw."

"Well, um, I noticed it getting more humid first, but there were touches of colder veins in the air. Then, after it started raining, a crack of lightning backlit what looked like a funnel cloud. I've only ever seen them in books and reels, but as unreal as it seemed, the shape and conditions matched what I learned about them. From that point, we took cover in my friends' apartment."

Astor didn't break his gaze. She continued, apparent that he expected more information.

"The sound was deafening. It was like an engine getting closer and closer, and it rattled everything. The lights were popping in and out and went out for a minute before flickering back on. We didn't know if the apartments were going to stay standing."

The furrowing deepened across Astor's face as the scientists poked rapidly at their datapads, taking notes, looking back and forth between Iridienne and their screens.

"That will be all, Iridienne. Thank you for your information." He began to turn without another glance.

"Governor, can I ask you a question before you go?" she stammered.

He turned back, a bit surprised. "Yes, quickly though."

"The Zephyr Squadron flew out before Sun Shower this afternoon; were they safe from the attack?"

Astor paused, frowning, eyes uncomfortably tracing her expression. Her feelings made their home directly on her face, and there was no use hiding it now, as he had already seen them.

"Yes, they exited the atmosphere range safely before the attack. They should make port by early morning."

Relief poured out with a massive sigh. She didn't realize she'd been holding her breath. "Okay, thank you."

"Who is he?" Astor asked bluntly.

Assuming he would have walked off once he answered, Iridienne was taken aback by his question; she stuttered, "Oh, Cyrus Codere. He's the squadron Captain."

"Yes, I know him. Excellent pilot." Without missing a beat, he followed with, "Interesting that I don't see any of your new comrades here tonight, but tomorrow's starting time doesn't change. Don't be late." Again, without another word, Astor turned and headed off, pointing and issuing orders, questions, and motions as his voice faded into the darkness beyond the flares of the lights.

Iridienne stood there, unsure of what to do next. She looked around; no one paid her any attention anymore, all busy with their own tasks and thoughts. As she turned to go back to her friends, she saw who she could have sworn was Donar off in the shadows speaking tensely with someone taller and even grimmer looking than him. A Taxalis scientist, she noted by the emblem on his lab coat.

Donar stalked off, and, to her surprise, the sinewy man Donar was arguing with looked right at Iridienne, like he felt her staring at him first. Iridienne looked down and moved ahead quickly, but the weight of his eyes followed her into the rows of people still craning and looking for answers.

The skin prickled on the back of her neck. She hated that she acted so skittish, but she wanted away from whoever that was. Once Iridienne made it to her friends, they moved toward the back of several dozen people and soldiers who still made a barrier to the fields. "What did he want to ask you?" Cirro prompted as they settled in a tight circle. Beads of sweat were forming on their foreheads and lips. They swiped uncomfortably, unaccustomed to the humidity.

"Just if I saw anything from The Compass before the storm hit. I just described what I saw, what it felt and sounded like."

The others nodded. Iridienne paused briefly. She didn't know if she wanted to plant this seed in her friends. She felt a swelling need to protect them. But they didn't seem satisfied with just that answer.

"He, um, also mentioned something about it really being an attack, like that announcement said. And that. . .well, I overheard something about the location of the storm was intentional." Iridienne felt her stomach drop. Her throat tightened, words shrinking behind her teeth as the field lights blurred into halos. She always imagined being named Immune as a once-in-a-lifetime chance for her to keep her friends safe. Now it just felt like it was dragging them closer to the unknown.

Eyes widened, and the group fell silent, the reality of the statement landing. Up until a few hours ago, the biggest concern anyone had in Tabrass was when Iterum would be ready for inhabitants, for the Exodus. Now, the potential of weaponized weather unpredictability loomed, raising unsettling questions about who had shattered this fragile sense of security. And why.

Cirro coughing into his shirt was the noise that jarred the silent heaviness as each of them wrestled with theories, minimizations, and worry.

"You solid?" Rhomy nudged him.

"Yeah, I'm solid. The dust in the air has been messing with my throat lately."

"Or maybe you still have food sitting as high as your throat from earlier," Cirrus broke the weight of the moment. Cirrus was joking, but Iridienne noticed the concerned look on his face he tried to hide so well. It was the same unspoken dread they were all trying to stifle.

"I wasn't the one passed out on the table." Cirro lunged slightly, punching his brother in the arm, smiling, still clearing his throat.

They all laughed, needing the relief of a light moment. Iridienne glanced at her watch, the leather strap well-worn and faded, and groaned, "I have to get some sleep. I apparently still have to be at the Taxalis by nine. . .despite," she waved generally, "everything."

"Oof. Yeah, let's get you home. I think maybe we all could use some sleep. . ." Rhomy eyed Cirrus, rubbing his eyes with the heels of his hands. The adrenaline was dropping, and they were exhausted.

Iridienne and Rhomy walked arm in arm, the brothers close behind. No one spoke; they listened to the soft pattern of their gaits along the road. Iridienne tried to keep her mind from wandering as it so often did. But she found herself jumping between what-ifs and a growing desperation to make the most of the hand she was dealt. She couldn't save her parents. Or the thousands of others that died. But there had to be something she could do for Cirro. And the countless others who could be protected from the coughs. Iridienne realized she was squeezing Rhomy's arm, the tension from her brain making its way down to her fingers.

"Sorry, Rhoms," Iridienne said, loosening her grip.

"No need," Rhomy said, as she gave her a knowing squeeze back.

The twins split off first, waving goodbye. Rhomy took a right at the bench where they always met, heading toward her apartment. A couple of minutes later, Iridienne made her way into her own home with the feeling she had been gone for months rather than just the day.

She collapsed into bed, suddenly aware of her exhaustion. But as much as she longed to disappear into sleep, she lay awake fighting away the gnawing fears and questions.

She looked at her watch again. Six more hours. Six more hours, then the rest of everything would change.

CHAPTER 5

IRIDIENNE MUST HAVE DOZED off at some point because the faint glow of morning crept in through the curtains. The hazy light through the fabric made everything a warm, deep orange as she stretched the stiffness from her joints.

Then reality hit her, nerves dropping into her stomach. Caffeine wasn't going to help the jitters, but the comfort of her morning habits won out over logic. She shuffled through her routine, making sure not to be late.

The picture of her and Cyrus the day he made Captain smiled back as she adjusted the frame on the counter while gathering her things into her bag. He should be back that day or the next at the latest. So much had happened in the short time since she saw him last. They had already made plans to meet up with some friends at their usual spot around the Pit on the outskirts of the fields when he got back, but the idea of waiting until then felt like years. She could almost smell the singe of smoke and ashes from the fire, could see the flames dancing across her friends' faces. She cherished those nights, unrushed by the day, wrapped up in laughter and stories. In a couple of days, hopefully, they'd be back there again. But for now, her Sun Shower invitation beckoned her to a building she'd only seen but never entered.

The Taxalis sat like a covering above the rest of Tabrass, two semicircles of metal, concrete, and glass that looked like the lids of an eye juxtaposed against the neutral rural landscape. From the outside, the glass was black and shiny, reflective, with no possibility of a glimpse inside. However, the glass was fully transparent from the interior. In the center was a carefully crafted courtyard that boasted some of the few flowers that still grew in the region.

The way the Taxalis was built, though, nothing was out of its view.

Iridienne took the path north toward the building, bag bouncing on her hip, strands of stubborn hair floating across her face that refused to stay in the low, wrap bun she twisted her hair into that morning with a final glance in the mirror. On her way, the stares of others on the street lingered longer. She nodded and flashed a half-smile self-consciously, adjusting her strap as she quickened her long strides.

Up ahead, she saw a group of field workers, not from her own unit, but they all knew of each other, walking towards her. Swarms of gruff jokes and good-hearted grumbles kicked up like dust around them.

Ranto, a sandy-haired man with deep wrinkles made from decades of smiling in the false sun, shouted to her as they closed the distance.

"There's our field girl!"

The tension in Iridienne's shoulders lessened as cheers and claps from the mixed group grew louder the closer they came up the road.

"Morning, crew. Looking dashing as always," Iridienne said.

"That is our defining quality," Ranto quipped back.

"No argument here," Iridienne conceded with a wink.

"Looks like you're headed in a new direction today, yeah?"

Iridienne sheepishly nodded back.

"Well, then, do us proud, Iridienne. Like light." Ranto patted her shoulder and the group nodded goodbyes as they went their separate ways on the road.

Iridienne blinked back tears, surprised by the tenderness of this tough bunch and the undercurrent of guilt she felt for leaving them.

"This is for them. . ." she reminded herself hoarsely as she closed the distance to her destination.

The Taxalis glared down at her, unflinching.

Steadying herself on the landing, she surveyed the front of the building, but there were no handles on the outside, she realized, glancing around for a way in. Suddenly, an automated voice greeted her, "Good morning, Iridienne Voht. Welcome to the Taxalis." Then the door opened.

Blinking and surprised, she mumbled a thank you to the disembodied voice and walked into the foyer, feeling the immediate contrast of the cool, triple-filtered air.

Where the rest of Tabrass was muted dirt and dust, the Taxalis was its opposite. The massive foyer stretched out to display multiple stories with open walkways, all stark and sterile. Metal, concrete, glass, grays, almost blue in some parts. The windows had to be tinted to scrub the yellow-brown haze outside, turning it bright, almost cerulean, from within. Lights from the floor cast a rippling effect up the smooth concrete walls. It looked almost like. . .water.

With her chin in the air and brain processing the influx of sensory experiences, Iridienne didn't notice the lithe woman walk up behind her. She jumped as the woman greeted warmly, "Hello, Iridienne. I'm Soleil. I've been assigned as your attendant. Think of me as your shadow with answers."

Startled, she subconsciously smoothed her tunic and adjusted her bag as she said, "Oh, okay, thank you. And ma'am isn't necessary. Just Iridienne is fine."

"I insist, ma'am. Please follow me."

Formal niceties aside, Iridienne's shoulders eased as Soleil led the way; at least there was someone to follow.

"One other is here already, though I expect the remaining three to be here soon. As I said, I'll be attending to you today as you're introduced to the next steps. First, we'll meet with the Governor. He insists on being the one to show the newest additions—that being you—the highlights of the Taxalis, and to wish you luck on your tests."

"Tests?" Iridienne asked, confused. No one had mentioned tests. "What kind of tests?"

"Comprehensive workups to collect data and genetic samples. The various branches of scientists use the data pulled from the Epitopes for botany adaptations, weather regulation, and, of course, genetic modifications to create a better world '*for the days to come*', ma'am."

"Oh, um, are they. . .Do they. . .?"

"They are a series of physical tests, blood samples, psychological screenings, and intelligence workups. Nothing painful aside from a needle stick or two and maybe some exertion. It's two-fold. It provides invaluable and necessary data for the Taxalis and will determine the sector to which you're assigned now that you're here." They kept a steady pace during the conversation, Soleil guiding Iridienne around effortlessly. Up the stairs and through the halls.

"Okay, thanks." Iridienne's head was swirling a bit, already imagining what the tests could possibly entail while being overwhelmed by the sleek interior of the building. A whole new world.

"Ah, here we are, ma'am." Soleil gestured. Azileh was already standing there with who Iridienne assumed was another attendant like Soleil. Azileh seemed at ease, natural at making situations feel comfortable even when they weren't; Iridienne noted how Azileh held her hands in front of her, not gripping her fingers like a lifeline, but gently and reposeful. She was nodding and adding to the conversation she was having with none other than the Governor.

"Iridienne, welcome." Astor turned and greeted her, scanning her up and down with swift precision. Azileh watched Astor with a passing shadow of concern. She then turned and smiled with a warm nod at Iridienne.

"Thank you, Governor. Soleil was a wonderful guide," Iridienne said politely.

"It's my pleasure, ma'am." Soleil clasped her datapad to her chest and gave a half-bow.

Iridienne appreciated Soleil's proximity in a place that was so foreign. A ding came through Astor's datapad, and with a couple of quick clicks and swipes, he announced the other three had arrived and were on their way.

Iridienne stood politely and tried to engage in the surface-level conversations; she would hum in agreement and nod her head, but her brain was taking in all of the peripheral information she could. Her new environment was an ocean of details. Then, she saw over Azileh's shoulder the other three Epitopes, all being escorted by their own chaperones.

"Ah, here are Elio, Adad, and Donar. Welcome to the Taxalis. Now the five are together, we can begin."

Astor led the five of them with their attendants through the wide, echoing halls with the ease of someone obviously familiar with the layout, but his tone carried the practiced polish of someone used to impressing newcomers.

Iridienne was toward the back of the group, straining to hear what the Governor was saying. He would turn back to the group as he spoke, and she would catch a few words then lose even more as he would turn forward again.

Soleil noticed and quietly said, "He's giving a passing history of the governancy, his predecessor, and the hierarchy of command here. A quick summary."

Iridienne breathed deeply, filling the edges of her lungs, and nodded through the exhale.

"Thank you, Soleil. Truly. So, basically, all decisions come through him, and he doesn't miss much?"

"He's known for not having a blind spot, correct. And governing with a ruthless loyalty to his vision of Tabrass."

Iridienne raised an eyebrow at Soleil's response, but she didn't say any more because they were coming to a stop at their first sector.

Astor's voice carried easily through the open space. "Governing and Functionality," he said, his tone practiced, reverent. "Every detail you see, weather cycles, crop health, transport routes, is calibrated to keep Tabrass stable."

The first room they entered thrummed with quiet light. Maps floated above the tables. Not paper maps but live, adapting ones, their cloud layers shifting and folding like real sky. Analysts moved between them gracefully, fingers tracing invisible patterns that changed the terrain beneath.

Astor spread his arms as though the room itself applauded him.

"Every cycle you see, every cloud layer, every calibrated shift in humidity, that's my administration's work. Stability isn't luck. It's precision."

Iridienne noticed the way he watched the group as he spoke, waiting for admiration to land. Beside her, Donar's jaw tightened. Azileh gave a polite nod; Elio leaned in like a child eager to please his dad.

A technician glanced up from a flickering amber display, her brow tight. She whispered something into a partner's ear, too low for Iridienne to hear. Both stiffened.

Astor continued without noticing. "If one variable changes, food yield, infection rates, atmospheric coding, my team recalibrates it."

Iridienne swallowed. *Except the tornado? Who was able to bypass the system then?*

Soleil shifted beside her, eyes flicking toward the frozen techs before smoothing her expression back into neutrality.

Astor moved on as though nothing had happened.

"Equilibrium is. . .delicate," he said. "Which is why I don't tolerate incompetence."

He didn't look at the technicians, but they still flinched.

"Except for an extinct occurrence like a tornado," Donar gruffed. Astor was already through the threshold, talking with his own attendant, and didn't hear the comment.

Enough did hear it though. Elio's mouth settled into a thin line, his body rigid. Adad snorted at the boldness. But Azileh leaned over to Donar and whispered, "Tread lightly," edges soft with concern rather than chastisement. He voiced, though, what others were thinking.

The rest of the group filed through the door, and the introductory march through the Taxalis continued at the next wing. It hummed at a lower pitch, like the silence between thunder and its echo. The walls narrowed into hard angles, the air trimmed clean. Iridienne's footsteps sounded too soft against the floor. Everything else in the space moved with purpose: pilots sliding into simulators, engineers speaking in clipped bursts, a fleet of holographic skies flickering above them.

Astor slowed his pace. "The Military and Terraplanning Division," he announced, his voice carrying the weight of habit. "Here we see not only how we protect the region, but how we shape the next."

Iridienne's gaze followed one of the projected flight paths looping through a digital atmosphere. The tiny craft shimmered, pivoted, and vanished into another sky. A single gesture from a technician redrew the route. The efficiency made her stomach tighten.

Astor raised a hand, and the room fell silent as if conditioned to obey him. Iridienne's neck tingled. The order here was sharp and precise. This was what control sounded like when it breathed. The undercurrent of command and hierarchy was palpable.

"This is where Tabrass breathes," he said. "Every launch approved, every video feed monitored, every secure channel filtered through my oversight."

He said it like a boast. Iridienne wasn't sure it should be.

Elio's hand shot up. "Sir, how does one, um, qualify to work in this sector?"

Astor smiled in a way that didn't reach his eyes.

"Competence," he said. "And loyalty."

Elio straightened, standing a bit taller, fists clenched. He couldn't drink in the room fast enough. His exuberance was amplified here, eyes wide and mouth slightly agape. Elio was the youngest of the group, barely old enough to participate in The Letting. He was the color of sun-warmed sand with brown eyes that surveyed, curious and hopeful.

A pair of officers in sleek black uniforms nodded as the group passed. Their eyes flicked toward the newcomers, measuring, assessing, then away again. Iridienne caught Donar's scowl in the reflection of a monitor. He rolled his eyes and muttered something about "puppets."

As the group was directed onto the next leg of their tour, Elio shook the hand of one of the military personnel, and Adad commented to Elio when he filed back in the group, "Wasted no time, huh?"

Elio just shrugged, face still flushed from the excitement, mind wandering with hopeful ideas.

Iridienne did a double take towards Donar, arms crossed as tightly as the frown between his eyes. "*He's angry,*" she thought to herself. "*Why though?*"

Leaving this sector, the group was becoming more at ease with one another as well as their attendants as more side conversations and questions began the game of bouncing back and forth between partners.

But Iridienne could feel an indeterminate shift as they closed the distance to the next stop. A faint vibration hummed through the floor, alive and rhythmic, like the exhale of something larger beneath them.

Warm light spilled from the ceiling as they entered, soft and gold, too perfect to be real sunlight. Not that she knew what that was like. The air was sweet, humid, heavy with chlorophyll and wet earth. Rows of hydroponic beds climbed the walls in miniature terraces, roots trailing into thin streams of water that pulsed in timed intervals.

A mist hissed from hidden vents, beading on Iridienne's skin. She brushed her arm, half expecting the moisture to sting. Astor slowed his stride.

"This is the Environmental Division," he said, voice turning reverent. "Reclamation. Detoxification. Rewilding. Your data will help determine what grows where and for whom."

Iridienne's gaze drifted to the far wall where glass cases held plants labeled with codes and shifting charts. Her breath caught when she recognized the deep red sorghum fronds. Their stalks were tagged, severed cleanly. She hadn't expected to see them again.

Astor's tone carried a thread of pride as he noted her attention on the specimens.

"Intuitive, Ms. Voht. Those are your Toppers. Already under analysis."

One of the older scientists glanced up at her, too quickly, his eyes studying her face instead of the plant.

"Voht?" he said quietly, then looked back at his screen.

Iridienne's pulse flickered. Something about the reaction didn't match the sterile calm of the room.

That scientist is old enough to have known him. My dad.

The thought settled heavier than she expected. Images surfaced without invitation. Her father coming home quiet, hands washed too clean, conversations that never finished. The way certain questions had gone unanswered about work, especially after her mom became sick.

The Taxalis had known his name.

And maybe why this scientist recognized hers.

Iridienne held the scientist in her peripheral vision a moment longer. He didn't look up until she turned away. Then, she felt it, the weight of another glance, before he shuffled toward a different group of data to study.

Further in the room, Adad, hands clasped behind his back, circled a set of glass cases.

"Do they use comparative samples to identify differences?" he asked.

Astor inclined his head, faintly impressed.

"Yes, something like that. Sometimes, though, there are other anomalies identified in some of the crops. We have digital DNA scanner drones that track the growth and basic data as the crops mature. They typically are launched at night."

That was news to the group. Astor seemed pleased with the notable surprise on the Epitopes' faces, save for Donar, who could at least be commended for commitment to his signature scowl. Iridienne felt an attendant shift beside her, the smallest tightening of posture, caught, then smoothed over. Donar noticed it too; his expression deepened.

Astor clapped his hands lightly.

"As refreshing as it is in Enviro, it's time to move on."

Adad gave the room a sweeping, final glance, and the group obediently began to file out of the main room. Iridienne stole a final look at the Toppers and sighed louder than she meant to.

Soleil, patient as a statue, said quietly, "Information overload, hm?" She kept her eyes forward.

Iridienne glanced over, embarrassed, and then back ahead as they continued to walk. "Mmhmm. It's a lot. A couple of days ago, I was hands-deep in soil. Now, I'm looking at things I didn't know existed until. What good am I here?"

Soleil's face twinged into a passing smile, a brush of empathy.

"Don't count yourself out yet, ma'am. The day is young."

The unintelligible conversations continued on their trek to the next sector when Astor and his attendants' datapads dinged politely with identical messages. Astor announced, "Zephyr Squadron returned safely. Mission successful," proud as if he completed the mission himself.

A smile stretched across Iridienne's face as Azileh gave her shoulder a quick pat. Before the Governor turned to continue, though, he shot a look at Iridienne. She involuntarily flushed a bit for the attention but was grateful for the perceived thoughtfulness, nonetheless. Breathing a sigh of relief, Cyrus was back on planet.

The last corridor narrowed into silence. Even the hum of machinery seemed to lower its voice here. The air smelled faintly of antiseptic and something metallic, clean, and absolute.

Every surface was white or glass. Light pooled coldly across the floor, reflecting the movements of technicians who glided between sealed workstations, a dance of shadow and light. Some bent over vials under sterile lamps; others studied pulsing displays from genome readers that blinked in quick, symmetrical rhythms, like heart monitors with no heartbeat.

Astor's tone softened, almost ceremonial, as he gestured toward the glass wall.

"The Genetic Division. Here, your DNA becomes the future of Tabrass."

Iridienne's eyes caught on the reflection of her own face in one of the glass walls. Blurred, translucent, ghostlike among the other samples. Her chest tightened.

"Your bodies' adaptations will guide future formulations: weather resistance, medicinal design. In essence: hope," he said simply.

A nearby technician fed a vial into a processor, and the machine whirred to life. Light flickered in sequences Iridienne couldn't follow, like a coded language meant for anyone but her. The air itself felt heavier, as though the room was holding its breath.

Astor gestured to the team beyond the glass. "These are the Geneticists of the Taxalis. They work to decode your immunity, the key to survival on Iterum." A few looked up, eyes detached behind transparent visors. The rest never stopped moving.

"Dr. Calen?" Astor called.

From the far end of the lab, a man straightened, unfolding from his work. Tall, lean, deliberate. He approached with the annoyance of someone who disliked being interrupted. Astor smiled, oblivious. "This is Nyx Calen, transferred from Enviro-Horticulture after his most recent discoveries. Dr. Calen leads our immunity research now in Genetics."

Nyx stopped beside the glass, his white lab coat draping on his ropey frame. The light caught the harsh angles of his face, black hair pulled back, eyes and skin both the color of burnt honey.

Astor continued, "Dr. Calen will determine which of your genetic profiles have the. . .greatest potential."

That phrasing chilled her.

Behind her, Donar muttered something she didn't catch, but it made Elio stiffen.

Nyx finally spoke, voice like a jagged blade.

"Some profiles are more useful than others."

Iridienne's stomach dropped. The shadows from last night flashed in her mind: the swarm of confusion in the damaged fields, the half-heard side conversations that left her with more questions than answers, the tense conversation in the edges of the chaos. Nyx was the man she saw Donar arguing with in the shadows the night before. And he must have recognized her, too, because he was looking right at her. Again.

CHAPTER 6

Iridienne swallowed, and she tried to hide her toes fidgeting in her shoes. A lone muscle flexed in Nyx's jaw. Astor, preoccupied with something his attendant was showing him on a datapad, dismissed Nyx and broke the frozen stand-off between him and Iridienne.

"That's all, Dr. Calen. Just a quick introduction. You can continue back to the labs." Astor resumed, voice smooth as the glass surrounding them, already guiding them to the next doorway. He was unaware of the static between the scientist and Iridienne.

Nyx's stare lingered on Iridienne a beat longer before nodding to the group, giving a fast flex of his mouth, a failed attempt to emulate a smile. He stalked off, now clearly annoyed he was called over to begin with.

Iridienne inhaled deeply through her nose, steadying her pulse.

"That one's a bit intense, hmm?" Azileh whispered, leaning over as they continued to follow the tour.

"Hah, you could say that." Iridienne liked Azileh. There was something comforting about her, a quiet surety in her words and movements. The two women walked side by side, behind Astor and in front of the three men behind, like an arrow pointing the way. The attendants followed behind.

Elio piped up, "Excuse me, Governor? I am grateful, of course, to be brought in as an Epitope, but how are other Tabrassians selected to work here? I'm assuming some are Epitopes from years past, but what about the others?" They continued walking as the Governor responded.

"Observant question, Elio. The short version, since we're nearing our final stop in the tour, is that you are correct in assuming that some of those working here are fellow Epitopes; however, non-immune citizens are filtered into their professions here via data compilations and invitation based on that data and internal needs," Astor answered vaguely but offered nothing more.

Elio frowned and glanced around, as if the rest of the answer he hoped for was floating around in the air. He didn't broach the subject again.

As they continued, Adad complained quietly about his feet aching from the walk, bending down to retie a loose lace on his boot. "We've been walking and standing for a few hours now. Based on the light." Adad snorted and kicked at the ground.

From what Iridienne could tell, they had navigated through most of the Taxalis, around both lids of the eye-shaped building. The light through the windows had transformed from a golden haze to a dusty flare almost overhead, the brightest part of the day.

"Ah, here we are," Astor broke in. "We've arrived at our last destination: the Trials Quarter. I'm sure your attendants explained the point and importance of today's introductions. We will run you all through a series of tests to determine in which sector of the Taxalis you will serve based on your skills, talents, and proclivities, both known and unknown."

A couple of them shifted uncomfortably, but not Donar. He stood boring a hole into Astor's face, feet glued to the ground.

Iridienne flexed her fingers, trying to dry the sweat slicking her palms. Her thumb found the faint ridge of an old scar and traced it out of habit, a quiet rhythm that steadied her even as the knot in her stomach synched tighter. Questions swarmed her mind faster than she could swat them away. *Were they measuring instinct? Seeing how we handled pressure without a briefing?* Maybe this was the test before the test.

Ahead, the corridor narrowed into a pair of steel doors, each stamped with the Taxalis insignia. The doors were guarded by a humming retinal scanner. The faint buzz of machinery filled the silence. Iridienne straightened, rolling her shoulders back until the fabric of her tunic pulled across her shoulders. Whatever waited beyond those doors, there didn't seem to be an option to decline.

Astor continued, "In totality, the tests will consist of three portions: a physical workup, genetic collection, and an intelligence analysis. We'll begin with the physical portion."

From somewhere behind him came the shuffle of feet and muffled voices trading clipped words just out of reach. Iridienne caught herself glancing toward the sound before Astor stopped, the irritation plain in the tension of his face.

"Any questions?"

Eyes snapped forward. Heads shook.

"Very well." He turned back, scanned his eye, and the left door released with a hiss. "Ladies first."

Iridienne took the first step forward, and they filtered single-file into a massive room with a quarter of it partitioned with lab equipment, computers, and test tube storage racks. The rest of the room had treadmills, flight simulator pods, and what looked like sensory deprivation chambers. Techs and attendants stood by.

"Whoa," Elio breathed out. Iridienne felt protective of him. Elio was young himself, but he had several younger siblings, and being selected as an Epitope was not only an honor but a financial gift to his family. She could only imagine the pride and pressure he felt.

Giving the group a moment to take in the scene, Astor introduced a shorter, fatherly-looking man, complete with a black lab coat and datapad. "This is Mazen, Trials Director. He is the Master of Ceremonies, so to speak, and will oversee the tests and results. I'll leave you all to get acquainted and then get started. You can expect to see me later."

With that, Astor and his assistant exited through the same doors they came in.

"Ah, well, welcome to the Trials Quarters of the Taxalis. It's my pleasure to be your guide," Mazen said. "Without further delay, let's begin. Please hand any personal items to Brisa," he paused, glancing down at Iridienne's wrist. "Watch included." Iridienne frowned but tucked the watch in her bag before handing it over.

"First, we'll take a baseline blood sample before the physical tests. Additional samples will be collected after each portion."

Five seats and phlebotomists were ready for them. The snap of rubber tourniquets punctuated the hush of the room, followed by the faint sting of needles sliding beneath skin. Iridienne felt the pull tighten around her arm, her pulse pressing against the band until the first rush of crimson filled the tube.

"Your blood, as you know, holds the answers to a better, controlled future where immunity isn't randomized but computable, so we will analyze the informational variants based on your bodies' responses to different activities and stressors," Mazen explained. "Each test, each reaction, gives us more to build from."

This situation was already so unexpected, Iridienne just accepted the reality that she couldn't predict or plan for anything that was happening or would happen. Shallow breaths wracked her lungs. She picked at her scarred palms as she held her hands behind her back, trying to keep her anxiousness at bay.

"Excellent. Now for the warm-up. Let's go on a jog, shall we?" Mazen's eyes were beginning to flash with the excitement of potential data. "We're going to hook you all up to sensors to monitor your bodies' reactions and the psychology of your choices to a variety of terrains on the specialized treadmills."

Iridienne scanned the treadmills; they were each equipped with large screens, headphones, and the running pads were twice as wide with small, flat, articulated squares covering the surface. She'd never seen anything like that before, and judging by the looks of the others, they hadn't either. They were each ushered to a treadmill where they climbed up and waited for instructions.

The five looked around uneasily. Adad shifted from side to side, fidgeting. Elio preemptively stretched his quads. Iridienne chewed on the inside of her lip, eyes scanning the complicated interface in front of her.

Mazen continued, "These treadmills are unique in that the belts here, as you can see, are much larger and those little segmented squares can mimic any terrain programmed into the system while you are moving. They can ripple, stack, dip. . .You'll experience that momentarily. Essentially, it adapts as you, in theory, will adapt. You'll also be given headphones to help with your focus, provide more holistic immersion, as well as monitor electric impulses neurologically. The instructions are simple: react to the situations presented, which will adapt based on your choices, and data will be collected. Now, proceed." He waved a thick hand forward.

The lights in the room dimmed; the scientists' datapads underlit their emotionless faces.

Suddenly, a jarringly loud timer blared, "Three, two, one. Begin."

Iridienne could feel the articulated belts whirr into motion as their screens flashed into an image. From the two on either side, it looked like they all were in different geographical settings. The rolling portion began to move slowly and flatly under her feet at first, then the quicker it became, the bumpier the terrain did, too, like she was running over a rocky path.

In her periphery, she could see the intensity increase and change with the other Epitopes, too. At one point, she was bounding and jumping from boulders and another running down a steep and unstable path, trying not to crash.

She saw Adad on her right, thrown from the back of his treadmill first; it slowed to a stop. Iridienne was realizing the finish line equated to failure. Sweat began its trek down her temples and spine as her muscles ached under the strain. She stole a quick glance to the left with the remaining ones; Elio's lithe and young limbs adapted to more complex scenarios, as if made for this type of test. Concentration marked his face. Azileh was the next to go down. Donar fought along, practically climbing up hills at one point before jumping off the back. He stayed on all fours with his forehead on the floor for several minutes to keep the room from spinning.

That left Iridienne and Elio. She couldn't help but feel like this was a competition, even though she wished it wasn't. Her only saving grace was the fact that she was taller and had longer legs. Elio was leaping beside her; he was certainly a sight. She swelled with pride for him, but she also hated how much she wanted to win something she didn't even understand. If any of this was something that could be won. At that moment, her toe clipped a square on the treadmill mimicking a rock and ended her run. Elio won.

Adad retching and the others panting and gasping echoed through the room. A couple of the Epitopes clasped hands over their heads, heaving, while the others were doubled over sucking in air.

The attendants wasted no time ushering the fatigued crew to the back of the room. Their clothes clung uncomfortably to their backs as they sat down in the hard chairs. Iridienne caught glimpses of purple shadows already forming in the crooks of arms as sleeves rolled for more samples, tourniquets snapping, vials filling again. The process blurred together: run, bleed, breathe, repeat.

"Very good. Very good. Quite impressive, mister. . .um. . .Elio, yes," Mazen said as he glanced down at his datapad. "The rest of you, we appreciate the data collection you've provided. Now, we move to the Intellect and Analysis portion of the day."

The group stood around uneasily, scanning the giant machines and screens, wondering what they were expected to do next. Some of their hands were shaking. They didn't know if it was from the adrenaline, exertion, blood draws, or a combination of the three.

After leading the way, Mazen turned cheerfully, datapad in one hand and proudly gesturing with the other. "Now, this particular test may seem similar at first to the last one. Unfamiliar settings. Unpredictable scenarios. However, we are measuring different adaptabilities, variables, and outputs. The hows and whys, if you will." Mazen paused, like he expected the five to clap at the opportunity. Instead, they just stared back, tired and exasperated. Mazen ignored them. "You'll each be positioned in a flight simulator pod, similar to a cockpit, and we will measure your choices and critical thinking among other collection points. The techs will settle you in. Happy flying. Proceed."

"Contribute to what? He realizes we're human, right? Not just data points," Azileh said under her breath, her distrust of Mazen clear in her inflection.

"Wait. None of us knows how to fly. How are we supposed to perform well at something we've never done?" Elio asked.

"You're not being awarded medals, my dear Immune," Mazen quipped. He seemed to be almost euphoric from watching the tests and reviewing the preliminary data, unaffected by the Epitopes themselves standing in front of him. "You five, and those who have been identified before you, have already won the greatest genetic prize." The lighting overhead caught on his glasses as he talked, giving him an inhuman flare. "Do your best. That's all we ask. You each have something unique to contribute."

The five were ushered over into their own simulators, which were built to look like a cockpit, as Mazen said, completely outfitted to function like a realistic fighter jet. In place of the windshield, though, was another massive screen, curved to fit the window. Iridienne stepped into her simulator, unconsciously buckling in as the finishing instructions were given. Her attendant handed her a helmet equipped with a headset and microphone. She wished Cyrus were here. But then again, she thought, if she failed miserably at whatever they were going to ask them to do, she was a bit grateful he wouldn't be here to see her crash and burn.

She scanned the myriad of lights, some blinking, some stationary, levers, switches, monitors, and gauges in front of her, trying to familiarize herself as quickly as she could before they began. She noticed a "Release" button and another one labeled "Arm." *Release what? Arm? Weapons?* She remembered Cyrus talking with Rafferty about something with the yokes and pedals in their aircrafts before. She wished she had paid more attention now.

She scanned the maze of lights, some pulsing, some steady, spilling color across the panels in erratic patterns. Rows of levers jutted like metal ribs, switches flicked between positions she didn't understand, and the hum of machinery vibrated faintly through her palms. Every monitor blinked a different warning, data scrolling too fast to read. Her breath quickened as she tried to make sense of it all, eyes darting from gauge to gauge, searching for something familiar.

Her pulse thudded in her throat.

Mazen's voice crackled in her ear, "Now that you all are ready. Proceed."

"Ready is a relative term here," Iridienne thought. Her jaw was already throbbing from clenching her teeth, her temples beginning to share the ache that split up her face like a fissure.

Suddenly, a reverberation began underneath her. The overhead lights dimmed, and the buttons and lights flared like hundreds of eyes blinking awake. The arrows on the gauges sprang to attention, and the smaller displays flashed to baseline. The screen that stood in place of the windshield came to life with an image of her on one of Tabrass's runways. The vibrations increased as the simulated engine roared into takeoff, shoving Iridienne back into her seat. The sky rushed into view as the plane took off down the runway. She instinctively grabbed the yoke, not that she knew how to fly, but she didn't know what else to do.

At first, she was speechless at the visual splaying out in front of her. She had never seen an aerial view of Tabrass like this before. A patchwork of neutrals with intermittent green patterns, it was like seeing someone's face for the first time after only hearing their voice.

Initially, she sat taking in the view when suddenly an alarm started going off on her screen. A digitized voice announced: "Threat impending." Her eyes began darting around the screen, not knowing even what type of threat she was looking for. Then the screen zeroed in with red brackets around nothing more than a speck out in front of her. Again, the voice announced: "Enemy fire incoming."

Quickly, she remembered the Arm button she had seen earlier. She pushed it, and the voice alerted, "Gunner's armed. Scan for collateral before release?"

At this point, Iridienne realized she hadn't spoken a word yet. Shakingly, she said, "Yes, scan for collateral."

"Thirty-two collaterals detected. Proceed?"

Her head was reeling. She blurted, "What are collaterals?" Then it clicked. "You mean. . .people?" she shouted incredulously.

The voice didn't answer.

"Do not release!" She pressed the button again, hoping that it meant it would disarm the missiles.

Suddenly, she had an idea. *What if I flew away outside of the populated region?* She turned the yoke of the plane, and it darted hard to the right. Alarms from the plane started sounding. She gritted her teeth harder. She had no idea what she was doing, but choosing to kill innocent people, even in a simulation, wasn't a choice she was willing to make. Her simulator was shaking when it abruptly jolted.

"Aircraft hit. Defensive failure likely. Mission compromise imminent. Brace for impact. Aircraft hit. Defensive failure likely. Mission compromise imminent. Brace for impact."

The voice blared through the cabin, fractured by static, then drowned out by the shriek of alarms. The harness bit into Iridienne's shoulders as gravity wrenched her sideways. Then downward, her whole body hung at a near-vertical angle. The lights strobed red, flashing across her vision in violent bursts. A roar filled her ears, metal screaming, engines choking, her own breath ragged and loud against it all. The world tilted; the horizon spun. The last thing she saw before she squeezed her eyes shut and screamed through clenched teeth was the ground rising fast to meet her. A jolt rattled her bones as the aircraft simulated the impact.

Panting, she opened her eyes to see the simulator moving slowly to an upright position, the cockpit powered down, and overhead lights on.

"What fresh death was that?" she yelled. She slammed her hands on the yoke. And then, "I wonder what data that gave them?" she asked herself bitterly. "Collaterals. Seems like an easy way to forget people are people."

She sat motionless, the hum of the simulation chamber still ringing faintly in her ears. Her hands lay limp in her lap, but her mind replayed every flicker of the scene, what she could've done differently, the split-second decisions that slipped away from her. The phantom jolt of the crash still rippled through her muscles, a reminder that her body hadn't yet caught up with the fact that none of it was real. When an attendant approached to retrieve her, she didn't speak as the whoosh of the door's release invited her back out into the expanse of the room.

Once she was out, she noticed two techs standing comparing datapads. One tech straightened. Another glanced sharply at her and subconsciously angled the datapad away from her.

Iridienne lingered on the techs until they both shuffled away to where Mazen was standing, his focus fixed on a glowing datapad. Lines of text scrolled faster than she could read, and his lips moved in low, clipped murmurs to the aide beside him. Pretending to attach her focus somewhere else, she drifted a step closer while adjusting her sleeve, slowly, quietly, just near enough for his words to cut through the hum of machinery.

"Adad Abras. . .unsuitable for Field Clearance. Iridienne Voht. . .refused engagement. Preserved ethical protocol. Risk index: moderate. Elio Roth. . .flexible imprint. Potential defense recruit. . ."

She felt disoriented. *What were they classifying exactly? Personalities?* Her own name echoed in her head: refused engagement. *Was that an accusation? A red flag? Or just a note in a string of others?*

The group emerged one by one from their simulators, sweaty, wild-eyed, and shaky-legged. None of them spoke as they were shuffled past the phlebotomy chairs again, sleeves pushed up almost automatically. Bruises bloomed beneath their clammy skin, purple rivers chasing shrinking veins. Lost to the mental processing of what they just experienced, they sat quietly, staring distantly at different parts of the room, replaying the scenes and choices in their heads. Mazen stood off to the side, still taking notes, glancing up and back to his datapad as his attention bounced from Immune to Immune.

"Well done, group. Very well done. I'm not often this intrigued by our findings," Mazen broke the silence.

"Was that thank you on behalf of the Taxalis or just you?" Donar rasped out. Eyes darted back and forth between the two men.

"Both," Mazen said simply, not picking up on the sarcasm. "Follow me, please. Our last trial will be quite different, intentionally so, than the last."

"Our?" Adad mumbled sarcastically. Morale was declining rapidly.

At this point, they were all feeling hollow and shaky from the repeated blood samples and shocks of chemical dumps in their brains from the tests. Adad was bent over, holding his knees, swaying slightly. Azileh closed her eyes, breathing deeply with her hands on her hips, trying to fight the dizziness. Iridienne leaned against the wall, head tilted upward, counting ceiling tiles to distract herself. In addition to the physiological toll they were feeling, there were no windows or clocks. They had no idea how long they'd been in this room, but Iridienne wagered it had to be hours.

Despite their declining physical states, the group was led to the Sensory Deprivation pods, their final trial. It was no mistake of the Taxalis to measure the reactions of the five in the abruptness of deprivation juxtaposed to the overload they had just experienced.

"After the previous measurements, some of you may find this final trial. . .restful. Others may not. You will be in sensory deprivation tanks, and your reactions measured. The salt will keep you afloat. Try your best to just. . . be. The aides have a change of clothes for you over there behind the curtains." Mazen gestured them to another part of the room. "Proceed."

As the group moved toward the curtained alcoves, the sound of water sloshing in the tanks filled the silence, rhythmic and unnerving. They changed into their clothes, some thankful to get the sweaty fabric off at least for a minute, and were ushered into the tanks.

Once inside, some panicked, like Adad. Again. The physically taxing tests were not his forte. When they finally released him, it was because he had begun screaming and pleading to be let out.

Others had their coping mechanisms.

Azileh sang, the smoky timbre in her voice calming not just to her but the Taxalis attendees who could hear her. It almost felt like eavesdropping on a private conversation, as they could tell the words and songs meant something to her.

Elio's stomach spoke for him instead. His hunger became his sole fixation; he began rattling off the menu from The Compass and the nuances of seasoning from each dish.

Iridienne, meanwhile, floated in near silence. The water hugged her ears, muting everything but her own heartbeat. She focused on each breath, slow and deliberate, the way she'd trained herself to do when panic banged at the door of her mind. Thoughts of Cyrus. . .his contagious laugh, how the corners of his mouth turned down slightly when he concentrated. She tried to conjure memories of her mother's voice, how she would sing quiet, floating notes when she cooked or rubbed Iridienne's back at bedtime. . .

Mazen apparently decided when to pull the five out because Iridienne didn't ask to be removed but was told they collected enough data from her. When she asked how long she had been in there, all Mazen said was, "Long enough."

Aside from Adad, who was rambling about the stress of the tank, Elio and Azileh apparently were released via Taxalis request. And then, finally, at no fault or acquiescence of his own, Donar was eventually tapped out by the staff as he outlasted everyone else. He evidently preferred the isolation.

As the five gave their final vials of blood, the techs chased dehydrated veins under the surface of the Epitopes' tingling skin. Whether it was from mental and physical exhaustion or anemia, they were depleted.

"Very good. Very good, our newest Immune. We will process the results and provide a detailed workup of our data and findings. Now, I'm sure you're all quite starved, so let's bring in some food, shall we?" Mazen tapped rapidly on his datapad as he spoke.

Elio perked up immediately, and Donar's stomach rumbled, betraying his rejection of any kindness or support from the Taxalis thus far.

The giant doors they'd walked through that same morning opened again with a low mechanical groan, and in came carts of food. The scent hit first, savory and rich, steam rising in curls that carried traces of roasted herbs and bread still warm from the oven. It wasn't as lavish as the meal in The Compass, but it certainly wasn't everyday fare either.

The group sat in silence at a long table off to the side, the soft clatter of ladles and spoons replacing conversation as they passed the dishes along. There was more than enough, another contrast to the just enough that many experienced daily. Porcelain tapped faintly against metal trays; someone exhaled a quiet sigh after the first sip. The rich soup spread warmth through their bellies, the heat blooming outward until even their fingers stopped trembling.

Donar huffed quietly as he ladled thick broth into his bowl. "Funny how generosity shows up when they need something from you."

Azileh raised a brow. "Need? Or took?"

Elio looked between them, confused. "I mean. . .The trials were hard, yeah, but they're trying to place us. Help us contribute."

Donar scoffed. "Right. Because nothing says *treasured Epitope* like bleeding you out six times and throwing you into a death spiral simulator."

Adad, still hunched over his bowl, said, "I thought I was gonna die in that tank."

Donar rolled his eyes.

"No one died," Elio said, though it sounded less confident now. "We signed up for this, didn't we?"

"No," Azileh said, the patience in her voice softening the response. "We were identified. That's not the same thing."

The room grew quiet again, but the silence felt heavier, not just with fatigue but the suffocating questions mounting in everyone's minds.

Iridienne stared down into her bowl. "They're not just testing us. They're watching how we react to being watched," she said quietly. She glanced over just as Mazen looked up, light catching on his glasses again. The same reflection catching off the dome-shaped cameras monitoring from the ceiling.

Elio's brows furrowed. "What do you mean?"

"Like we're part of a design. Inputs, outputs. Every move, every choice, they take more blood to study it."

Whatever the Taxalis wanted from them, it was more than just their special blood.

The group sat quietly and finished their food after that. The entirety of bread, roasted vegetables, and warm tea was gone in less time than it took to complete one of the trials. Elio sat back, hands folded behind his head, eyes closed, and breathing deeply. Adad was wiping the inside of his bowl with the last piece of bread from his plate, and Donar was rubbing his face with both hands, trying to coax the fatigue from the muscles. Iridienne could have easily fallen asleep at the table herself. Azileh sat with her cheek propped on her fist, humming softly. "I'm ready to see my kids," she said quietly to herself.

"Do any of you know what time it is? How long have we been here?" Iridienne asked no one in particular. She rubbed her wrist, uncomfortable with the absence of her watch. The rest shook their heads or shrugged, unsure themselves. No windows, no clocks, no clear passage of time.

Mazen walked up again after giving them time to settle. "Now that you all are satiated, we will show you to your rooms. It's quite late now, and it's been a long day," he announced. They all looked around, confused. No one had mentioned staying at the Taxalis. Iridienne just assumed they'd go home and report back the next day.

"Excuse me. Rooms?" Azileh questioned.

"Yes, rooms. We will naturally provide a change of clothes, necessary toiletries, and bedding items," Mazen said directly.

"No one mentioned anything about us staying here," Adad added.

"Are we obliged to stay?" Donar rhetorically sneered.

"It is our honor to have you as our guests in the Taxalis. You know you are quite important," Mazen remarked, again unfazed by the edge in Donar's voice.

Before anyone could respond, the doors opened again. Couriers stepped in swiftly, depositing a bag of hygiene items, neatly folded black clothing and shoes which would be the standard uniform of those within the Taxalis, and a bundled stack of bedding to each Epitope. No words were exchanged. The five stood motionless, watching as the doors shut just as quickly as they had opened.

They shared glances, like passing notes between quiet hands, the weight of fatigue pressing heavily on their shoulders. None dared speak what they were all beginning to feel as they stood awkwardly with their clothes and bedding in their tired arms. The gesture was framed as hospitality, but the sterile efficiency of it all felt like containment.

Donar scoffed, eyeing the stack of necessities in his arms. "Guests? More like prisoners."

CHAPTER 7

LONG INTO THE NIGHT, vent fans burred through a clockless dark.

Mattresses creaked as the Epitopes' restless bodies adjusted throughout the hours that strung together. Maybe this turn, this side, this sigh would help them sleep. Nothing worked for long though.

The next morning, they all dressed quietly, uniform in their black jumpsuits emblazoned with the Taxalis logo on the lapel. The logo was primarily stitched in tan and made up of two hands cupping a single stalk of wheat between them, while a lone drop of blood in red thread hung suspended underneath. A homage to Sun Shower and the offering the citizens of Tabrass bled each ceremony.

After an uneventful breakfast, they were ushered into what looked like a meeting room with long tables, more sterile colors, a large screen, and a row of various scientists and official-looking leaders lining the front, spearheaded by none other than the Governor himself.

"Good morning, everyone." Forced smiles rippled through the room as many sat up a little straighter, chairs adjusting.

"I trust you all slept well," Astor began. The bags and dark circles under the troupe's eyes answered differently.

"We'll make this quick as there is work to be done. Thank you for your efforts yesterday in the Trials Quarter. I'm sure Mazen explained, the data provides invaluable information that proves useful in numerous sectors."

The various leadership representatives bobbed their heads in agreement, waiting for him to continue.

"In fact, you are in good company. Let's have the previous Epitopes present in the room stand in solidarity with you. As they know firsthand the unique mantel you bear." Astor gestured for the others to rise.

Scattered across the room, a couple dozen Epitopes stood to face their newest members. They exchanged brief nods and acknowledgments and scattered, wary glances. A solemn hush fell over the room until one of the older Epitopes took a seat and the rest followed. The Governor stood presiding over his curated flock.

The five were then ushered to the front to stand beside the Governor, who drank in the attention from the room.

"In light of the unprecedented attack, your contributions are more critical than ever. As every Epitope before you, as is tradition and obligation to Tabrass, you have the opportunity and privilege to contribute to your region in new avenues. Now, we will announce to which sectors of the Taxalis you will serve and belong."

The five shifted a bit. Iridienne felt her stomach flutter. Elio sniffed and cleared his throat, straightening a bit taller.

"Without further delay, let's begin. Iridienne, you will be with the Governing and Functionality Division. Elio and Azileh, you will join the Military and Terraplanning Division. Adad, you'll be assigned to the Environmental Division, and Donar, you'll be with the Genetic Division."

Iridienne was standing closest to Astor, who kept his eyes forward as he spoke quietly to her under the applause echoing in the room.

"You've lived where policy meets soil, Iridienne. We could use the perspective of someone from the fields in governing. Plus, it's evident you're well-liked in the community."

Then he turned his face ever so slightly to her and added, "I can see why." His gaze lingered a beat too long. Then he signaled for the noise to die down and announced loudly to the rest of the group, "Your leaders will collect you and begin the acclimation process. Like light," he ended. Iridienne's skin crawled from the encounter.

"Through water," the collective group responded.

So, that's it? I wonder if they'll explain what the results said, or that's that? Iridienne thought to herself.

Each leader from the sector groups then went to collect their latest additions. She stole a glance back at the other Epitopes. Elio grinned excitedly, and Azileh stood with signature stoicism. Donar was difficult to read as his resting face typically included furrowed eyebrows and a scowl. Adad looked a bit shell-shocked, and Iridienne was trying to control the wild look of being overwhelmed and yet curious about what the Governing and Functionality Division would hold.

She was folded into her new group, and they were paraded down the hallway as people stopped to turn and look at the newest recruits. They were moving past the Genetic Division entry point when she saw Nyx holding the door open for the group. In the compact filing through the door and chattering of multiple conversations within the pack, it could have been easily missed. But Iridienne swore she saw the smallest piece of paper trade hands between Donar and the grim scientist at the entryway. Then they disappeared behind the door with a sharp click.

Iridienne couldn't unknot the questions that mounted with the interactions between Donar and Nyx. First the field in the middle of the night, now this? *Maybe they knew each other before Donar was picked?* Iridienne tried to reason. *That makes sense. They definitely had kindred personalities.* Maybe their odd interactions meant nothing, but she couldn't shake the distant nagging of intentionality.

After Donar was left at his new post, next, they moved towards the Military and Terraplanning Sector, and up ahead, coming from the opposite direction, was a flight crew walking towards them. Iridienne immediately broke into a wild smile, a sob unexpectedly catching in her throat. She could almost smell the fuel and dirt on his skin as he moved closer. Cyrus. How many thoughts had rattled through her mind of him over the past days? His expression on the day of Sun Shower. Her new assignment to the sector. Her data results. The attack. She longed to sit and work through the questions, fear, and excitement, untangling the knots of emotions that wove themselves tighter with each new circumstance that seemed to present itself. She wanted the comfort of his rough hands holding her own and the wisdom and advice he always seemed to have.

He caught her stare almost immediately after she spotted him, his dark eyes widening then creasing from his smile. She stepped out of the group, away from someone next to her who was rattling on about something on the datapad they were holding, hurrying forward to meet him.

Grabbing his forearms, and sliding into an embrace, the chaos of the last chain of events seemed to stop, if just for a moment. He squeezed her, smelling her hair, hand rubbing her back.

"Hey, Rids," he said deeply.

All the words they wanted to say were traded in a lingering look cut short since both parties accompanying them halted awkwardly for the reunion.

"I'll find you," he said. His volume rose, voice commanding attention with an order as he fell back in with his crew as they headed in the opposite direction. Rafferty stole a smile at her as he nodded his head. He had an air like a younger brother that could charm his way out of any predicament. Torrey and Rays, other members of the squadron, gave a wink and a wave as they carried the back of the group.

Iridienne could breathe easier just having seen Cyrus with her own eyes. The longing remained, but she managed to stifle it and lock into the information and questions from the group around her. Not long after, they rounded a corner where Soleil was waiting at attention at a hallway intersection, a folder and datapad tucked in the crook of her arm. The group stopped once they reached the woman, blonde hair slicked back neatly with a sharp part.

Iridienne smiled at the familiar face. "Glad to see you, Soleil."

"Same to you, ma'am."

"Please call me Iridienne. Rids, even, if you like."

Soleil smiled. "Iridienne it is then. Now, we have much to cover. That'll do, everyone. I'll take her from here."

The group dispersed with nods toward Soleil; Iridienne noted the apparent authority Soleil carried that she hadn't seen before.

"I'm sure you have a litany of questions since we last saw one another. Where would you like to begin?" Soleil asked, essentially reading Iridienne's mind.

"Well, uh. . ." she stammered. "I guess let's start with how I did on the tests? I mean, I know I was assigned to a particular sector, but they didn't explain why or what we're doing. . ." she said, trailing off. It was hard to verbalize the swirling thoughts, one question birthing another.

"That is actually why you're with me again. Once the selection announcements are made, the Epitopes come back to their attendants who brief them on their results, sectors, and expectations. So, here we are."

"Oh, perfect. Could we maybe go somewhere and sit? Is the center outside area an option? I only saw it as we were walking the sectors yesterday, but being under the open sky sounds like room to breathe for a minute."

"Yes, of course. This way."

Soleil moved like wind across the tops of a wheat field, like an easy whisper, her countenance just as gentle. Although soft-spoken, she carried an authority and adeptness that was evident in her interactions. They made their path to what would be the pupil of the eye-shaped building, the warm air greeting Iridienne like curling steam from a cup as they crossed the threshold outside. She and Soleil settled into bronze-colored metal seats near a grouping of lavender and yarrow. Iridienne was mesmerized by the purple and white flowers, the fragrance swelling in the air.

"I trust you're comfortable here for our discussions to continue, ma'a—Iridienne," Soleil caught herself.

"Yes, this is lovely. Thank you, Soleil." Iridienne reached out and touched Soleil's shoulder briefly in gratitude.

Soleil smiled, then cleared her throat, and was back to business.

"An item I believe is important to make you aware of now that you're a sanctioned Epitope is your visibility."

Iridienne stared blankly. "I don't understand?"

"You are being watched because you are precious to the Taxalis. You are afforded freedom to go out into Tabrass, but you are not permitted to discuss anything coming from the Taxalis internally. You are also being watched by friends, family, acquaintances from your old life who will see you differently. . .because you are now different."

Iridienne shifted uncomfortably on the metal chair, suddenly feeling clammy and exposed.

Soleil continued, "As you know, you were selected, based on your results, for the Governing sector, which is quite the placement. Not every year is someone selected for that sector. This particular division has a unique functionality in that it isn't just policy and paperwork. It's the spine of the entire region. Think of it as the quiet command center behind every field tilled, every ration calculated, every transport route cleared. But it's not just administration. You'll be looped into projections for Iterum, settlement modeling, atmospheric compatibility data, and resource allocation planning. That means your decisions won't just affect Tabrass today. They'll echo into our off-world future. You need to understand the reports and data compiled from the other sectors, but you also need the personality to not only disseminate the information, but make difficult decisions for the greater good, while recognizing the rapport needed to maintain peace and progress for the future of Tabrass."

The two sat in silence for a moment.

"That's. . .a lot," Iridienne said slowly. "So, I guess I tested well in those things? How did they even test that on a treadmill and flight simulator, and blank tank?"

Soleil smirked at the term. "Blank tank, hmm? That's a new one. I like that." And then she looked up. "And that, ma'am, is an excellent example as to why you were selected. In essence, you're charming, humble, and you don't miss a detail. From the data results, you could have also been picked up by the Military Sector; however, based on the notes here that I'm reading, it seems Astor himself requested your appropriation to the Governing sector." Soleil tilted her head slightly.

Iridienne shifted self-consciously in her seat. "I was just trying to survive in there, nothing special. . .I did talk to him the night of the, um, well, the night of the attack. My friends and I headed to the fields after the storm cleared to see what happened, and he saw us standing in the crowd and called me over to give an account of what we saw. Maybe that's why," Iridienne offered.

"Certainly a possibility. He highly values loyalty and commitment to Tabrass. Aside from that, though, your test data is undeniable. You are a prime fit for this sector." Soleil flipped her datapad around to display a screen full of charts, percentages, and summaries. She explained each breakdown for each portion of the tests to Iridienne while Iridienne's eyes looked back and forth between the screen and Soleil, drinking in the information. Iridienne felt like she was reading information about someone else entirely rather than herself.

"The 'Blank Tank', as you called it, showed your ability to control your mental faculties and maintain control in a situation that can often cause panic and even hallucinations." Soleil mentioned.

"I guess that's what Adad was explaining after, why I overheard people mention he was screaming."

"Yes, exactly. But for you, that obviously wasn't your experience. Based on the information collected, even when you seemed to initially register stress, you were able to manage yourself quickly and even eventually get to a state of hypnagogia."

Iridienne nodded, remembering it all.

"You also did well on the physical portion, too. Your adaptability scores were particularly noted. It seems what ended your run was not hubris but celebration about another Immune's success." Soleil smiled.

Iridienne's ears perked at the hum in the air growing closer. A pack of drones whizzed overhead; her eyes tracked the noise until they were out of sight. Soleil politely cleared her throat.

"Sorry, Soleil. I'm listening."

"Now the one I wanted to save for the end included the more complex results: the flight simulation. Your critical thinking, and again, adaptability and concern for others, ranked you highly for this sector; interestingly, however, it seems a growth point is being able to ask for help or receive assistance from others. According to the data summaries, you're willing to be self-sacrificial before you would ask for help, based on the simulations at least."

Iridienne's face and the tips of her ears burned with truthful embarrassment. The data wasn't wrong. She was never good at asking for help, and she hated the idea of feeling like a burden, or worse, the possibility of rejection. She fidgeted in her seat, waiting for Soleil to continue.

"We all have weak spots, ma'am. You'll have plenty of chances to sharpen your strengths and grow. But if I may, needing others isn't a weakness. The combination of each individual's strength compounds to outweigh the strength of one," she paused. "These were overarching discussions of your results, but I'll provide you with the detailed report to look over later."

A ding from Soleil's datapad interrupted their conversation, but her words were already ruminating in Iridienne's head.

"It looks like you're being called to your first briefing. I'll send you these detailed reports once your datapad is assigned and prepped for clearance."

"Mhmm. Thank you," Iridienne mumbled as she stood and followed Soleil to the door.

Soleil navigated them to a room with a soldier stationed at the door and a retinal scanner to gain access.

"After you, Iridienne." Soleil nodded to the scanner.

"Oh, me?" Iridienne fumbled and leaned forward tentatively, the blue laser covering her vision briefly.

"Welcome, Iridienne. You may proceed," the digital voice chimed as the door clicked open.

She exchanged a look with Soleil mixed with excitement and anticipation. "We'll see each other soon. Like light," Soleil said.

"Through water," Iridienne finished as she walked tentatively into a meeting room. With a giant illuminated screen at the front, the tables curved inward like a half-moon amphitheater, all eyes were directed toward Astor, which he relished.

Iridienne slipped through the back aisle like wind through the fields, settling into her seat.

Astor announced, "The information covered today is still developing. Under no circumstances are you to discuss what you've heard here unless first prompted. Understood?"

"Yes, Governor," rumbled up in unison.

"Very good. We must discuss the most recent attack. While the two others were much smaller and further from the Tabrass center, it is apparent these are a hijacking of weather regulations, and it is paramount to eliminate this threat to Tabrassian citizens and the environment," he said.

Iridienne felt like she was back in the flight simulator again, trying to make sense of all the new information being hurled at her. *Most recent? Two other attacks? A threat?*

Astor continued, "We all experienced the bold attempt at weaponized terror. But," he turned to look at them all, scanning the room, "how many of you came down to the fields to see the damage that night?" He waited.

The room murmured awkwardly. People whispered next to each other; shrugs and questions rippled around the room. Less than a dozen raised their hands. Iridienne was one of them.

"The Taxalis is meant to lead Tabrass. How can we lead what we do not protect? What we do not monitor!" His abrupt crescendo startled several in the room.

"Even one of our newest Epitopes—Iridienne Voht," he gestured to Iridienne, "was at the fields to survey the havoc! Just hours before, she was a field worker who tended to those same crops. She had not even *entered* the Taxalis, yet she understood where she needed to be!" Chairs scraped and bodies shuffled, turning toward her. Expressions ranged from curious to jealous. Her face and ears burned with embarrassment. She clenched her teeth and tensed in her seat.

"You must ask yourselves where your priorities are rooted. To whom your loyalty belongs. It belongs to the Taxalis and Tabrass!"

Astor made the room sit in admonishment and scolding a moment longer before moving on.

"Now that we are all of the same mind, based on the limited information collected from these events, we are working under the assumption that these attacks are being perpetrated by a group that has hacked the geoengineering protocols. We cannot assume these attacks will stop, but, in fact, worsen in severity. They have yet to provide a reason or purpose behind the attacks."

"It's a power play, obviously. To prove they can. It's the start of a coup," a man barked. Iridienne flinched at the jolt of the man's voice.

"They could be setting a precedent to then ask for a ransom or a request of sorts," another offered.

Astor held up a hand to silence them. “Yes, those avenues have all been noted and are being explored. With the terraforming of Iterum nearing completion, my assumption is that the attacks are connected to the Exodus.”

“What we cannot afford,” Astor continued, “is civil unrest. The balance of Tabrass is delicate but a well-functioning system, and so we must adapt under the agreement that this enemy, this *Hostis*, is the greatest threat to Tabrass’s peace and progress.”

Nods and hums of agreement reverberated through the room. For Iridienne, she sat as if seeing through what was apparently a thin veil for the first time. She could feel whatever semblance of predictability or foundation she still had shifting under her like the rusty dirt blowing outside.

CHAPTER 8

As much as Iridienne hated to admit it, she found a sense of importance with the attention and compliments she hadn't had before from working in the fields.

But she did miss working under the open air, even on the dusty days. The fields felt like home, the shifting of the crops like quiet whispers spoken back to her. Some days out there, she would daydream of what the mornings would look like with blue skies instead of brown and real sunlight instead of hazy glows from behind the smoggy clouds.

So, when she could, she would take her lunch out into the middle courtyard for whiffs of lavender and speckles of color in the petals.

And without a doubt, the thing she missed most was her friends.

On the way down the steps leaving the Taxalis that day, Iridienne closed her eyes and took a deep breath. She had been waiting for tonight. It had been too long, postponed with increased travels and work around the region due to news spreading about the Hostis attacks. She and Cyrus and their friends finally found a night when they could make it to the Pit, their spot on the edge of the fields. And her request for special leave was approved.

Epitopes had to submit leave requests for special circumstances, a realization she frowned at when she was initially told. She moved through life freely before. The permission slip left a bitter taste in her mouth.

She was guardedly excited about the night in the previous days this week, but now that it was actually happening, Iridienne was outright giddy. The people she loved, all in one place, under the blaze of the smoky flames, songs, and stories. She couldn't wait for the patchwork of voices and laughter that wove together like a comfort and covering.

Cyrus was supposed to pick her up at dusk, in a couple of hours, which gave her enough time to get home and change from her now-typical black jumpsuit into her familiar dusty-colored tunic and boots and finish up the sun tea she was bringing for the group. Although there wasn't direct sunlight, there was enough light and warmth for the tea to steep in the window throughout the day. A few drops of almond oil, and it would be ready to go.

She finished changing her clothes and prepping the tea, and timely as he ever was, Cyrus was knocking his familiar waltzing rhythm at Iridienne's door right as the light began to wane.

"Come in!" she called, finishing up gathering her things.

Cyrus's shadow filled the doorway as he came inside. "Ah, you made sun tea. Rafferty will be excited. Rhomy, too. That's a favorite of theirs." He wrapped himself around her as she stood at the counter, setting his chin on her shoulder. She tucked her head in the curve of his neck, holding the warmth of his embrace.

"Mhmm. I was craving the nostalgia of it tonight." Iridienne's mom had made the same recipe on special occasions throughout her childhood. She finished screwing the lid on the tea container as Cyrus moved to the side.

"Here, I'll carry that." Cyrus reached out, grabbing the overhead handle of the jug.

"Thanks. All ready here. Time to head out?" Iridienne turned to him.

"Yeah, we're solid. Let's go."

As they navigated through the grid-laid streets, far behind them, a low hum lingered. Maybe a generator, maybe a patrol drone, but Iridienne chose not to look back. In her mind, she was clocked out.

Cyrus and Iridienne headed out to the upper range of the fields towards the Pit, hand in hand, catching each other up on their days at work. Iridienne told Cyrus what she could about the meetings and briefings, excitedly rattling off people's names and summaries of conversations and all the new things she was learning. Cyrus listened intently, sharing in her excitement, his eyes roaming over her face as she talked. He would then explain how his crew was doing on flight simulations, how Rafferty was growing into his own as second in command of the crew, and how others like Rays and Torrey, who would be there tonight too, were a hilarious duo on long flights to the drop posts.

When the conversation lulled a bit, they walked quietly as the brown sky deepened where it met the earth, the sounds of the fields alongside them carried on their own conversation, punctuated by the crunch of the ground beneath their feet.

"Hey, Cy, I've been meaning to ask you. The day of the Sun Shower, when they called my name, your expression wasn't. . .what I expected, I guess. You seemed, I don't know, worried? Upset? I couldn't read it."

He was quiet for a moment as he gathered his words.

"Oh, it's not that I'm not excited for you, Rids. I am. You're a solid fit for the Governing sector. There's no doubt there. You're just the mix of things that place needs. I. . .there are. . ." He sighed and stole a glance at his watch, an issued comms piece, and lowered his voice a bit. "The closer you are to the Taxalis and the inside of Tabrass, the more I can't protect you."

She wasn't expecting that.

"Can't protect me? From what? The attacks?"

"Yes, those for sure. There's chatter now about the inevitability of more. That moment when they called your name, I was so proud of you, but I couldn't help but feel like I couldn't keep you safe. Rids, once you know things, you can't unknow them."

"But safe from what, Cy? If anything, it feels like knowing more about how the Taxalis works, the findings they are constantly trying to decode and perfect, the safer we *all* will be. And the more information we'll have to make sure Iterum is a better version of Tabrass," Iridienne reasoned.

"I'm just saying, Rids, being nearer to the information doesn't make you safer; it's the opposite. The more you know, the more responsibility you carry," Cyrus said.

The edges of his mouth turned down slightly, forehead wrinkled with concern. His eyes surveyed the landscape but were buried deep in larger worries.

Cyrus had been picked early for military service and rose through the ranks easily, gaining a reputation as a respected leader and excellent pilot. He couldn't share much about the details of his job; Iridienne knew it weighed on him at times.

"Is there something I need to know? Things are different now that I'm working in the Taxalis. Surely there aren't secrets between sectors, right?" Iridienne looked up at him. Cyrus's eyebrows were run together, eyes tracing the falling clouds. The crescendos of voices and laughter of their friends surrounding the Pit floated to meet them up the path.

They stopped walking in the middle of the rusty dirt, shouldered to the right by fields and open air to their left, the Taxalis and other buildings sitting in the distance like alien mirages. They looked down to their friends and then at each other. Cyrus sighed, but not releasing much of the weight that seemed to rest heavily on him.

"I'm not ending the conversation, Rids, but it's more than we can cover in the distance between here and everyone else. Later? On our way back home?"

Now Iridienne sighed and dug at the dirt with her foot. She hated loose ends and unsaid words, but she agreed there wasn't time now.

"Sure, sounds solid. You'll have to make those long legs walk slower." She nudged him, teasing, trying to lighten the mood as they started walking again.

"I'll walk backwards, forwards, slow, fast, or to Iterum if you asked it, Rids." He pulled her in, kissing her, his free hand cupping the nape of her neck. She sank into him. He was her safety as much as she was his home.

They were pulled back to the present by loud cheers, clapping, and whooping from their friends who were close enough to see them now. Cyrus and Iridienne pulled apart, laughing to themselves and yelling out to the group who were still relentless in their teasing as Cyrus and Iridienne came fully into view. Then Rafferty came striding up, his long, lean frame dodging the legs and drinks of the others. "Is that *sun tea?* Rids, you shouldn't have!" Rafferty bearhugged her, swinging her around in a circle before setting her down and heading straight to the jug Cyrus had sat down next to the other random collection of snacks and drinks. Iridienne laughed, patting him on the back as her eyes surveyed for Rhomy, who was already standing, waiting for her hug with open arms and a smirk.

The friends embraced with arms wide before swaying back and forth in a tight squeeze.

"Rhomy, how is everything? I've missed you!"

"Oh, you know. Same old dirt. Especially with these two." She nodded over to the twins, Cirro and Cirrus, who sat tag-teaming some wild story to Torrey and Rays.

"Those two always tell the best stories. With new details every time." Iridienne winked.

Rhomy gave her a look of agreement as they made their way to the makeshift benches surrounding the fire. Rafferty and Cyrus came over not too long later, Rafferty on Rhomy's right while Cyrus sat in between Iridienne's feet, arms draped over her knees.

Late into the night, the group of friends ebbed and flowed in stories, catching up on each other's lives. Most had grown up together and had a lifetime of funny memories, heartbreak, and familiarity to share. But the others, like Torrey, Rays, and Rafferty, had been around long enough now that this group was interwoven. Laughter caught up in the sky like sparks from the fire. The flames danced shades of orange across their faces as smoke embedded its smell in their clothes. If they could've seen the moon or stars, the lunar watchman would have made its arched shift across the deepened sky.

"Anyone object to me polishing off the tea?" Rafferty stood, eyebrows raised, looking around. Everyone knew how much he loved it, and no one objected to him filling his cup with the last bit.

As he sat back down, he turned to Iridienne. "So, Rids, I gotta ask, how's it feel to know you're the newest batch of 'Munnies? It was pretty wild to see you up there that day."

The others shifted their attention to her.

"Oh, um, I mean, I don't feel different. It's just a lot of information to take in and learn now." Iridienne tried to deflect because she didn't like being the center of attention, "Plus I get to wear basically my version of a flight suit, so I can't be jealous of you guys anymore," pointing a free finger at Rafferty as she held her cup while she tickled Cyrus in the ribs with the other hand.

"Ah, well, they are pretty dashing." Rafferty laughed, sitting up and straightening a pretend collar. He was charming, with a boyish grin that most couldn't help but return.

Rafferty's parents both died when he was younger of the Cloud Coughs, and so he was adopted into military school, sworn into a life of service to his new family, the Tabrassian military, and now Cyrus's squadron. He gave off an air of being carefree, but if you caught him when he thought no one was watching, he looked longingly, as if towards something he could not have.

"Have you heard anything else about the attack after you talked to the Governor that night?" Cirro broke into the conversation. Eyes darted back to Iridienne. Cyrus turned a questioning face back up to her. There was still so much they hadn't talked about yet.

"Some," she answered honestly. "But I'm new, so I don't know much other than what we already suspected the night it happened. I know the Taxalis is putting resources into determining if there are any more potential threats."

That seemed to satisfy the bunch, who then jumped into exchanging descriptions and satisfying acknowledgments of who had seen what that night. Cirro and Cirrus, of course, started regaling everyone with details and expert storytelling that kept their attention as the tension of the retelling rose and fell. Iridienne sat and watched, soaking in their expressions, movements, and voices. She could sit here all night if it meant making this last.

Torrey broke into the dialogue, "I've never seen a cloud pattern like that from an aerial view. We were already in orbit, taking the latest drop to the depot, when we saw swirling clouds. Normally, the coverage is pretty opaque, plain, ya know? But this was spotted with lightning and a moving circle. It was wild for sure."

Cyrus glanced up at Iridienne, confirming the description. She rubbed the outside of his shoulder.

"I didn't think about what it looked like from above," Rhomy said distantly, her mind conjuring up the image.

"Our view was much more docile than your experience, no doubt," Cyrus added.

"It was unreal. . ." The twins jumped back into retelling the night at The Compass when the storm hit, leaving no part out. They would throw in, "Right, Rhomy? Rids?" to confirm they weren't exaggerating, and the friends would nod, agreeing, adding their bits of details. The four military members sat engrossed in the story.

"I doubt that'll be the last one. . ." Rafferty said half to himself.

"Raff." Cyrus shook his head, signaling for him to stop.

"There *are* rumors already that there might be more," Rhomy added tentatively.

The group sat quietly, torn between secrecy sworn to their sectors, fear of the unknown, and wanting answers.

Iridienne broke the silence, "Here recently, so many things have changed and been unpredictable at best, but there are some things that are still solid, that we can still count on, though. Rain, tornadoes, or whatever else can't wash off what we've got here."

"I'll cheers to that. . .even if my cup is sadly empty." Rafferty raised an empty cup, and the rest lifted theirs.

"Like light," he said.

"Through water," they echoed and drank what was left in their glasses.

For the better part of an hour or more, Cirrus propped up the guitar he brought on his knee and began picking a familiar tune as side conversations fell into flow again. He began to sing softly, almost as if he were talking to himself, a low and raspy liturgy of memories. Cyrus picked up the harmonies of the familiar song, and they fell into the tune with quiet hums from the others.

Smiling at one another through the lines, Iridienne's chest ached for the family that sat around her. This had to be what the Taxalis was working towards, to preserve this. People and times like this. At least for her, that had to be her intention, no matter how close to the internal information she had to get.

Eventually, hours after the crew of friends arrived, the fire started dying down, and the group started picking up the space around the Pit. They decided not to throw another log on, as many of them had to be up in just a few hours for work. As Cirro dumped dirt onto the embers, a coughing fit hit him, but he blamed the smoke and dirt kicked up in the air. Cirrus offered him a sip out of his thermos, and his coughs settled a bit. No one wanted to name the fear that settled in everyone's mind. Cloud Coughs. Iridienne made a mental note to ask Soleil about medicines and progress on that when she returned to the Taxalis.

"We're going to stick back for a bit," Cyrus said to the group as they gathered their things to leave.

"Ooohhh." Nudges and winks ensued again as Cyrus rolled his eyes and laughed. Iridienne and Rhomy hugged again, making plans for an early morning breakfast before work this coming week. She hugged Cirro and Cirrus and shared some final jokes and grins with Torrey and Rays. Rafferty picked her up in another bear hug, thanked her for the tea, and mentioned something about needing to press his flight suit so she didn't show him up. Cyrus and Iridienne stood with his arm around her shoulder, and hers around his waist, as the remaining friends headed out down the path they came, leaving swirls of dirt in the wake of the lantern light.

Once the group's light faded further away, Iridienne and Cyrus sat back down on the felled logs surrounding the Pit, picking back up where their conversation left off.

"I needed tonight," he said. Their lantern light cast deep shadows across their faces.

"Me too," Iridienne agreed.

They sat for a second, and Cyrus broke in, "Rids, I know you already know this or have at least heard rumors, but there were two other smaller attacks that were dissipated, but the most recent one was way bigger than the others and much more destructive. They think a group is responsible for the hijackings called. . ."

"The Hostis," she finished.

He stared and hung his head. "I couldn't keep you safe from the air, Rids. All I could do was hope and pray that you were solid. . .safe."

She laid her head on his shoulder, letting the ache sit heavy in the smoke of the fire. She understood now what he meant earlier while they were walking to the Pit, that he had no time or opportunity to even warn her before everything happened.

"Cy, based on where we both are now, we're stronger together. What you know and hear, and what I'll learn, together we can help. Maybe we can figure out who this group is and why and how they're able to break into the regulatory systems." She reached for his hand, weaving her fingers past his calloused and scarred palm. Together, their strengths and weak points were complemented and filled in by the other. They both knew that. Apart, they were strong; together, they were better.

"You know that's not the last attack. The likelihood of another is almost guaranteed, but we don't know when or what kind. We're one of the last functioning regions, so my guess is that it's not an outside attack. The thing that's just sitting in the back of my head is that they have to have someone on the inside. Like in the Taxalis. How else would they have access to the data and systems to pull this off?"

Iridienne sat back. She hadn't even considered it could be someone from the Taxalis. Tabrass always drove home the value of unity and working for the benefit of the whole. *Why would someone try to attack or distract from the work of getting off planet, especially when they were so close to being ready?* She felt dizzy, grappling for a reasonable explanation. But the more she considered it, the more it made sense. It would have to be someone with access. With knowledge. With motive.

Cyrus and Iridienne sat in the quiet, bearing the weight of each other's worries. The crackling of disintegrating wood was the only punctuating noise in the night.

The more you know, the more responsibility you carry. Cyrus was right.

CHAPTER 9

"IRIDIENNE? IRIDIENNE. IRIDIENNE, HELLO?" The spike of vocal agitation jerked her back from her roving thoughts.

Astor was staring at her with piercing annoyance as Soleil ever so gently placed her hand on Iridienne's knee as a reminder.

Steady.

One recurrent expectation that was driven home during Iridienne's last few weeks with Taxalis training was that a citizen, an Immune at that, assigned to her sector in Government was expected to be a calming, reassuring presence, unstartled and prepared. Personal emotions and reactions were discouraged. The region looked to them for leadership.

So, she had to be a leader they could trust and follow.

Her eyes flared wide just briefly before she took a deep-lunged breath, her shoulders settling like stone with the exhale.

"Yes, Governor. I was considering a possibility, an origin theory. My apologies."

"Yes, yes." He waved off the apology. "Since it was so engulfing, please share." Evidently, the expectations of neutral responses expired with the Governor. Astor had been increasingly agitated, especially since the last weather attack in the weeks prior, which left the region without power for days. Lightning had caught a portion of the field on fire and almost waterlogged another section of the fields that hadn't rooted quite yet. They were able to pump most of the water off the crops and extinguish the flames, but it was no secret that the Taxalis and Tabrass as a whole were in reactionary protocol. Sitting, waiting ducks, as it were.

Iridienne stole a glance at Soleil as she straightened, with Soleil giving the briefest nod back.

"Of course. It's worth coming back to the consideration that these attacks are not external. Rather, they have an internal origin, sir."

A cacophony of voices rose, arguments, affirmations, unintelligible disagreements from across the room. Apparently, reactionary emotions were fair game now. Soleil raised an eyebrow. Iridienne took mental notes of responses, trying to piece together some hint or trail of *who*. Maybe an answer to *why* would come once they found someone to ask.

Astor stood forcefully from being hunched over the table, propped by his arms at forty-five-degree angles, immediately knotting his hands behind his back as he paced the front of the room.

"Enough! You forget your posts!" he boomed. Silence suffocated the heightened conversations mid-phrase. Some embarrassed and others haughty, people started shuffling back into more comfortable positions as Astor continued.

Iridienne took another deep breath and waited for what came next.

"This isn't the first time this idea has been proposed, but if my memory serves me correctly, Iridienne, you have not wavered from this theory, yes?"

"That's correct, sir."

"Very well." He paused, wheels turning. "These meetings have proved fruitless so far. So, we are building two committees. One to investigate the external avenues and one to investigate the possibility of internal interference. If you are needed, you will be notified today. Dismissed."

Stunned by the abruptness of his statement, the room cleared quietly with a few side conversations mumbling on as they filed out of the meeting room. Iridienne and Soleil walked down the hall without talking until Soleil broke the silence.

"From what I understand, most of the new Epitopes will be assigned to the committees because they believe you will carry a fresh perspective and relevant connection to Tabrass versus those who have been in a Taxalis longer," Soleil said. Then she added carefully, "Although. . .Astor seems to have taken a particular interest in you."

Iridienne shifted uncomfortably. She traced the scars on her palms again, the familiar trails like raised berms on her hands. She didn't want the attention; she didn't know why Astor would have any investment in her specifically. Her body temperature rose a bit, just enough to make her skin feel clammy. There was nothing she could do about it now, and she honestly didn't want to deal with the gritty unease of the implication, so Iridienne changed the subject and said, "It feels like the sector is segmenting."

"I would have to agree. Consider your side, Iridienne."

Suddenly, an alert came across her datapad. Iridienne read the quick message with a sigh, biting the inside of her lip.

"We weren't wrong, Soleil."

Soleil shook her head.

"Well, let's go see who the other lucky members are. Like light, Soleil."

"Through water, Rids."

Iridienne looked up, visibly touched. Soleil had never called her anything other than "Iridienne" or "ma'am." Soleil didn't like to make a fuss of things, so Iridienne didn't make one, but the gratitude of Soleil's friendship and concern settled tenderly.

Iridienne headed off down the hall, up a set of stairs, to a floor above as she neared closer to the unveiling of this new team. She found the room detailed on the digital note and headed inside.

They were given just enough information to know where to go and when, but she had no idea what to expect when she walked in.

"Azileh? Donar?" Iridienne half laughed. "Soleil mentioned some of us newbies were going to be assigned. Do either of you know anything about this?"

"No, no clue, actually," Azileh said.

"Sentiment shared," Donar replied.

"Friendly as ever," Azileh added jokingly. "Iridienne, it's good to see you. I hear you've done well in Functions," referencing Iridienne's sector placement. Iridienne was immediately reminded about why she liked Azileh and why Azileh had probably done well herself in the Military sector. She was direct, honest, and kind.

"Cyrus said you've fallen right in lock-step yourself, Azileh. I guess their tests had some merit, hm?" Azileh made a face in agreement.

As they stood there, a couple of familiar faces and others she'd seen in passing but didn't know personally came into the room. Ten now.

"So this is a combo committee?" Azileh looked around.

"Looks like."

Then the door opened, and in came Astor with two more members of the committee from the Genetics and Military sectors.

"I see you are all here, twelve in total. Three from each sector. While you all are not the only ones in your respective areas that have voiced agreement on an internal concern, you are the ones who have been chosen to ultimately uncover if you're wrong or if you're right. Ideally, if you're right, you will also have found names. There's an identical setup for an external investigative committee as well. Let's waste no more time, shall we?" Astor bluntly explained, sentences bumping up against each other with little room for more than an inhale between.

Astor continued to explain that the point of the committee was essentially to become detectives amongst the sectors in the Taxalis. If the attacks were coming from an internal group, it was their job to find them. There was a higher-ranking official assigned to the group to organize approaches and assign tasks from within. For theirs, it was Anatole, whom Iridienne recognized from her own sector. He was incredibly smart, detail-conscious, and not easily rattled.

"Without further delay, Anatole, the room is yours. I'll be expecting the first report soon." Astor gave a cordial nod and exited the room.

Anatole exhaled, set his shoulders a bit, and turned to the group. "This is going to be a dig. I hope you're all okay with getting dirt under your nails."

Some of them exchanged glances.

His baritone voice was a comforting note compared to Astor's directness as Anatole explained that there would be three smaller groups composed of a representative from each sector, and they would work together on individual smaller hunches, theories, and threads to pull as they arose. Then, he began matching up the sub-teams.

"Donar, Iridienne, Toril, and Solanna, you all will make up the next group."

Iridienne didn't know Toril except by face; he was probably a decade older than her, freckled, with a close buzz cut. He was the Military representative, a high-ranking field commander, and probably bled dirt; he had dedicated his life to the service of Tabrass. Solanna, who sat nervously twirling her long, dark hair, was the Environmental member, and then Donar in Genetics. The four grouped up and made their introductions, sharing their initial concepts and thoughts about where to start looking for potential answers. Donar contributed very little, but Iridienne noted he was intent on listening to every word.

"Alright, folks. Here's the first question: Do we look for motive first, and maybe that will point us to those responsible? Or do we look for questionable people first?" Toril proposed.

They *hmmed* in agreement and consideration. *How do you know where to start looking if you don't know who or what you're looking for?*

"Maybe we don't pick a focus yet. It seems like we could start sleuthing through documents and reports to see if there's something there. Infractions or write-ups. . .problematic people? Or maybe even contextualized anecdotes or history of the region that could shine some light on the motive?" Iridienne offered. She couldn't think of anywhere else to start.

Toril agreed, "That seems like our best option so far, short of interviewing every person connected with the Taxalis. Solanna, Donar, thoughts?"

Solanna was incredibly quiet, dark eyes wide as she answered, "So far, I think that would be best. I primarily look through data in my area already, so I can be quick but thorough."

Toril and Iridienne nodded. "Donar?"

"Sure, this shouldn't be like looking for a seed in a storm," he answered sarcastically.

The three shot each other glances, but at least they had a tentative direction.

"Okay, maybe we can all start to look into those things or people in our own areas first. We have a mid-week check-in, so let's bring what we find then, and see what we come up with," Iridienne suggested.

They all agreed. At least Iridienne thought Donar did. He didn't have much of a choice to be there, but she hoped he would contribute anyway.

"Okay then. Let's do some digging."

CHAPTER 10

IRIDIENNE GATHERED HER BELONGINGS to head home for the day after her sub-group decided on a plan of action. As she opened the door to exit the Taxalis, she saw Cyrus waiting for her at the bottom of the steps. She broke into a bright smile, the sight of him igniting a flutter in her stomach.

He was leaning against the railing, still in uniform, grinning as he saw her.

She skipped down the steps into an immediate embrace, burying her face into the brown and tan camouflage of his jacket.

"This is a nice surprise," she said, looking up.

"I wanted to see you," he replied simply. "We finished our rotations and reports early, surprisingly, so I headed over here to catch you before the lockout period kicks in. How was," he paused for dramatic effect, "the *inner sanctum*?" Cyrus said jokingly.

Iridienne snorted. "I'm not sure that's what it is, but there definitely are some different things happening," she added carefully.

"Mmm?" Cyrus looked down, serious now, concern and curiosity mixed on his face. There was still a faint layer of dust in his hair and on his uniform.

"Mhmm," she confirmed. "Can we swing by my place so I can grab a drink, set some of this down, and then I can explain?"

"Yeah, of course, that's solid."

Cyrus and Iridienne headed down the path south towards the city center, making a sharp left into the neighborhood district, weaving a bit through the identically laid streets, to her place.

Once inside, Iridienne pitched her bag and datapad onto the counter, and Cyrus laid his keys down and slipped off his standard-issue military watch, both message relay and leash. They were required to wear it while on call. Only those connected with the Taxalis were allowed messaging equipment, but it also meant privacy was, at best, partial. He rubbed the pale band of skin on his wrist a bit as Iridienne moved into the kitchen to make some tea. She caught Cyrus watching her. She suddenly blushed, feeling self-conscious.

"What?"

"Nothing, it's just nice to watch you," he responded. Eyes lingering, unfazed by her pause.

She laughed and threw a tea bag in his direction, the string and tag fluttering to the ground, not anywhere close to him.

"Oh, really?" he cocked an eyebrow and nimbly dodged around the counter to catch her from behind, his arms wrapping around her. She could feel the stubble as he sniffed into her neck, trying to tickle her. She was squirming and squealing for him to stop, both of them laughing.

"Okay, yes, ma'am. I'll let you finish." He brushed his hair back with his hand.

"Mhmm. That's what I thought." She smirked, tightening the lid to her thermos. "Ready?"

"After you, Rids," Cyrus said, half bowing, gesturing with an open hand to the door.

She opened the door and walked out into the dusky light. She let Cyrus lead the way, walking side by side with her hand gripping the crook of his elbow by his bicep. The sky and surroundings weren't much to look at, the same hazy, dusty tans never changing, but she still preferred being outside. It felt free.

They were headed out past the fields, beyond the Pit, to a dried-up creek that had a ledge that overlooked the cracked bed where water cut through the ground decades ago. They found it exploring a couple of years back, and it was their little secret where secrets could be held.

They settled on the edge, legs dangling, and sat in silence for a while.

Eventually, Iridienne said, "They assigned some of us to two committees today to try and find any information on who's responsible for the attacks. One group is investigating external possibilities, the other is looking internally." She explained who was in her sub-group and who made up the rest of the groups, and how the meeting in general went on earlier that day.

"Oh, wow. Seriously? That's bold. All hands on deck, it sounds like," Cyrus said. "Wait, *you* were assigned, weren't you?"

Iridienne made a face to indicate that she, in fact, had been chosen. Again.

"For internal review, of course," she clarified.

"Of course."

Silence again filled the space with swirling thoughts from both of them, only to be tangled more by the crescendo of a tracker drone duo buzzing by in the air.

"The more you know, Rids," Cyrus echoed and trailed off. He sounded sad, almost.

"Well, we don't know anything yet. I guess I'll start my. . .*investigating*. . .tomorrow." She shrugged. "I'm not sure what I'm even looking for."

"Anything that looks off, I guess," Cyrus said. "Speaking of, Rafferty has been acting strange lately. I saw him sneaking off the other day after shift ended. And you know how he's always joking and pretty happy? He's been kind of prickly. Real short fuse, like he's mad about something."

"Huh? That is unlike him," Iridienne contemplated. "Maybe he has a secret girlfriend?" she said half-joking, nudging Cyrus's arm.

"I mean, maybe? I don't know why he'd be secretive about it, but maybe he's trying to avoid getting hassled all day about it by the guys."

"Yeah, could be. Something happen at work that could've put him in a bad mood?"

"No, at least not with me. I don't know. Could just be a mood, or he's tired. We've definitely been ramping up security and upping the shipping progress, too. Everyone's doing more, been ordered to finish projects quicker. I've noticed they've been asking the mechanics to tune up the faster jets. Our commanding officers have been in more meetings, too." He paused. "Stuff's changing, Rids. Even the Iterum ships have round-the-clock attention now."

"Yeah, it is. I want to believe things will calm down, go back to normal once they—we—figure out who's responsible for the attacks. Or the terraforming will finally be finished. I just don't know if normal is even realistic anymore."

The wind picked up a bit, bending the scraggly grass sideways. Cyrus looked up, eyeing the sky.

Iridienne continued, focused on unwinding the thoughts in her head, "I know I've said this, but what would someone gain from attacking their own region and people? And if it is someone from the inside, there has to be more than one." She trailed off because the wind was blowing and not relenting at this point.

She and Cyrus stood up, eyes still glued to the sky, turning slightly to get a wider view. Then Cyrus pointed out past them, northeast. The sky was always hazy and dirty looking, but billowing up from the horizon point was a darker wall that looked like an umber wave.

The sand and dirt were stinging their skin and eyes at this point as they tried to shield their faces while still looking out. The wall continued to grow, threatening to eclipse the skyline at the rate it was moving.

"It's a sandstorm. Rids, we can't get stuck in this."

"We're too far out to run back. We'll get caught in it," she said back, voice straining over howling air.

Cyrus looked around the mostly flat land. There was no coverage, no trees, no buildings close enough to run to. Then, he looked down. The dried-up creek bed walls would have to work.

"Down here! We need to slide down and hunker against the walls! Quick!" Cyrus was yelling over the wind. He slid down the rocky dirt wall first, reaching up to help Iridienne down. The sandstorm was getting dangerously close. Any grass or stray foliage was whipping angrily in the air that was now almost impossible to see through. The wave of dirt was about to envelop them.

"Hurry, Rids, now!" Cyrus pulled her against the wall, pushing her down into the dirt. "Get down!" He wrapped his body around her back, covering what he could with his jacket, pressing his weight into her to hold her down.

"Close your eyes!" he yelled over the top of the noise. He buried his cheek against her, facing the wall of the creek bed, eyes squeezed shut. Then, the storm was on them. Stinging and thick, the dirt rolled past them with force as the wind gathered more and more grains with each gust. It was almost impossible to breathe. Dirt caked their nostrils and gritted in their teeth. Both Cyrus and Iridienne were choking in the thickness of the air. Still, they held onto each other, praying it would pass soon.

They took short breaths, trying to breathe into the fabric of their clothes to help filter the air, and their legs ached against the rocky ground as they continued to press into that and each other. Then they could feel the pressure of the wind start to lessen barely, pressing past them. They stayed in the bundled layers of limbs until all that hung in the air was dirt. Iridienne and Cyrus unfolded, joints aching with the uncomfortable pressure and position they sat in, piles of dirt sliding off their clothes.

Their eyes were red and involuntarily watering to expel the rogue granules that kept falling past their eyelashes, creating muddy trails down their dirty faces.

They had to figure out a way up the creek wall. Further down the dried bed, the distance from the top was only about eight feet. Cyrus hoisted Iridienne up first so her top half was folded on the bank. Cyrus dug his boots into the dry wall, anchoring in some stray roots as Iridienne offered him a hand. Once they were both up on the bank, they tried to get the excess dirt off, patting their clothes and shaking out their hair.

Now that they could see the landscape better up on the bank, Iridienne turned to look towards the fields.

"If that hit the crops, it could cause scarring or abrasions. . ." Iridienne trailed off.

"No doubt we are both getting messages, and all our stuff is back at your place," Cyrus said.

"We need to get home," Iridienne agreed.

Heading in the opposite direction, there were already personnel moving towards the fields again. They both wondered out loud what kind of damage they were assessing.

As soon as Iridienne and Cyrus made it through her door, she saw her datapad lighting up and heard the repetitive buzz of messages coming in. She picked it up and swiped through the alerts to the message of mandatory attendance that evening for updates and check-ins. Committee members, sector leads, and high-ranking military were noted in compulsory attendance. Cyrus checked his watch, which was full of messages, too. He gave her a look and moved into the other room to issue a call back to his commanding officer.

She could hear fractioned parts of the conversation. "*Yes, sir. No, sir, I understand. It was off because I was clocked out. Well, sir, Iridienne and I. . .caught out in the sandstorm. Yes, I understand. It's mandatory at all times now. Tonight? Yes, sir.*"

He came back around the corner, and Iridienne glanced up from her datapad. "Sounds like we're going on another adventure together tonight. I've been called in, too."

Cyrus grunted. "I need to get cleaned up. You, too." He winked. Iridienne smiled as she glanced down, lifting her arms and stirring up a cloud of dust as her hands clapped her sides.

“I don’t think you have any of your uniforms here. Do you want to run home and shower, and then meet me at the top of The Compass? We can head in together?” she suggested.

“That’ll work. See you soon.” Cyrus wrapped her in close, kissing her with a long linger. Neither cared they tasted like dirt. “Like light, Rids.”

“Through water, Cy.”

CHAPTER 11

He was already waiting for her where the road to the Taxalis connected to The Compass, freshly showered with a clean set of fatigues on. His hair was still damp, but the loose waves were beginning to dry.

"It took three rinses to get the dirt out of my hair. I'm not sure I even got it all," Iridienne said as she walked up, her long hair still wet. "Obviously, I didn't have time to dry it."

"I don't think they'll mind much. I have a feeling this is going to be. . .tense. You solid?" he asked.

"As ever. Let's go get a good seat."

They headed up the road and then up the stairs towards the black-glass building that always seemed to be watching. Now, though, as much as it seemed to be surveying, the Taxalis wasn't seeing what it wanted to see.

The automated voice welcomed both Cyrus and Iridienne, and the door clicked open. There were already workers on site, and there were varying shades but a universal look of concern on most everyone's faces. The couple moved towards the largest conference room, the one that held all of the leaders and commanders of their areas. Iridienne was still not entirely sure why she was asked to come, other than being appointed to the internal committee less than twenty-four hours before. Soleil's uneasy comment about Astor's piqued interest in her flitted like a gnat in her ear.

Dozens of higher-ups grumbled in low, territorial knots, muttering in their own side conversations. Most everyone knew Cyrus well, his reputation preceding him. Most knew *of* Iridienne simply because the latest Sun Shower ceremony was not even a distant memory yet.

Iridienne surveyed the room and noticed most of the internal committee members were there. Solanna was already seated, and Toril came over to say hello. Solanna glanced up at him sheepishly through her dark lashes and laughed at something he said. Iridienne smiled to herself at the vignette of something blooming despite the turmoil.

Cyrus gave nods and shook hands, and Iridienne acknowledged the few she knew as the two milled through the aisles to a set of chairs towards the left with a good view of the front of the room. Some in the room eyeballed the duo's matching wet hair and shared exaggerated looks. Cyrus and Iridienne chose to ignore the dramatics. After they sat down, they saw Rafferty come through the doors, eyes scanning for someone.

Cyrus lifted up a hand to wave, and Rafferty made his way over.

"What do you make of all of this? This is wild!" Rafferty said as he settled into the chair next to them.

"We were stuck out in it. I've never seen anything like it."

"*What*? Where? How? They're saying it sandblasted some of the crops. How did you guys not lose the top layer of your skin?"

Cyrus explained where they were and what happened with Rafferty listening intently. He glanced over at Iridienne, impressed, eyes wide and eyebrows raised, from time to time.

Rafferty leaned back, arms crossed, resting his ankle on his opposite knee. He had an appeal about him, even now. "Well, that explains the damp hair. I figured y'all didn't get freshened up just for this impromptu gathering," he joked. "But truly, I'm glad you two are solid. Something's in the works. . ." He trailed off.

The room had filled up to almost capacity when Astor came in through a side door with some attendants, moving with intention.

"Good evening. Your haste is noted, considering the increasing frequency of the attacks. Make no mistake, these are uncharted times, and we are under imminent threat. We are now facing pressure from two directions: preservation in our current location while expediting the final processes for readying our Exodus to Iterum. Now more than ever, the burden is shared for the days ahead." He paused for effect after quoting Tabrass's motto.

"We are all needed. The region can expect increased work hours and output, as well as an expectation for cooperation during the continued investigation into the origins of the attacks. I am confident the persons responsible will be found and held accountable according to Tabrassian law." He paused again then added.

"In this case, unto death."

A murmur of shock vibrated quietly in the room.

"There hasn't been an execution since that uprising more than fifty years before, right?" Iridienne whispered to Cyrus.

"Right," he said back, face serious as a scar.

Iridienne began thinking back to the history lessons in school. From what she remembered, it was because of food and medical resource shortages. When she asked her dad about it, though, he said the Cloud Cough cases had escalated and citizens demanded resources to test for treatments. These stories were the ones shared around tables or across cups of tea in the quiet of people's homes. Citizens began to question why the Epitopes were protected and elevated, through luck so it seemed, but those given an eventual death sentence of the coughs felt as though they were expendable.

Iridienne's dad explained that, initially, there were relatively peaceful protests, but then a group tried to set fire to the fields. To make a point that disunity would not be tolerated, the ones the Taxalis caught were hanged in front of the fields they tried to destroy.

The gallows, past the fields close to the far southern border, were still standing, like a distant reminder in the back of everyone's minds. She remembered seeing their shadows, skeletal ghosts haunting the planted ground.

"*What's going to happen to the ones they catch now?*" Iridienne thought.

"Stay in the room," Cyrus whispered as he nudged her gently, knuckles brushing hers gently under the table, his eyes not leaving the Governor, who continued his filibuster for his captive audience.

Rafferty smirked, unfazed by the Governor's volume rising through his speech, but more amused at Iridienne's propensity to get lost in thought.

". . . once discovered, the accused parties will face a tribunal and be prosecuted accordingly," Astor said, then his face hardened. "Codex 19 has not been enacted since the coup half a century ago. But, we are sitting on a precipice," he boomed, volume almost too loud. "Either we are destroyed or they are. We cannot and will not weather attacks like this indefinitely."

"That last pun might've been a little on the nose, but we'll allow it," Rafferty mumbled. His comment was woven more with bitterness than humor.

Cyrus was right; Raff was acting a bit strange. Iridienne tried to shrug it off as different reactions to stressors, but it was off-character nonetheless. She found herself longing again for the past, when things were simpler, easier, predictable. When things were the same. That was a different life now.

Astor continued, "As you know, we have appointed multiple mixed committees for internal and external investigations. Finding the sources of these attacks is paramount and of the utmost priority. However, we will *not* slow our work for Iterum in lieu of the imminent attacks on our doorsteps. Our capacities will grow because they must."

Uneasy shifts rippled through the attendees. Iridienne glanced around through the waves of faces and noticed Nyx, the geneticist, was in the room, grim as ever. He drilled holes through the Governor as he continued his speech.

"Failure to identify those responsible is not an option. You all know your roles." Astor concluded, "For better days to come. For Tabrass. You are dismissed."

The room began to stand, chairs skidding back, noises of people stretching and starting conversations amongst themselves swelling in the room. Rafferty, Cyrus, and Iridienne sat for a bit longer before they stood to leave.

Rafferty turned to the couple. "Are we still on for the Pit in a few days? I think it would do us all some good." He eyed Iridienne. "Especially if some certain tea was involved. . ." He trailed off, glancing around jokingly.

"I'll make you some tea, Raff." Iridienne patted his knee.

"Yeah, it's a go unless something comes up," Cyrus confirmed. His statement, heavy with other implications, hung there for a minute.

"Well, that's solid then. I'm glad for something to look forward to," Rafferty said, standing. Suddenly, he cleared his throat, throwing a look at Cyrus and nodding past his head. Cyrus caught it and turned, looking. Their commanding officer was making his way to them, face unreadable. The three friends stood, Cyrus and Rafferty at attention, and waited.

"At ease, gentlemen," he said to Cyrus and Rafferty. He nodded at Iridienne. "Ma'am."

"General, what can we do for you?" Cyrus asked.

"We've received orders that the Governor wants the storehouses and next supply cache delivered ahead of schedule. There is concern, chatter, of attacks that may compromise the Iterum supplies. The frequency of the trips is likely to increase too. Regardless, this latest order means we leave tomorrow, first thing. 4:00 AM report time."

"Yes, sir, understood," Cyrus responded. The three men exchanged a salute, their right arms bent diagonally across their chests, hands angled like knives.

When the general was out of earshot, Rafferty sighed and rolled his eyes. His cheekbones were more pronounced, as if he hadn't been eating. "So much for sleep, eh, Cap?"

Cyrus raised his eyebrows in response but frowned when Rafferty looked away with his hands on his hips, surveying the room.

"Raff, you solid, man?" Cyrus asked.

"Oh, yeah. Sleep's actually been a bit elusive as of late. I'd probably be up anyway, no problem," Rafferty responded.

The uneasiness of the unspoken sat there between the three like an item out of place. Iridienne changed the subject back to something simpler.

"Well, if your team leaves tomorrow, we all should still be solid for the Pit in a few days, yeah?"

"Wouldn't miss it. I'm going to head home. See you in a few, Cap," he said abruptly, like he suddenly needed to be somewhere. He shook hands with Cyrus, gave Iridienne a tight side hug, and weaved his way through the remaining attendees in the room. Iridienne noticed that as he headed to the door, he nodded ever so slightly to Nyx. Before Rafferty left the room, Nyx rose rapidly and made his way in that direction too. The two men left in single file, mixed in with the others exiting.

Iridienne turned back to Cyrus. "Do you know Nyx Calen? He's a geneticist. I cannot get a read on that guy, but I keep seeing him in. . .I don't know. . .weird interactions." She trailed off.

"I know of him, but I don't think I've spoken to him personally. He has a reputation for being short with people, but other than that, I don't know."

Then Cyrus added, "I did see Raff talking with him briefly the other day, actually."

"Really?"

So what she saw wasn't a coincidence. Nyx. Donar. Raff. Maybe Nyx was a trail to follow.

"I wonder how they know each other."

"There's one degree of separation in Tabrass. There's no telling," Cyrus said distractedly.

She wrapped an arm around his waist, pulling him back to the present. "Will you message me when you get back? I know you need to get some sleep, and I need to sort out some trails I'm following, but I'd like to talk them through with you when you get home."

"Of course, Rids." He smiled down. "Guess we're done here," he said as he looked around. "I'll walk you home."

As they made it to the exit, the Governor was standing close to the door, talking with one of his attendees. "Good night, Governor," she said as they continued forward.

Astor looked up. "Good evening. From what I understand, you two were caught in the sandstorm." His eyes dragged them up and down, resting on Iridienne.

"We were," Cyrus confirmed. His voice short, body rigid and on alert.

"That would explain the wet hair." Astor gently scooped a damp strand from Iridienne's shoulder, lingering half a second before letting it float back down.

She blinked a frown and pulled her shoulder back slightly. Cyrus stepped forward like a barrier.

"Until next time, Governor," Cyrus said directly, holding eye contact.

A muscle in Astor's jaw flexed. "First thing, your group reports their latest findings, Iridienne. I hope to hear something of interest."

She nodded as they exited. Cyrus intentionally positioned himself between Astor and Iridienne on their way out. Her stomach dropped. Her skin crawled, and she felt dizzy. *Why did I freeze like that? Why did he touch my hair? Why didn't I say something?* Her lungs suddenly felt full of dirt, suffocating in a way that even the sandstorm did not. She gripped Cyrus's hand until they made it outside.

She had nothing to show for the last couple of days, aside from the dirt on her scalp and the feeling of his fingers on her hair.

As soon as the quiet of the night hit her face, she gasped, sucking for air like breathing through a wall of dust.

CHAPTER 12

Donar was already waiting in the meeting room the next morning when Iridienne came in. He stared Iridienne down from the door to the table where she put her things down. Iridienne had become accustomed to Donar's moodiness and mysteriousness, but that familiarity certainly did not make her trust him any more. The other groups huddled closely over papers or datapads, passing them back and forth, voices low, eyes glancing around sporadically.

Swirls of questions moved through her mind. Her pulse ticked in her ears as she scanned the other tables. *What did they find? Have I been approaching this wrong? Are they going to penalize us?* A situation like this felt like her worst nightmare, underperforming at something that mattered. She took a breath and steadied herself.

"Morning, Donar," she said as she sat down.

"Mm," he grunted in reply.

She took a sip of her tea. "Found anything interesting?"

Donar simply shrugged and said nothing. The two sat in silence, waiting for the other half of their team.

Thankfully, Iridienne thought, Toril and Solanna were not far behind. They came in together, chatting about something serious, some findings perhaps. Hopefully, they had something to contribute because Iridienne had come up with minor leads that led nowhere and could feel the pressure mounting.

"Hey, Iridienne. I heard they sent out your Captain's crew this morning. Another load delivery already," Toril commented as he sat down. Iridienne smiled and nodded in acknowledgment. Toril continued, "My bet is that they're trying to speed up stockpiles because of the attacks. . .which means someone has to figure out a lead sooner rather than later. I don't want the Governor breathing down my neck. More than that, though, I want to catch the ingrates that started this whole trash fire. I've racked my brain trying to come up with some motive, and I got nothing. They're smart, whoever they are, and good at covering their tracks. But damage for the hell of it?" he scoffed. "Cowards in my book."

Donar snorted at that.

The uncertainty and threat of the unknown made her uneasy, and Donar's passive-aggressive reactions lit a fuse in Iridienne. Before she even realized what she was saying, she snapped.

"Donar, do you have something to say? I know small talk and being generally positive isn't your default, but if you've got something to say, out with it."

Now it was her turn to stare at him.

He drummed his fingers on the table, adjusted in his seat, and propped his forearm on the table to turn toward Iridienne. Toril and Solanna sat watching; Toril was intrigued by what was unfolding. Solanna was deeply uncomfortable.

His voice was low and even. "Has it ever occurred to you that your precious Governor is just that: a role. That he's playing a part?"

She wasn't expecting that. She sat blinking, feeling like she was standing on shifting sand. "He's not my 'precious' anything. It's his job to care for and lead the region."

"If you say so," Donar replied and moved back to face the table, their brief conversation obviously done.

Toril and Solanna shifted as Iridienne navigated a mixture of rage, frustration, and the worst additive: doubt. *What if there was merit to what he said?* That tiny seed, not unlike the seeds in the fields the citizens bled over just weeks before. *What if?*

Toril broke in, "Mm'kay. We need to get a plan together here, yeah? The Gov' will be here in a minute, and we can't tell him we got nothing."

They all agreed and readied themselves to organize what little they brought to the table. Toril took the lead, and they each shared the ideas they were currently chasing.

Toril started with Donar. "Donar, you have anything to report?"

Donar chewed on his cheek for a second, wrestling with the words he wanted to share. "Well, I am relatively new to the Taxalis because of my special blood, as you know." He shot a look at Iridienne. "But what I think is interesting, in my brief forays into the genetics records, is that we haven't found a cure for the coughs even with all of the genetic testing and engineering efforts elsewhere. Based on the information that I've seen, it's not been. . .a *priority*." He waved his hand and sat back, arms crossed.

They all sat with the information. Again, the only thing anyone could really expect with Donar was shock value and negativity, but he had proven to be rarely wrong. The coughs were a sensitive subject because most people had lost someone, or many, to the sickness. They all sat uncomfortably.

"Alright, that could be an interesting motive to consider for why the attacks are happening. Donar, you want to keep following that lead? See if there's a name or names connected with that?"

Donar gave a sarcastic salute, and Toril moved on to Solanna.

Solanna was very soft spoken, gentle, and incredibly astute in her work and came prepared. She also hated being the focus of attention. She pulled out her datapad with screenshots she scrolled through, explaining, "We have been working on some GMs in the lab," and was met with confused glances. "Sorry, GMs—genetic modifications—to the genomes of sorghum and wheat seeds to help with the sustainability of the crops. But as I was pulling data from previous splices and experiment cycles, I noticed that the same identification code, 0998–34XN, had accessed all of the experiments. Like, *all* of them. Even years and years back, which is unusual. But the first four numbers of the ID are for the upper-level Genetic Sector, like lead scientists are given. At first, I thought, maybe, it was someone from Genetics from these groups," she gestured around the room, "but it would have been someone higher up." She inhaled. Talking this much in front of people was taxing for her. "It may not be much, but why would someone care to look at all of those?"

"That's good, Solanna. Very good," Toril replied, the wheels in his brain already turning. Solanna notably blushed and tucked her head, glad to be done with her piece. If Iridienne didn't know better, she'd say Toril had a soft spot for this quiet woman who spent more time with plants and pipettes than she did people. Iridienne smiled a bit to herself.

"Okay, so we need to figure out whose number this is, then, right? Maybe that will open up a lead?" Iridienne offered, hopeful.

"Sounds like," Toril agreed.

Collectively, it wasn't much, but Toril had an easy confidence and a way of presenting information, so it seemed better or more than it was. Iridienne was grateful for that; at least it would buy them some time.

"Okay, we have a potential *why* and *who* from different directions. That's something. Good job, team." Toril nodded.

They barely had a minute to breathe before the door hissed open on the back wall. Astor came in with an entourage of attendees, scientists, and others scampering in his wake. Everyone in the room shifted, sat up a little straighter, faced the front a bit more, even Donar.

"Good morning, teams. I hope you have something for me. One by one, the groups will be called into this backroom for a brief report, then excused to carry on with your work."

Someone from a different group raised their hand. "Excuse me, sir?"

"Yes?"

"With all due respect, wouldn't it be more beneficial for the groups to hear each other's reports? The collaboration might spark some new ideas."

Some nodded in agreement; others glanced around, uncertain how the Governor would respond. Iridienne couldn't remember anyone directly questioning the Governor's orders. The room was notably cinched.

Astor smirked, an angry hairline fracture showing on his polished facade.

"Perhaps, Mister. . .Anil, is it? What I don't want, and what, quite frankly, Tabrass and her citizens don't have time for, is everyone chasing each other's trails instead of their own. Everything that is decided for Tabrass is done with thorough consideration and not just for her survival but betterment." Astor had been pacing slowly, words deliberate, then he stopped. "So, no, this is not show and tell with the class today."

Anil sat without another word, face visibly incredulous, but he bowed his head in understanding and acknowledgment of the Governor's statement.

"Now that is cleared up, Group One, you're up. Move with purpose, please." Astor held his hand palm up and gestured for them to follow. A couple of his security attendants were left in the room by the door. Even still, the room breathed a sigh of relief once they separated into the next room.

"Well, that was tense," Toril said what they were all thinking. Today had almost been too much for Solanna. Iridienne put a hand on Solanna's shoulder, hoping to extend some resolve to her.

In her head, Iridienne tried to find the silver lining, tried to maintain hope. But she couldn't get Cyrus's words, now more like a prophecy and promise, out of her head: *The more you know, the more responsibility you carry.*

"I'm sure he has his reasons. We all want the attacks to stop, for Tabrass and our people to be safe. There are just different opinions about how to go about it," Iridienne offered, half trying to convince herself. Her teammates considered what she said, but doubt's quickly growing seed had taken root, and Astor's response watered the ground.

"After all, why would he lie?" Iridienne asked.

Donar replied, "Why would he not?"

CHAPTER 13

Outside, her thoughts didn't feel suffocating.

After being in a string of tense meetings and coming up empty-handed on her search for answers, being in the courtyard made her feel like she could think. She could release the ideas to the sky when she was ready, like she could breathe without sucking in the recycled thoughts again and again.

Iridienne sat next to the flowers outside after the group had given their report and then split up to go about their own work and simultaneous investigations. She was replaying the interaction back in her head, trying to reconcile her perceptions with others' comments and the incoming reality of the situation.

Astor had seemed pleased with Solanna's findings, encouraging them to pursue those avenues further and offering a meeting with one of his security personnel to cross-reference the ID number. But Donar's contribution was received more like an accusation in the small meeting room.

Iridienne watched Astor's reaction intently, partially hoping to quell the uncomfortable bubble of wariness. As hopeful as she was, she also knew she had to be as objective as she could, even if the nudges were pointing her in a direction she didn't want to go.

She wanted to give Donar credit; he delivered his part as diplomatically, albeit as succinctly as possible, but it still struck a chord.

Astor stared at Donar and then said, "If my memory of our history serves me correctly, those types of thoughts turned into an invitation to the gallows. Tread carefully." The four of them, even Donar, were shocked at the directness of what was a thinly veiled warning.

Her temples throbbed at the memory of Astor's threat as she held her head in her hands. Then she shoved the stubborn stray strands behind her ear that escaped her low twisted bun at the memory of Astor's hand touching her hair. If motive is one of the things they were supposed to uncover, the only thing becoming clear was that motives were murky at best.

"I thought I'd find you here," Soleil said gently, trying not to startle Iridienne.

Iridienne looked up, shaking free of her own thoughts.

"Oh, Soleil. I'm really glad to see you." She reached out to touch her arm. She laughed a little to herself. "I am that predictable, aren't I?"

Soleil smiled as she sat down. "I assume you can't spend years working under the open air and not still long for it at times. The sky doesn't have a ceiling." She glanced up. "Well, not entirely anyway."

Iridienne suddenly felt the abrupt burn of tears brimming along the edges of her lids. She was grateful for Soleil's tenderness and friendship, for someone was who they were without the undercurrent of other intentions.

The tears came quietly, rolling rivers that tracked the curves of her face, disappearing in the black fabric of her uniform. Iridienne didn't bother to stop them, and Soleil stood quiet guard as Iridienne cried, mourning for things she didn't quite have words for yet.

"I just expected things to be so different. Every other year, Immune are picked out, and then it's just. . .normal. And now? Nothing is the same. Nothing," Iridienne said when she was able to find her voice, sorrow cracking in the syllables. "I don't know what I'm doing. I don't know how or why we're being attacked at all. It feels like everyone—my team, my friends, the Governor, for sky's sake—expects me to have answers. And I have none. I'm just a field worker!" Then quietly, "But all I know is the more I hear, the less it seems Tabrass is functioning for the good of *all*."

"It's not fair. But it's the lot that's been rolled," Soleil agreed solemnly. Then, boldly for her, she added, "But if someone can navigate the coming storms and not lose sight of what's at stake, it's you, Rids."

Iridienne sat there shocked, salty trails still drying on her face.

Soleil continued, "Others see it too. Which is understandable, but remember who was there in the beginning. Those are the ones you trust because where you're headed, you can't go alone." She reached over and took her hand.

"There are still answers to find. And this place and its people are worth protecting. Maybe the greater good is allowing others to be part of the solution with you."

Iridienne lunged into a hug, burying her face in Soleil's shoulder. Soleil laughed, a bit shocked, and then returned the embrace.

When Iridienne pulled back, Soleil reached into her pocket and slipped something small and metal onto the table.

Her voice was barely above a whisper, gentle and constant still, but there was a weight of urgency in the tone. "There is a place that may have some answers for you. There's a storage room in one of the lower levels that has undigitized documents that contain information not in the main databases. Level X is logged as a route to bulk storage, so foot traffic is sparse and camera sweeps are batch-reviewed, not live. Level X, Room 1013. Here." Metal scraping metal. Simple, worn brass. A key.

Soleil added, "They monitor the door logs, so you need to have a reason to go down to those levels. But attendees are given master key logs for 'emergency access to secure areas.' I served in Logistics before being promoted to Attendancy, so I have a better understanding of the channels than some other attendants. Down there, this level's doors are. . .analog, if you will. Hence, *that*." She eyed the key.

"If this is a door you choose to open, we can go to the subterranean loading levels together, and if anyone asks, it's because you wanted to understand the shipping frequencies as part of your sector."

Iridienne blinked rapidly to keep her eyes from widening into saucers, locking her lips together in a thin line to keep from gaping. She looked up at the muddy sky, flashes of Cyrus, Rhomy, Cirro and Cirrus, her parents circled in her mind like fragments in a current.

What answers did they deserve?

Soleil took her fingers off the key, and Iridienne replaced them with her own, scraping metal backwards to her, slipping the key into her bag.

"Keep the information close for now, Iridienne," Soleil said as she stood. In a louder, more formal voice, she added, "Per your request, we'll tour the shipping and loading levels tomorrow. Like light, ma'am."

Iridienne snorted at the formality. "Through water, Sol."

CHAPTER 14

Iridienne's eyes stared wide at the ceiling long into the night after she was home, replaying her conversation with Soleil. She wondered if she said too much, if she let her emotions get the best of her. She trusted Soleil, but most things felt complicated now. She kept revisiting the image of the key Soleil gave her. Where did she get it, and why were there documents that were undigitized? She pulled her familiar tote from beside the bed up on top of the rumpled comforter. Her fingers visited the brass key in her bag, tracing the teeth like braille, hoping for an answer.

Once she eventually dozed off, Iridienne dreamed about Cyrus, his broad body still in his fatigues wrapped around her as she slept, her back to his chest. There, her breaths didn't snag like being caught in her ribs. She woke up missing him, feeling the weight of his presence with her.

"*Today,*" she thought. "*He should be back today.*"

For her though, today was the day she and Soleil would visit the shipping levels in the Taxalis.

Iridienne could make the walk to the giant inky eye-shaped building without a second thought, so her brain wandered, skipping between thoughts and questions like a stone on water. Worn buildings, shifting dirt, kids laughing, a song being hummed in the distance. Her concentration broke when she registered the familiar silhouette on the bench up ahead.

Rhomy.

Iridienne broke into a jog towards her friend, who sat ever faithfully at their typical meeting point.

"Hey! What are you doing here?" Iridienne said, catching her breath. Then suddenly, "We didn't plan a meet up, right? I didn't forget?"

Rhomy laughed and shook her head. "No, we hadn't planned anything. I knew you came this way, so I figured I could catch you on the way to work."

The two friends embraced. Iridienne felt a lump form in her throat. There had been so much happening that they had hardly seen each other. An ache for simpler times lingered between them.

"I think everyone is still planning to make it to the Pit tomorrow; are you still coming?" Rhomy asked as they sat back on the bench together.

"Yeah, I wouldn't miss it. I already put in a special leave request that was approved before the latest order of increased hours. Cy should be back today, too." She sighed. "Something normal sounds really nice."

"I mean this in the nicest way possible, but you look tired, Rids. Everything solid?"

Iridienne smiled weakly back at her friend and then to the ground. "I am. Very. I can't talk about it much." She trailed off. Then suddenly, she blurted quietly, teeth clenched, "I almost wish I had never been chosen. This wasn't what I thought it would be. I have no idea what I'm doing, and all I want is for the people I care about to be safe, and that's proving to be the one thing I can't control."

Rhomy put her head on Iridienne's shoulder and her arm around her back. "You are not in this alone, Rids." The friends sat shoulder to shoulder, Iridienne roughly wiping her nose and Rhomy gently rubbing her back. Once the tears stopped falling, Rhomy looked over at Iridienne and added, "You know, solving the world's problems is more of a collective effort anyway," nudging her friend.

Iridienne shook her head and groaned. Wasn't that what Soleil told her the day before? "You're right. You've always been the wise one in this friendship." She looked up and sighed at the sky.

"Well, I mean, if you insist. . ." Rhomy jokingly flipped her hair and made a face, and the two laughed like the world wasn't upending, at least for a moment.

"Thanks for waiting for me, Rhomy. I've missed you."

"Anytime, friend. I got you. But for now, we both better be off to work." Rhomy patted Iridienne's knee as she stood. Iridienne sighed again and pulled herself off the bench.

They hugged a final time, Iridienne squeezing Rhomy extra tight, and they were off in their separate directions with promises to see each other the next night.

As Iridienne finished the distance to the Taxalis, she headed inside and to her office for a quick check-in. She logged into her messages and alerts, seeing an update from Solanna on their review team's channel. Iridienne's eyes scanned the screen, as the soft blue glow haloed her face.

A rap at the door made Iridienne jump. As she straightened her collar and her spine, she raised her voice. "Come in."

The door opened to reveal Soleil standing, poised with a faint composed smile. "Good morning, Iridienne."

"Morning, Sol. Come in, please."

"Very well. Are you ready for our tour this morning?" she asked as if she were taking Iridienne on a tour of the bathrooms.

"Yes, let me finish this message, and we can go." Iridienne finished typing her response to Solanna and the rest of the team. She grabbed a journal and pen off her desk and added them to her bag with the key still tucked safely inside. Before they left, Soleil handed Iridienne a faraday bag, nodding to her datapad. Iridienne frowned but didn't question it, slipping the device into the pouch and closing the flap.

Then, Iridienne and Soleil made their way to the levels underground.

Whether Soleil was nervous, Iridienne couldn't tell. Not a hair was out of place, not even a nervous tremor shook a finger as she poked and swiped on her datapad. Soleil regaled Iridienne with background information on the shipping and loading protocols and frequencies, mundane information to anyone catching a wave passing by and covering their real reasons pretty well. Iridienne was hoping to move through the hallways without garnering too much attention, and thankfully, it seemed like it worked. Once they were in the elevators, Soleil punched in the code for the shipping level. The elevator sank slowly, humming past the main lab levels until the panel flashed Level V: Loading & Freight. Soleil glanced over her shoulder. "Ready, ma'am?"

The doors opened to a wash of mechanical noise and cold, metallic air. Soleil punched another quick code in before they stepped out. Once the doors closed, they could hear the elevator ascend back up.

Crates stamped with supply numbers were being slid across the bay by a pair of loaders in uniform. The space was cavernous and heavy with the smell of ozone and lubricant, the sound of pulleys and docking clamps echoing off the walls. Soleil moved with the poise of someone who belonged there, issuing a few clipped instructions to a nearby technician about delayed shipments, something about atmospheric filters being logged incorrectly. Iridienne realized it wasn't small talk; Soleil was manufacturing a reason for them to linger.

When the technician turned to check his console, Soleil leaned close and murmured, "Access door behind the compressor stack. It'll take you to the lower maintenance stairwell. Trust this next part, please. You'll need to act dizzy."

Iridienne blinked. "Okay."

"Ma'am, are you okay?" Soleil elevated her voice to catch the room's echo.

Iridienne snapped into character. Her eyes fluttered, and she stumbled, trying her best to look disoriented. Some of the technicians paused their movements to look over.

"The ozone filtering seems thicker down here. She's not used to the density of the smell," Soleil explained with believable concern.

Iridienne had her hands on her knees, taking exaggerated breaths.

"Excuse me, a response, please. She's one of the newest Epitopes! Can we get her some air. . .is there an exit close by?" Soleil's voice carried with urgency.

That revelation made several workers jump to attention, and a gangly man closed the distance to them in three strides, stumbling over his words.

"Yes, of course, the air filters down here are due for a swap. Uh, yes, right over here, there's a stairwell that's connected to a different filtration system. Please. . ." He gestured over to a door close by, glancing back nervously as Soleil collected Iridienne who still was feigning being faint.

"Right here, ma'am. There's a landing with a bench here she can rest on. One floor up, you can access one of the main elevators back to the surface floors."

"This will do. Thank you, Mr.," Soleil looked closer at his badge, "Mr. Braon."

"Thank you for your kindness," Iridienne added, with breathy sincerity.

The man nodded his head and stumbled over some more formalities as Soleil ushered Iridienne through the door and to the bench. She made sure the door closed with a haunting echo before they broke character.

"I can't believe that worked. How did you know that was going to work?" Iridienne whispered sharply.

Soleil paused for a moment and said, "I didn't. It was a calculated risk."

Iridienne stared wildly, mouth agape, studying Soleil's face. Soleil simply offered a prim shrug, and Iridienne sat back, head on the wall, snorted softly and shook her head.

"Well, here we are. Where do we go from here?" Iridienne eventually asked.

"You'll go down one level, turn left when you open the door. Look for Room 1013."

Iridienne sat up abruptly.

"That was singular, Soleil. Are you not coming with me?"

"No, I still have my datapad with me, and I have a scheduled meeting in an hour. I'll go back upstairs, and confirm the story if anyone asks," Soleil replied.

"Why the faraday bag?" Iridienne asked.

"Just being prepared," Soleil said simply.

Iridienne exhaled hard and stood up. "Well, this is it, I guess. . .Wait, how do I get back? I can't exactly go through this door again." She threw a hand up at the door in front of them.

"No, you can't. If you go up seven levels from here in the stairwell, you'll come out on the datacenter floor. I'll see what I can do to get the camera in the hallway offline for a bit or scrub the footage. It has limited traffic, so slip in through the door as quickly as you can. Then. . .carry on."

Iridienne's head swirled with information and questions, about Soleil, about this room, all of it. She opened her mouth twice, hoping words would pour out in a pattern that made sense. Even with all the uncertainty, she knew she couldn't go back because she didn't have the answers. But maybe this room down there did. Like a branch rubbing on the window, the nagging won out in her mind. She stood with a resolute sigh.

"Okay then. Like light, Sol."

"Through water, Rids."

The two parted in opposite directions, and Iridienne descended the metal stairs, one cautious step at a time, until the hum of machinery thinned into silence and the lights above her faded to amber.

Level X was not frequented and, from what she could tell, was a glorified storage floor. This space had the staleness of an uninhabited home. It was a little dimmer, a little duller, a little sadder. Further down the hall, she found the door waiting for her.

Room 1013. She unlocked the door and opened it slowly, trying not to wake the hinges. Once inside, she pulled it closed with a soft click and locked it from the inside.

Motion-sensored lights buzzed on, sleepy from a long hibernation. Boxes upon boxes in rowed shelving units met her as she surveyed the room. "*If anyone asks why I was here, I can always say I was chasing leads related to the attacks,*" she reasoned. The rub of her shoes on the floor even felt too loud in the stillness.

Iridienne walked slowly down the aisles, eyes moving methodically up and down the boxes. She noted the label names were mainly date ranges, some reaching back decades. She fought the feeling of real vertigo at the overwhelming task waiting for her under the lids.

Iridienne decided to survey the room, get an idea for at least the label names, and then decide where to start from there. Once she made her way further in the dimly lit room, she noticed a few toward the back were labeled differently. Some had names instead of dates. *Project Silver, Lux Iterations, Iterum Schematics. Bioethics II.* A few others had combinations of letters and numbers; Iridienne assumed codes for. . .something. She sighed. Starting here with this stack seemed more manageable, and if she were being honest, more interesting—at least based on the names—and she could cross-reference the date ranges from the other boxes if she found anything in this stack. As good a place to start as any.

She grabbed the top box of the six sitting there, *Lux Iterations,* and positioned herself on the floor under the direct overhead lighting to see better. Lux. Iridienne immediately thought of the old rhyme they would sing as kids playing next to the fields:

Lux is bright and lights the way,
We'll see it soon, soon one day.
Give your drop and close your eyes,
The crop still grows, the storm still cries.

They would sing and dance in a circle, and after the last line, they would let out big, fake boo-hoos and fall down and laugh. Iridienne remembered asking her mom one day what "lux" meant as she skipped and sang around their little apartment as a girl.

Her mom smiled and said simply, "It's an old, old word. From long before our time. It means 'light.'"

Back in the present, Iridienne rubbed her hands across her face and through her hair, bringing herself back to the task at hand.

"*Lux Iterations. Versions of light. . .*" she thought. Maybe all the box contained was boring strains of weather algorithms, but she was curious, nonetheless.

Once she pulled the contents out and scooted the box away, she immediately noticed she wasn't wrong about the strains of algorithms. The majority of the information looked like reports and memos with formulas. Chemistry and weather engineering were never something she particularly cared to study at length in school, but these were definitely trials for something. One particularly thick folder she pulled out of the box was labeled: *Iterations 1–2,418*. Iridienne looked through the sheets and then fanned them out like a flipbook. Every single sheet in the folder was emblazoned with a red stamp that read: FAILURE.

I'm guessing these are formulas they were testing? For. . .?

She kept searching through the papers and files looking for an answer but was coming up short on what the 2,418 failures were for. She checked her watch; three hours had passed already. She let out an audible exhale.

"Okay, Lux. Seems like it wasn't working out anyway. Let's table you for a bit and see what else we can find," Iridienne mumbled to the stack of papers she was reloading back into the dusty box and set it off to the side.

A muffled rattle from outside the room seized her chest, tight and sharp as pointed anxiety coursed through her body. She froze. Ears straining to hear any semblance of a threat just outside the wall. Blood thumped in her ears as she reasoned maybe it was just the pipes or clanking from another floor through the vents.

Once she realized no one was coming on a raid through the door, she picked up the next bunch in the stacked tower labeled *Project Silver*. Iridienne opened the lid and thumbed through the folders stuffed full of papers, pulled out a stack, and began her search.

Once she started looking through the papers, she realized they were heavily redacted, too. Memos, research, various correspondence, reports, they all dealt with the same rejected experimental findings different than the Lux formulas, though. Again, so much of it had been blotted. The only decent information she uncovered was a date range that started over two decades before and spanned roughly eight years.

Was this an experiment for crops? More weather experimentation or coding? She had flipped through almost an entire folder, skimming the words that were visible until one caught her attention: "patient."

"So this was an experiment with people? Experiment for what?" she thought to herself.

Iridienne was trying to hold on to a hem of hope that she wasn't going to find something ominous, maybe she'd find that Tabrass and the Taxalis tried to help their people in whatever this was, but she couldn't shake the weight in her stomach that the more she dug, the more dirt she would find.

This was more than what she found in the other box, so at least she had a hint of something, a thread to pull. She began back at the top of the stack of papers she had been through, this time looking for information that involved people specifically. So many of the papers were blacked out to the point that the document was pointless. She scanned documents and took notes of even the smallest finds. After flipping through countless papers, she found one that mentioned "treatment" and another that was dated much later in the experiment range that noted "symptoms," although those were redacted, too.

"Okay, fresh eyes, fresh eyes. What am I missing?"

Iridienne leaned against the wall behind her, letting out a massive sigh. Her hips ached from sitting on the ground, and the prickly sting of blood returning to her feet traveled sharply up her veins as she stretched her legs out over the piles of blacked-out lines.

She subconsciously checked the time on her old watch, which triggered another memory of her mom. Maybe it was a combination of the what-ifs and treatments she was looking for or just the watch itself, but she thought about the last time she saw it on her mom's wrist. It was the day she died. Her mom was insistent, as much as she could without being able to breathe, about staying home where she was comfortable.

They're not doing anything for me at the medical center anyway, she had said.

Iridienne's dad, doing his best to curb his grief, acquiesced to his wife's request. A final show of dedication for the great love of his life.

Okay, Iris, we'll keep you right here. I won't leave your side, Iridienne recalled, her father, Avi, telling her mother. Iris patted his hand and smiled through the wheezing.

Iridienne remembered sitting vigil by her bed, telling her mom stories by request, and her dad holding her mom's hand until her lungs didn't fill with a shaky breath again; although, the sickness made her skin look blue-gray and lifeless long before.

Iridienne missed her parents terribly, even after all these years. After her mom died, Iridienne's dad never really recovered. He did his best to take care of her, but once Iridienne turned eighteen, the birthday he gave her the watch, he disappeared a week later with a simple note: "*I've gone to where the Irises grow.*"

For years, she'd believed grief was what finally broke him. Sitting among sealed boxes and redacted lines, she wondered if her mother's death had simply been the last thing the Taxalis asked of him.

Iridienne rubbed her hands across her face and strained eyes. Her story was just one of countless in the Tabrass community. She couldn't change the past, but she could honor the ones whose stories were just another footnote or memory or maybe even a redacted line.

Iridienne pulled herself back from the edge of grief.

"Okay, back to this. I need to reevaluate. What do I have? Is there another direction, another variable?" Iridienne mumbled to herself. She sat there waving her feet, eyes staring distantly at the ceiling as her thoughts roved from place to place.

Iridienne spread the folders across the floor, pages overlapping like scales. Black bars swallowed entire paragraphs; only fragments survived, dates, initials, the occasional word that meant nothing on its own. She angled her datapad for better light.

The device blinked once, then again. A quiet chime broke the silence.

"Unidentified checksum detected. Attempt to decrypt?"

Her pulse jumped. She hadn't initiated any scan. She hadn't even touched the screen.

The line blinked again:

"Unidentified checksum detected. Attempt to decrypt?"

She hesitated, then tapped *yes*. The datapad processed for a breath and projected a skeletal string of data, partial code, broken slashes, and a header half-visible:

/Iterum/Project-13X: Restricted

Before she could blink, the screen dimmed and asked for authentication:

"Decryption requires passphrase."

A passphrase. For ancient paper? She almost laughed. Then she saw it. The uneven lighting in the room made it hard to see. The faint phrase embossed lightly in the bottom margin of several pages, decorative, almost invisible under the grime: "*For the days to come.*"

Her breath caught. Soleil had said those familiar words recently, almost prayer-like.

That guess was as good as any. Iridienne typed the phrase in.

The datapad pulsed, light rippling outward like water. Files unfolded across the screen, schematics, medical logs, and a single document stamped in red:

HUMAN TRIAL SERIES: EPITOPE / EXODUS

She stared until the glow burned her eyes. *Why were these things hidden? With passwords or encryption? What are they hiding?* There was a date range she noted on one of the research reports, which means there was an end. She let out a quick huff, mustering up another surge of energy now that she had a new trail to chase. *How and why did the experiment end?*

The box had been relatively organized chronologically, and there was a final stack of papers and a thin file she hadn't made it through yet. Despite the minimal information she had found so far, she was hopeful for another crumb of intel.

The majority of the stack wasn't any help, but the second-to-last paper had an interesting partial line: "Bioethics transfer" and "Exodus Protocol."

As in "the" Exodus? Like what we're prepping for now? Transfer. . .? Could that be how this finished? They switched directions? So, they. . .gave up on finding a treatment or a cure?

Iridienne checked the time; hours had gone by. She needed to go back upstairs. She made a few more notes in her notebook and began tidying up the years of paperwork back into its familiar container. She stood and stretched her arms out over her head, bent over, and lugged the box back to its stack. Dust scattered as she dropped it down on the top.

Then, she slipped the datapad in her faraday bag. Hopefully, that would keep the files safe until she could look at them again.

A mixture of excitement and dread settled in. This was something, but these answers were essentially just questions multiplied. She felt like she was chiseling at mortar, soon to start moving the stones that held the foundation of what she thought she knew about her home.

CHAPTER 15

The beads of sweat formed on her forehead, others traveling down the road of her spine almost immediately as Iridienne stepped outside.

Her senses went on high alert; the humidity was like trying to breathe through a wet cloth.

"A storm?"

Then a low growl in the air caused Iridienne to turn and put her hand up as an awning over her eyes. It wasn't thunder that she heard, though. A smile fanned across her face as she exhaled a sigh of relief. It was Cyrus's squadron descending to the flight platforms. If there was a storm, an attack, coming, he was back at least. He was home.

It would be a couple more hours at least before he was finished with the digital records and debriefing, but she was glad she picked up a tin of his favorite tea because he always came to see her first when he landed.

Then, her datapad dinged a polite alert from her bag. She slung her tote around and dug the tablet out to see a flash on the screen.

Attention all Taxalis personnel: Storm watch until further notice. Response measures activated.

So, she was right.

Another attack must be forming, but they were attempting to counteract it, I guess? A gust of wind blew sideways across her face. The air pressed down like a held breath. The further from the Taxalis she walked, the more fatigue settled on her shoulders.

Once she was home, she dropped her items on the counter, made a cup of warm tea, and plopped down on the couch by the window. She dozed off almost immediately once she sat down. In the purgatory between dreams and reality, she felt the warm hold of a hand on her face, the stroke of rough fingers moving her hair from her forehead. She nuzzled in closer to the gentleness of the feeling on her cheek.

"Rids," the voice said softly. "Rids," it said again, unrushed.

Her eyes fluttered open to Cyrus kneeling beside her, his fingers tracing the soft curves of her jaw, tucking her hair behind her ear.

Iridienne breathed a smile at seeing his face and turned to kiss his scarred palm. "Hey, Cy. I'm so glad you're home." She held his hand in place on her face.

Cyrus's eyes creased with a smile. "Me too, Rids." He sat down next to her, moving her legs to drape across his. "Long day?"

Iridienne's eyes were still heavy with sleep, and she sucked in a breath as she readjusted a bit, her mind remembering the winding searches through the folders earlier that day. She propped her head on her hand, elbow resting on the arm of the seat. "Mhmm. Tell me about your flight. My brain is still waking up. . ." She trailed off.

Cyrus leaned his head back on the couch. "Sure, it wasn't particularly exciting though. Normal route stuff. Raff's still off, but a surprisingly easy flight."

Iridienne nodded, making a sound to acknowledge the Rafferty comment.

She added, "I'm sure you saw that alert that said 'response measures' were activated for some kind of storm brewing?"

"Yeah, I saw that as we were landing. From what I understand, the Taxalis is deploying countermeasures based on the weather modification technologies that got us here in the first place," Cyrus said. "It seems to be working for now," he added, "but it's a temporary patch at best."

Iridienne nodded.

"The depots are just about full, Rids. The Exodus Protocol has to be imminent. I'm not sure what else they're waiting on," Cyrus added heavily.

They sat quietly, both lost to their own thoughts for a minute, pondering the weight of what this meant.

"I wanted to process some stuff with you that I found, actually. I think it's something. . .something big." Cyrus sat back up and turned to her. "It's interesting that you mentioned that—the Exodus Protocol. I found something about it," Iridienne said.

"Found something? Where?"

Iridienne explained about Soleil and the key, Level X, the room, and the paper files she found. The longer she talked, Cyrus sat more erect, leaning forward, listening intently and asking questions here and there.

"Most of the information was redacted. Like so much, it was basically just pages and pages of black lines. I was hitting a dead end, but then I realized something: the reports had a date range, which means the experiment actually ended at some point. So, I started digging again, and near the end of the stack, I found something. Then—Cy, this is the unreal—there was physical metadata on the papers my datapad automatically picked up that required a passphrase. A phrase that was printed, like barely visible, on the papers. All of the content was encrypted. All of it surrounded these two phrases: 'Bioethics transfer' and 'Exodus Protocol.'"

"Wait, what? Why were they redacted, but then more information encrypted somewhere? *The* Exodus Protocol?" Cyrus was leaning forward at this point, brain churning through the information Iridienne was detailing.

"I don't know what else it could be," she confirmed. "But then—think about this, Cy—the document used the word 'transfer.' That sounds like they didn't just stop the research. They changed directions. Like they abandoned the whole idea of a cure entirely."

At this point, he sat back with his mouth open slightly, his dark eyes following some invisible pattern, trying to make sense of what this meant.

"Another question that I couldn't figure out was why these files aren't digitized and in the system?"

"I don't know. If they didn't want the information to be openly available, they could set the security clearances to limit the accessibility. This seems like they don't want people to know about this at all. And I can understand why. . ." Cyrus trailed off. Then quietly, "Rids, if this is true, how many people have died because of this. . .it would cause another coup if people knew."

Iridienne nodded past the grief and anger welling in her throat, at the loss of her mom, how many people who sat vigil while someone they loved died. "I think that's what is happening now. These attacks have to be connected."

"It sounds like it," Cyrus agreed.

"I don't know what they hope to gain—whoever Hostis is—from the storms and stuff unless it's punishment, but if the attacks really *are* connected, their anger might make more sense. Not their actions. But, wars have happened for less."

They sat for a bit in silence, her head on his shoulder, when Cyrus sat up abruptly, an idea downloading.

"Where did you say the room was? What level again?"

"Level X, Room 1013."

"1013?" he said again.

"Mhmm. Why? What's up?" Iridienne asked.

"It might be nothing, but you know how Raff has been. . .different lately? He's been reckless and mad, like defiant. But during a debrief last week, he was doodling on a paper, and he wrote and circled '1013X' in the corner. He was sitting next to me, and those debriefs can be. . .redundant. He was restless and sketching other schematics and notes in the margins. I wasn't intentionally trying to look, but normally, he just draws and sketches random things. Later, he ripped the paper out, tore it, and tossed it. I didn't think much of it at first, but now. . ."

"Peeking at papers, hm?" Iridienne tried to joke, but neither of them felt like laughing.

"That can't be a coincidence. 1013X? That doesn't connect with anything in our jobs."

Iridienne and Cyrus were both uneasy. It wasn't a secret that Raff carried wounds from losing his parents to the coughs, though he spoke little of it. If he knew that a search for a cure was abandoned, it might explain the additive of disdain.

"But where would he have gotten that information? The room and the content inside seem to be off record. At least to most. I haven't asked, and she hasn't offered, but I don't know why or how Soleil knew or why she chose to tell me. Do you think she's connected? Surely it can't only be her who knows about this?" Iridienne was beginning to spiral.

"Valid questions. I have no idea." He turned to face Iridienne, reaching for her hand to steady her before he asked the next question. "If we pull at this, are you ready for what we'll find?"

She sat quietly, sadly, for a moment, even though she knew her answer already.

"No, but we can't pretend like we can function in ignorance anymore either."

"More responsibility," Cyrus echoed.

"I wish we knew if we were opening something that couldn't be shut before we did it." Iridienne fell back against the couch.

"Would that change your choice?" Cyrus asked.

"No. But we'd know a little more about the storm that could come after."

Cyrus nodded, expression distant.

"Cy, I almost forgot. Sorry, I'm working through a backwards timeline, apparently, but I didn't tell you how my group's debrief went." She paused and continued slowly, "Which I'm realizing there's a connection here." Her brain was churning through the increasingly tangled implications.

Iridienne filled Cyrus in on the tense interaction with Donar, his perceived interest in cough treatments, and then Solanna's finding of the upper-level login accessing the testing files. Cyrus stared intently, soaking in the information, becoming more fidgety as she continued. He was obviously gaining speed in putting pieces of this abstract together.

"Rids, I have clearance to see whose ID number that is. I can look. And the Donar thing, that guy is. . .like swallowing sand, but it can't be a coincidence that he noted something with the cough cures too."

"Yeah, I know, you're right. Donar, the ID, the boxes, they're all connected, I think. The thing I can't square up, though, is how Soleil comes into all of this. She obviously knows more than she's told me."

Cyrus nodded. "It's a purposeful risk, but she's done nothing to make you distrust her. If anything, she's helping. I wouldn't trust her blindly, but she's not given a reason to warrant suspicion, you know?"

Suddenly, Iridienne had an idea. "I wonder if it was by chance at all that Soleil was assigned to me or if it was intentional," she thought out loud.

"Maybe, it's possible. At this point, we're dusting off the surface to a much deeper story here, Rids. I have a feeling we're going to find more than we ever wanted to. The thing we have to remember, what I tell my team, even, is that we have to remember the mission. Remember the 'why.' Why are we doing this? Why do we care? Why?"

"Because truth isn't a commodity. Or it shouldn't be. People are worth the truth and worth saving. If we say 'for the benefit of all,' then it should mean *all*. We don't have an 'all' without the ones who make it. A collective all, a collective 'better' means everyone, not just the special ones. The idea of the 'unified all' is nullified if some are exempt," Iridienne said back.

Cyrus smiled at her and lowered his head for a moment. He loved her. How injustice and integrity ignited that spark in her. How she believed every word she just said. She had a way of believing in a wild hope that made it seem reachable.

Cyrus looked back at her. "Okay then. I'll find the name, and you keep digging through those boxes."

CHAPTER 16

For the first time in their friendship, Iridienne beat Rhomy to the bench the next day.

The opaque sky was starting to dim, and Iridienne was feeling antsy in her apartment. She couldn't focus and found herself fidgety and pacing, so she headed out early, notebook in hand. It was easier to think, being out under the open air. She could find her way to the familiar meeting place in the dark, so she let her mind go on autopilot as she meandered to the worn seat she frequented through the years.

She dusted the rough surface off a bit and sat with an exhale. Iridienne flipped through the pages of her journal, dancing between her notes and ideas, each pairing resulting in more questions, pen spinning in her fingers. She was actually looking forward to digging through more files and boxes, and she was entertaining the idea of going in over her days off to keep momentum in hopes of finding an answer to the relentless questions. It was like she woke the dead, and they wouldn't let her rest until she settled the matter—whatever that matter was.

She tapped her pen, circling and recircling the words "Bioethics" and "Exodus." Those were the most distinct trails. Iridienne held them close, though. Like she and Cyrus talked about, she wouldn't share this with her smaller group, Donar, Solanna, and Toril, just yet. Give them just enough information to satisfy; don't overshare. She didn't like the feeling of partial truths, but she also agreed full truths weren't right here either. Not now.

Her concentration was broken by a familiar voice.

"Rids? First time for everything, huh?" Rhomy called to her, laughing.

Rhomy was notably shocked as she walked up to find Iridienne sitting jokingly smug at their familiar checkpoint.

"Seems like the theme nowadays," Iridienne replied, standing up to hug her friend.

"I needed some air to think, so I figured I'd wait for you. Cy said the guys were headed to the Pit from the platforms. I'm glad we get to head out there together," Iridienne said as she lay her head on top of her friend's as they started their walk to pick up Cirro and Cirrus on the way.

"Me too!" Rhomy said with a hop in her step. "Even if it's just a walk over there together, it'll feel like old times."

Before too long, they were knocking at the twins' door. "Headed out!" they heard a muffled voice yell inside the apartment. Then coughing. A ragged, wrecking cough. Iridienne and Rhomy shifted uncomfortably, glancing at each other. The coughing eventually subsided, replaced with the sounds of a throat clearing and hushed tones of calming assurances.

Rhomy chewed on the inside of her cheek, and Iridienne ran her fingers across the overlapping scars on her palm as they waited.

Cirrus opened the door with a wide smile and a tired face. Cirro was right behind his brother, eyes bloodshot from the coughing.

Rhomy wasted no time wrapping her arms around the first brother's neck. "There are my favorite guys!"

Rhomy had always been sensitive to protecting others, combating her fears with hopeful optimism that bordered on avoidance. Iridienne tried to hide the ache for her friends because even as close as they all were, they hadn't navigated sickness like this together until now.

The four friends exchanged hugs and made their way to meet the rest of the group. They walked leisurely, trying not to exhaust Cirro without making that reason obvious to him. The group caught each other up on their most recent days and peppered Iridienne with questions about the sandstorm.

Cirro, Cirrus, and Rhomy were enthralled with Iridienne's story, eyes locked on their friend as she layered the details of the storm. Iridienne's ability to note and retain details only aided her storytelling abilities. Her hands danced out in front of her as she spoke. At one point, she was walking backwards, facing her friends, eyes wide as she explained the most intense point of the storm.

The friends exchanged glances and offered acknowledgments of surprise and shock as Iridienne continued her retelling. She added particularly favorable descriptions of Cyrus and his chivalry, pretending to swoon as she described being pinned to the dirt. In reality, she and Cyrus were terrified, but sometimes stories needed to be an escape, so that was the gift she offered her friends, and they weren't the wiser.

"Then we were immediately called into a meeting back at the Taxalis. Cyrus cleaned up nicely. I'm pretty sure I still have grit on my scalp, though," she laughed, concluding her story.

"That is wild, Rids!" Cirrus laughed. "But, truly, I'm so glad you're okay. Finding out you've got special blood *and* getting caught in two rogue storms seems. . ." He trailed off, unable to find the word.

"It's something," she snorted, agreeing. "Not sure what to make of it yet, but as long as I can still make it to the Pit with you guys, I'm doing alright." She shouldered him a bit with a wink. Cirrus put his arm around her shoulder and squeezed while Iridienne walked arm in arm with Rhomy. Cirro was trying his best to hide the wheeze that had become his companion recently; he offered non-verbal responses, but the extended walking gripped the lung capacity he had left. Unspoken and organically, the group slowed their pace to accommodate their friend and brother while maintaining a sense of dignity. Cirrus noted the kindness, and it almost broke his heart.

Eventually, the group started to see the glow from the fire up ahead.

"Oh, someone's already here! Yay!" Rhomy hopped. Then the currents of conversation carried over, men's voices interchanging laughs and jokes back and forth.

"Well, hello, gentlemen. If it's not the best-looking flyers in Tabrass," Rhomy announced. "Thanks for starting the fire."

Torrey and Rays pretend-saluted with a "Ma'am." Rafferty bowed regally and came up with a wink. Cyrus flashed a grin as he loaded more wood on the fire.

The friends exchanged handshakes and hugs, and Cyrus wrapped Iridienne up in his arms and kissed her mouth and then her forehead before she settled around the fire next to Rhomy.

After everyone was settled, Torrey pulled out a battered deck of cards while Rhomy passed around cups. "Alright," he grinned, "same rules as always: if you lose, you owe the group a secret or a song." That earned groans and laughter, especially from Rays, who was infamous for an impressively off-key rendition of an old Tabrass folk song a couple of years earlier.

They had just started the first round when Cirrus noticed Rafferty zoned out, staring into the flames, and said quietly, "Raff, you good, man?" He shook the distance off his face and sat forward. "Yeah, sorry, just thinking about how bad the next surprise storm is going to be." Everyone paused mid-sip or shuffle, glancing at him.

Cyrus had seen an increase in these out-of-character episodes, so he slid in to help smooth it over, "Well, let's hope it doesn't hit tonight, hm? I have a feeling I'm going to win this round."

Torrey dealt the next hand, and Cyrus groaned, slapping down his cards in defeat. Instantly, the group jumped into a chant: "Secret or song! Secret or song!"

"Okay, okay!" Cyrus said, laughing with a sly smile. "Secret."

The group eyed each other, nudging and oohing to egg Cyrus on.

"Let's hear it then!"

Cyrus allotted a drawn-out pause. "I love Iridienne," he said with some theatrical flair.

Iridienne blushed and elbowed him jokingly with an eye roll. Groans were emitted from the group. "That's not a secret! Doesn't count!"

"I wasn't done!" Cyrus interjected. "I have a secret proposal. . ." He was laying the dramatics on thick.

And then he turned and said, "Marry me, Rids." The group fell silent, shocked, all eyes resting on the two of them poised in time. Rhomy stared in gleeful disbelief, and Cirro nudged Cirrus.

"What?" It came out as barely a whisper.

"Marry me, Rids," Cyrus said again, his broad smile widening across his face. "You are my favorite person. We're with our favorite people at our favorite place. Marry me, Rids. Right here, right now."

Against the crackling glow of the fire and the deepened sky, the group's eyes were wide and white, waiting for her second response.

Iridienne's gaze never broke from Cyrus. She traced his face, the lines forming at the corner of his eyes, the way his hair curled easily like a smoke trail. How he gently held her hand in his, and how she never felt safer than with him close by.

She glanced around for a moment before she replied, "Well, where do we stand?"

The group erupted into cheers and shouts of excitement and disbelief. She laughed, wrapping her arms around his neck; he picked her up, swinging her around, cheering himself.

Rhomy immediately jumped into action, organizing where everyone would stand while Rafferty stoked the fire for more light. Torrey stood playing guitar as Cyrus and Iridienne took their places facing one another, flanked on either side by their closest friends.

Cyrus began, "Rids, you are the first person I think of when I wake up, when I land, when I want to tell someone something. You are the complement to the spaces I'm not meant to fill, and I've seen over and over how we're strongest when we're together. I promise to cherish you, listen and support you, protect you with my life, and love you until my last breath."

Deep shadows danced across their side-lit faces. Iridienne responded, "Cy, you are who I trust most. You are my constant, where I feel safest and at home. You are *my* complement in those places I can't fill, and I love celebrating what makes you, you. I promise to honor you, respect you, and adore you all of my days."

They stood, facing each other hand in hand, etching the image of the other aglow with that night for another moment before Cyrus added, "I do have one final surprise."

"Oh?" She raised an eyebrow. "More surprising than a wedding?"

Everyone laughed and shifted where the gravity of the moment had held them.

He pulled something delicate from his pocket; holding the chain by the top, he let it drop, the necklace's charm spinning in the firelight.

Iridienne looked up at him in disbelief, tears beginning to brim. Jewelry was a luxury almost no one had in Tabrass unless it was an heirloom. Iridienne reached up, gently laying the suspended charm on her open hand. It was a golden sun.

"This has been in my family for generations," he said softly. "Now it's yours, Rids. Like I am. Like I always have been. You are my sun."

He draped the necklace around her neck, and her hands instinctively went up to hold it. "It's perfect," she whispered. "This is perfect."

A tear ran down her cheek as he cupped her face and kissed her as his wife by the firelight, surrounded by those dearest to them.

Cheers, shouts, and claps erupted from their friends again. They patted them on the shoulders and back, the light from the fire flickering off of smiles and eyes squinted with laughter.

The group spent the rest of the night telling stories, remembering funny moments they had recalled dozens of times over. Torrey and Cirro took turns playing ebbs and flows of songs that made them go quiet and then pick up into shanty-type work songs they would sing in the fields.

Through the evening, Iridienne traced the feeling of the golden sun in her fingers, feeling the slight weight of something so precious around her neck.

Eventually, they let the fire die down into smoldering embers, heartbeats of red glowing through the cracks of ash and burnt wood. Smoke billowed up into the dirty sky.

Cirrus slapped his knees and stretched his legs out. "Alright, friends, I think that's it for me. As comfy as this log is, my bed is calling my name. 'Ro, you ready?" His twin nodded back, and the brothers rose to leave.

Torrey, Rays, and Raff took note and announced their leave, too. In what had become a ritual at the end of each night at the Pit, the group each scooped handfuls of dirt onto the fire to kill the remaining embers. Their own version of The Letting.

The three airmen headed out first, and Rhomy and the brothers went next. Cyrus and Iridienne were left. He was still sitting on the log with Iridienne sitting on the ground, her head propped on his knee.

"Did you plan tonight?" Iridienne eventually asked.

"Hmm? Well, yes, and no. It's always been you, Rids. Of that, I've been sure. But tonight, it was perfect; it was us." He reached to stroke her hair back. "Whatever happens with all of this, I want you to know and to trust in my adoration of you. You have my heart, my protection—always." She was looking up at him as he spoke with tears forming in her eyes; she kissed his knee from where she was sitting. "Time to head home?"

They found their way home in the dark, a few hours before morning would greet them too soon.

Back in Iridienne's apartment, they felt no need to rush but stayed cocooned in the night and the unbroken attention. All the love, the trust, the adoration they shared, they now offered each other for the first time as their bodies met in wordless conversation, an exchange of souls.

In the haze of the next morning, Iridienne woke, tucked under Cyrus's chin, her own breath bouncing back off his chest. He was warm and smelled like the wind and the faint whisper of smoke from the night before.

"Mmm," he hummed above her. She didn't realize he was awake.

"How long have you been up?" she asked softly.

"Long enough to realize this is the best morning I've ever woken up to," he rumbled back, voice still raspy from sleep as he kissed her head. She smiled into his chest, and he thumbed the chain across the nape of her neck. They lay there, limbs tangled together in the sheets, when a muffled ding snuck out of the fabric of Iridienne's bag. Then, Cyrus's watch added to the discordant chimes.

"It's not a workday. We should be off," Iridienne mumbled, holding tighter to Cyrus's back.

"But the only reason it would be going off is if there was a problem," Cyrus answered, ever the pragmatist.

Iridienne groaned. "You're right. Will you grab mine too?" she said as Cyrus got up to get his watch and datapad.

She caught herself tracing the lines of his back as he moved, the endearing bedhead that stuck up at whim. He turned back and caught her staring, and gave her a look with raised eyebrows and a smirk. "Hm?" he asked as he sat back on the bed.

"Just enjoying the view," she responded and readjusted to a sitting position as he handed her the tablet, tucking the sheets around her to free her arms.

Cyrus let out a sigh. "Apparently, it *is* a workday. We're being called in. I would suspect it's to talk about the success of the counteracting measures they took against the latest storm." He put his head back on the wall, eyes closed, breathing heavily through his nose, notably frustrated that there was a required meeting.

"Well, this says we have another hour and a half, which is plenty of time. . ." she threw the covers over their heads as she finished, "to sneak in some more time here before we have to go."

"Oh, really, is that an order?" he teased as he wrapped his arms around her.

"It is, Captain." And then she kissed Cyrus under the veil of the simple white fabric, where they met in unison again before filtering back into reality.

CHAPTER 17

TUCKED SAFELY BENEATH THE inky, coarse fabric of her Taxalis uniform, Iridienne's sun charm laid gently on her sternum.

She pressed her fingers to the charm, a quiet reminder that something in this place still belonged only to her, knowledge she could retreat to in the midst of the tension. Cyrus had to go to his apartment to change before he came in but encouraged her to go ahead and that he would be ten minutes behind.

Once she was inside, she checked her datapad for any new information on the impromptu invitation. The location was updated: East Wing Conference Room. *Maybe this would be a positive meeting?* She could hope.

Soleil was waiting for her close to the door to the meeting room; she smiled as Iridienne walked up.

"Good morning, ma'am. Apologies for being called in on your time off."

"Hey, Soleil. I could say the same to you," Iridienne said as she gently squeezed her shoulder.

"Let's see what they have to say, shall we? After you."

Iridienne nodded and walked into the room. It was growing into the same group from the time before. Expected.

She saw Rafferty was already in the room, his angled jaw chewing on a pen. He looked tired. He wrote something on a piece of paper, pushed it down the table a bit where no one was sitting, and then got up to walk in the opposite direction.

He looked up, saw Iridienne, and his countenance changed to a sincere enough response, but Iridienne immediately noticed behind him that Nyx was walking from the front of the room, around the side of the rows.

He picked up the piece of paper Rafferty wrote on, smooth as a slice from drones on the Toppers, and continued snaking through the rows to his seat. She frowned, glancing past Rafferty's shoulder, as her stomach clenched, not because she knew what the note said, but because now Nyx did.

Rafferty noted her expression and checked over his shoulder, but Nyx had already slipped the paper into his pocket and was moving with his back to them.

He looked back at Iridienne. "Morning, Mrs. Captain! You're positively glowing," he teased.

"Mhmm." She swatted at him playfully. "You look lovely as ever yourself, Raff."

He ran his fingers through his sandy hair jokingly, like he was preening, when he spotted Cyrus walking in. "Ah, there's the mister." He nodded at Cyrus walking in, hair slicked back from a quick shower. "We can sit over here. Best spots in the house," he said with a quick, lighthearted eye roll. He waved Cyrus over, who made his way easily through the room.

Before Cyrus was within earshot, Soleil leaned over and quietly asked, "Missus? Mister?"

Iridienne laughed. "You're perceptive. Cy and I. . .Well, we're married."

Soleil's eyes widened, her whispered words direct. "Married? Oh. . .oh! That *is* so good, so right." Then she broke into a smile. This was the most emotion Iridienne had ever seen Soleil willingly offer. It made her wish Soleil had been there last night.

As more people filled the room, the hum of voices created a white noise in the background of chairs scraping. A cough punctuated the noise, causing ears to perk up and people to shift uncomfortably. Cyrus made it to the table where Iridienne and Soleil sat. Rafferty kicked back informally in his chair, hands tucked behind his head, surveying the room.

"I hear congratulations are in order," Soleil said to Cyrus.

"You hear right. Thanks, Soleil," Cyrus said back, shooting a look at Iridienne who smirked back.

Iridienne whispered to Soleil, "I'll tell you all about it after this." Gesturing across the room with her eyes. "Do you know what *this* is about? I was assuming because they counteracted the other storm, which is good news, yeah?"

Soleil's countenance had returned back to its stoic calm. "Yes, it involves that. They are almost certain these attacks are internal, so even though we're closer to answers, it hasn't quelled the growing unrest."

"Mm," Iridienne responded, looking around uneasily.

The rest of the room continued to fill up, discontent grumbles of having to be there coupled with general questions about the reason behind the meeting continued bouncing around the room until the metal clank announced Astor and his entourage walked in the door closest to the front of the room. Immediately the noise of the space obeyed and tempered down, backs straightened, rattles of throats being cleared.

"Thank you all for coming in on short notice," Astor began.

Rafferty mumbled under his breath, "Not that we had much say so. . ." Cyrus shot him a look.

Astor continued, "I won't waste time. We've begun countermeasures against the Hostis's recent attacks. Our teams have made progress, not just in cleanup, but in understanding how to intercept the storm system before it deploys. This marks a shift: we're no longer reacting. We're moving to prevention.

"That said, this next phase will require all hands. Mandatory overtime is now in effect for applicable units. Surveillance, environmental control, field intelligence, security, we dig out every last rat involved in this, and we do it with precision. One positive that has come out of this is that we are uncovering any inconsistencies and questions of dedication to Tabrass herself. I am confident we will eradicate this disease from our region."

Iridienne subconsciously touched the charm under her uniform. Astor spoke of eradication like salvation. She frowned, wondering when saving became the same as destroying. Astor's volume elevated, using the punctuated surprise to ensure his captive audience was listening.

"The objective hasn't changed: identify who's behind this. Isolate them. Eliminate the threat before they can strike again.

"I don't need to remind you what's at stake. You're here because you're trusted to hold the line.

"You will be contacted by your superiors promptly about overtime requirements and any shifts from your current focus. Special leave requests will be denied until further notice."

Astor then invited an environmental scientist up to show colorful and complicated maps and equations, explaining as simply as he could how they discovered the tell-tale patterns that helped identify the incoming attacks. Eyes across the room danced over the 3D maps that swirled and reacted, flashing complicated data and formations as the nervous scientist continued to sputter his explanations.

Eventually, they were dismissed from the meeting and told again to meet with their superiors about specific next steps.

Iridienne squeezed Cyrus's forearm as they all said their goodbyes to head in their respective directions. He pulled her in for a hug and whispered, "Remember what we're looking for" into her hair. They caught eyes, and she gave the briefest nod.

She needed to get back down to Level X.

CHAPTER 18

Iridienne fidgeted with things on her desk and lined up stacks of papers, adjusting the chair in the corner. When she couldn't stand to wait any longer, she slipped out the door.

She entered the Loading and Freight level, but this time without Soleil. The hum of machinery filled the air, and the scent of lubricant and ozone clung to the walls. Mr. Braon noticed her approach, eyebrows raised in polite surprise.

"Ah, Ms. Voht, feeling steadier on your feet today?" he asked, wiping his hands on a rag.

"Much," Iridienne said with a sheepish laugh. "Sorry again for the dramatic exit last time. I promise I'm not in the habit of passing out on the job."

Braon waved it off. "No harm done. The heat and mixture of smells down here gets to plenty of us."

She smiled and leaned against a crate, taking in the hum of activity. "I was actually curious about what you all handle down here. Last time, I didn't exactly get a chance to ask."

That earned a few laughs from nearby workers. One of them launched into an explanation about the new tracking software, and another pointed out the color-coded labels lining the walls. Iridienne asked follow-up questions, genuine and curious, and by the time she'd made a full loop of the area, she'd learned names, routines, and even a few complaints about outdated scanners.

After a while, she brushed her hands on her jumpsuit. "Thanks for letting me hover. You all keep this place running smoother than most people realize."

Braon grinned. "We try. Door's always open if you get bored upstairs."

"Appreciate that," she said. "I'll take you up on that offer soon, but I won't take any more of your time. I'll take the same exit, if that's alright? Like light."

"Through water," they replied and turned back to their tasks and chatter as she slipped quietly through the maintenance door leading toward the restricted stairwell, down to Level X. The worn brass key was still tucked safely in her tote pocket.

Once in the room, she scanned the labels of the boxes stacked towards the back.

Five boxes down towards the bottom of the stack was one box whose label was blacked out. "*Redacted. . .maybe? Might as well try this one*," she thought. She rearranged the pile to free the box and started looking. More and more folders of unhelpful black lines. Then, about halfway through the pile, she noted the word, "Exodus" again and several pages later, "Epitopes."

Not a new connection, but something. She continued to look. She kept seeing the initials EP scattered throughout the pages. She assumed, "Exodus Protocol." With each page she flipped, though, she kept trying to suffocate the gnawing, growing suspicion of something bad with feeble hope and weak explanations. "*We know that studying the Epitopes is meant to help Iterum,*" she reasoned. But then at the end of the file, her fingers froze on the page. The words seemed to hum, to blur, her eyes frantically rereading, hoping the connection forming was wrong.

"Epitope Priority" caught her eye. *Priority*? EP. Exodus Protocol. Epitope Priority. Her stomach dropped as she looked up from the folder. *Did someone figure this out before now? Is this the reason?*

Jarred from her search, Iridienne realized she had lost track of time looking through the files. She weighed the risks and decided to take the rest of the files from the box with her. She wrapped them in her jacket and stuck her datapad on top so that was, hopefully, the focus if she had to stop and talk to anyone before she got back to her office.

Thankfully, the trek back to her normal floor was relatively uneventful, and she moved about unbothered. Before too long, Iridienne's desk was covered in haphazard piles splayed out like an opened fan. She knew the system, but to anyone else, it just looked like a mess. She spun a pen in one hand, the other propping up her head on her closed fist. She could feel the throbbing of a headache starting to spread as she skimmed through the redacted documents in the blue glow of her computer and datapad. Her eyes bounced from screens and papers and back.

She was pulling at threads that all seemed tangled with the Cloud Coughs, but now, how did the Exodus Protocol and Epitope Priority connect? So much of the information was redacted, which wasn't a surprise, but how much information and the longevity of the time frame were what piqued her interest in this direction to begin with.

Questions paced in her mind: "*Maybe the attacks were from carryover sympathizers from the coup connected with coughs all those decades ago? But what would the attacks do? They're not helping. What does 'priority' mean? That the Epitopes were the new focus of research so we could eventually start over?*"

She was trying to avoid even thinking about this idea. She was afraid that once the seed hit the ground, she wouldn't be able to uproot it: "*What if the Epitopes are being prioritized for the Exodus?*"

The more she dug and traced her ideas through the files, the more that seed was watered. Some of what she could gather through the dizzying lines of documents was that the DNA donations of the citizens at the Sun Showers were much more heavily tested than she realized. She had always assumed just the DNA of the Epitopes was monitored, not the entirety of the population. She was finding that the Taxalis collected a myriad of data points on the citizens at each ceremony.

Priority.

Why is there so much data on this? Do other people know how much testing is actually being done on everyone? What does this mean for deciphering the natural immunity question?

Iridienne sat back against the chair, wove her fingers behind her head, and stretched between her shoulder blades, vertebrae cracking as she exhaled.

"*It's like trying to trace patterns through fog,*" she thought to herself. She was close to making a connection, seeing where the pattern overlapped, but she was missing something.

Her gaze flicked toward the datapad beside her, thinking back to when it blinked alive on its own in the Level X archives and the words glowing on the screen: *For the days to come.* That phrase had opened more than a file; it had opened a wound. The checksum fragment she recovered—*/Iterum/Project-13X: Restricted*—still lingered in her hidden folders, taunting her.

Whatever "priority" meant, it had roots in that same archive. The pattern wasn't new. It was resurfacing.

A sudden, abrupt alert caused her to suck in a breath sharply as the datapad clattered to the ground. She scrambled to pick it up, frowning with a huff at her own jumpiness. Her face illuminated with the digital light as she read the message, readjusting in her seat. It was from Soleil. Her eyes flared.

"*Cirro and Cirrus have been arrested. Be careful, Rids.*"

The throbs worsened as her head spun with different questions, now out loud. "Arrested? I just saw them two days ago. What could they have done? Where are they?"

"*Meet me in the courtyard,*" Iridienne typed out her response, grabbed her bag, datapad, a stack of files, and ran out the door. Her mind was focused on getting to Soleil as quickly as possible, and Iridienne didn't notice Donar just down the hall. The doors were supposed to automatically click closed and lock, but in the hurry of her exit, she didn't pull it hard enough for the door to shut all the way.

Donar moved through the bustling workers in the hallway like a specter, slipping in between the empty spaces toward Iridienne's door. He slid soundlessly through the threshold and gently clicked the door shut.

He eyed over the piles and layers of the files, making sure to leave everything as he found it. He pulled a notebook out of his jacket pocket, taking notes of what he saw.

Once he was done, he slid the notebook back in his jacket, straightened his shoulders, and turned the doorknob. As he walked out into the hallway, he turned to the empty room and said, "Thanks for the update, Iridienne. Interesting finds."

He gave a nod to a couple of workers passing by and filed back into the flow of the Taxalis corridors, unsuspected.

Once back in the genetics labs, Nyx caught Donar's eye as Donar sat his bag and jacket down by his workstation. Donar's scowl deepened as he pulled the notebook out of his jacket, gesturing slightly towards the book. Nyx's reptilian stare bore unwavering as he moved silently toward the table, scooping the notebook in his hands without a word.

Levels lower, Iridienne was almost to the courtyard. She could see Soleil sitting outside at their typical spot, waiting, poised as ever. Iridienne didn't break stride as she pushed the door open to swing into the outside air. Soleil turned to look at Iridienne, the worry having settled in darkened valleys under her eyes. Iridienne sat down hard on the chair, legs still turned outward, ready to move. Her eyes were wild with questions, searching Soleil's face.

Soleil reached over, tapped her own datapad twice, pushing it slightly into a better view for Iridienne. Soleil's eyes locked with Iridienne's, and Soleil shot a quick look at the datapad and then back to her.

In a hushed voice, Soleil explained, "Steady, ma'am. I can't say much, but I reached out to you as soon as I heard. The brothers have been arrested for fraudulent sampling at Sun Shower."

Iridienne swallowed. Her eyes flew over the screen, taking in the words, and all the swarming information halted into a terrible clarity. Tampering with blood samples at Sun Shower was unthinkable, like rewriting your genetic fate. Now, reading the screen, she realized how serious this was. It was treason. Sacrilegious even.

Soleil laid her slender, cold hand on Iridienne's. "Whatever you decide, I'll say again: Be careful. Everything is a magnifying glass."

"Heard, Soleil. Thank you. Truly." Iridienne placed her other hand on top of Soleil's and smiled sadly.

"Of course, Rids." Soleil weakly smiled back.

Iridienne left the Taxalis grounds, rushing down the steps and leaving a trail of dirt kicked up into the air as she ran. Her chest ached, mouth heaving for air, but at least that discomfort dulled her racing thoughts momentarily. She weaved, still running, to Rhomy's door, skidding to a stop. Resting one hand on her knee as she sucked for air, she knocked, dragging her knuckles across the door, and knocked again, her usual signal. Iridienne heard the doorknob creak; Rhomy's dark eyes were wide with fear, face contorted with worry through the narrow crack of the door.

"Oh, Rids, hurry get in." Rhomy opened the door enough for Iridienne to slip inside before shutting it quietly and bolting the chain. She had never bolted the chain.

The friends immediately embraced, Rhomy sobbing into Iridienne's shoulder. Iridienne turned her neck a bit to prop her cheek against Rhomy's head, quiet tears catching in the spirals of her coarse curls.

"Some soldiers came and pulled them both from work," Rhomy finally said quietly as she pulled herself from the damp spot on Iridienne's shoulder.

"They were saying something about fraudulent samples?" She glanced up at Iridienne, tracing her face, Rhomy's own begging for answers. "What does that mean?"

Iridienne's thoughts were air-tossed leaves, spiraling; she was grasping at where to begin, what to make of what was happening. "Soleil told me that they had been arrested and showed me these documents, flagged genetic reports, with their names." Iridienne paused. "They were accused of cheating The Letting at the last Sun Shower," she finished quietly. The weight of what this meant settled into the room.

Rhomy pressed her fingers into her temples, pacing in uneven lines across the small room. Her mind was spinning, her mouth barely moving, working out what Iridienne was telling her.

"It was because Cirro was sick, wasn't it? We all acted like we didn't notice the coughs and the wheezing," Rhomy said frantically.

Iridienne nodded. "Cirrus used his blood for both his and Cirro's Letting during the ceremony. He knew the blood reports and the crops both showed if people were sick."

"What does this mean? What's going to happen to them?" Rhomy asked.

"I don't know. I'm going to pull every favor, every thread I can follow. I'll ask to meet with the Governor about them."

"*The Governor?* You have access to him like that?" Rhomy's question felt like a void between them.

"I see him at work, that's all. I'll do everything I can, I promise."

"I know." Rhomy squeezed Iridienne's arm gently. "I didn't mean anything by it."

Iridienne gave a sad smile back. "Is there anything else I need to know? Did Cirro or Cirrus say anything recently?"

"Well, I did notice Cirrus had these black tablets once, a few days ago," Rhomy offered. "He passed a couple to Cirro after a coughing fit, but I tried not to make a thing about it."

"Black. . .were they hard? Shiny?" Iridienne asked.

"No, chalky, almost. Like charcoal," Rhomy said.

"There hasn't been any charcoal in Tabrass in forever, though?" Iridienne frowned. "The Taxalis banned it after people started using it to tamper with health scans. Anything that could distort a genetic read is locked down now."

"Yeah, I know. But there's a rumor. Rids, you have to be so careful with this. There's a rumor that—do you remember Maris, the old woman with the long white hair everyone thought was crazy—she has been treating people with the coughs, like under the radar." Rhomy trailed off.

"With charcoal? Do you think Cirrus went and saw her?" Iridienne asked.

Rhomy nodded.

"Do you know where to find her?" Iridienne asked.

"She still lives in the back of the residential quarter, building 42, top floor, last door on the right."

Iridienne looked over to Rhomy; they shared a knowing look. Iridienne sucked in a shaky stream of air, eyes rolling up for a moment. So, this was firsthand knowledge then.

"So you went with them?" Iridienne asked.

"Just once," Rhomy said quietly.

Iridienne swallowed hard. "Which means he went more than that."

Rhomy nodded again.

"Then I guess it's my turn," Iridienne said and headed to find Maris in building 42.

CHAPTER 19

Even with Iridienne's hurried steps, there was something comforting about walking through the rows of buildings, hearing the faint static of voices through the open windows, seeing the footprints of comings and goings in the dirt streets. It was an untouched ecosystem; at least she pretended like it was up until she climbed the last step to the walkway leading to Maris's apartment.

Her pace slowed a bit as she moved toward the door. The lights were dimmed behind the closed windows. The outside looked unsuspecting, worn brick and chipped trim like every other door, but Iridienne's pulse was beating into her temples, and her fingers were tingling with nerves. She was trying to rehearse the questions she wanted to ask in her head as she approached the door, but it felt like trying to catch grains of sand in the air.

Suddenly, before Iridienne had a chance to even knock, she saw the doorknob slowly start to turn.

She swallowed and thumbed at the scars on her palm as the door opened to reveal Maris, her long, coarse hair pulled into a thick white braid, reminding Iridienne of the cloud seeding trails from the pictures. The wrinkles in her skin held stories like rivers moving through ravines. She smiled, crow's feet fanning out around her eyes.

"Hello. . ." Iridienne said tentatively.

"Hello, Iridienne. I assumed you would find your way here sooner or later. Please come in." Maris opened the door further, gesturing her in.

The adrenaline was making her head swim as she swiveled to take in the apartment. It was meticulously neat and smelled like jasmine and mint from the kettle in the kitchen.

"Tea?" Maris offered as she pulled out a chair at the counter for Iridienne to sit.

"Um, sure. Thank you." She slid apprehensively into the chair and watched Maris make them each a cup, moving peacefully with hardly any noise. Maris set the cup down gently, and Iridienne smiled as Maris slid the cup to her. Maris stood stoically in front of Iridienne, cupping her tea with both hands, and waited.

"How did you know I was coming?" Iridienne broke the silence.

Maris took a sip of her tea, unrushed, and answered her question with a question, "Do you know where our farewell 'Like light through water' comes from?"

Iridienne wasn't expecting that; she shook her head, trying to get it to think. "Uh, something to do with light refraction, if I remember right."

"Mhmm. That farewell originated from the idea that refraction meant light changed direction when it shone through water." The steam from the cup curled upwards as she spoke. "We say it so that good fortune, or light, would follow the person regardless of where their direction led them."

Iridienne sat with Maris's response for a minute. She was uneasy as Maris was calm.

Maris continued, "So it seems your direction led you here."

"I guess that's true," Iridienne said slowly, feeling frustrated by Maris's opacity. "I won't tiptoe around why I'm here. Though I'm beginning to suspect you, somehow, have an idea."

Maris continued to stand, waiting for Iridienne to finish. She wasn't threatening, but Iridienne didn't like how in the dark she felt.

"What do you know about Cirro and Cirrus? I know they came to see you. What do you know about cough treatments and them being arrested?" Iridienne spit out.

It was then that Maris showed a change in emotion. She replied, "I didn't know they had been arrested. A frivolous display of power," she said, disgusted. "Although I can't say I'm surprised. Everything is shifting now."

Iridienne was becoming visibly agitated by the calm nature that permeated Maris's responses. "Yes, everything is unsettled. Everything is shifting. Now my friends are too. How long have they been coming to see you?"

Maris smiled sadly; the timbre in her voice had a rasp like dust being blown against brick. "Yes, I gave them charcoal tablets. It's not a cure, but it can offset the symptoms for at least a while. They reached out before Sun Shower, and I was doing what I could. But the brother, Cirrus, was eaten with worry for the other. Desperation is a poison in a way, you know." She took a sip of tea, eyes distant, remembering. "While the charcoal is a secret kept by the citizens, an old folk treatment, the tablets weren't the reason the boys were picked up. I think you know that, though."

Iridienne wanted someone to blame, to attach her fear, and as easy as it would be to make Maris the responsible party, Iridienne knew Maris wasn't. Her mind was working faster than the questions could fully register, but one stuck out above the rest now. "Wait. If there is at least a treatment, why don't they use it?"

The corner of Maris's mouth turned up sadly. "That is an important question, isn't it, love?" Iridienne sat with the realization heavy on her chest. The threads of that tangled connection were beginning to straighten.

"Those are the questions that will bring you to real answers. But if you begin to ask them, you have to be willing to unravel what was before."

Iridienne nodded weakly.

Maris continued, "Although they would've been in trouble for the charcoal if discovered," she paused, "I would wager they were arrested because the Taxalis caught them stealing from their most important resource: our bloods' data."

Iridienne sat silent for a moment. "How do you know all of this?"

"The answers might be closer than you think. The Taxalis has secrets, Iridienne. Make sure you're uncovering the real ones for the right people."

Iridienne contemplated Maris's words as she stood up to leave, feeling it was time. She passed her cup to the old woman's weathered hands. Then, Iridienne said, "Maris, can I ask you something? Does 'Project Silver' mean anything to you?"

The old woman's face dropped, her mouth into a straight line for a moment, as she swallowed. "That was a long time ago," she said thinly. "They allowed charcoal treatments for a time as a test group. . ." She paused. "When the Immune became the priority, they cut funding. Said it wasn't sustainable."

Priority.

"Wait, I remember my mom mixing black powder into her tea at night. Is that what that was? They were using it for treatment for a little while, then?" Iridienne was quiet, holding back the flood of emotions of remembering, but also realizing.

"Yes, they did for a while. Eventually, the treatments weren't deemed as worthy of the cost. . .or the admission of failure."

"Not cost-effective? Even though they helped? Why wouldn't they want to help the people who were sick?" Iridienne asked incredulously.

Maris shrugged slightly, her knotty hands turned up toward Iridienne. "The Taxalis shifted their resources. The Immune have always been the focus, not the sick. Maybe that's your next question."

Iridienne nodded quietly, her mind wheezing with the implications of what Maris was hinting at, "Thank you, Maris."

Maris dipped her head and smiled and walked Iridienne to the door.

As Iridienne turned the doorknob to leave, Maris said, "Say hello to Donar for me."

Iridienne spun, eyes wide, confusion wrinkling her forehead. "What? How do you know Donar?"

Maris said simply, "Donar is my grandson."

CHAPTER 20

Iridienne felt like the secret she was holding was plastered all over her face as she sat down with her internal investigation team to discuss what they had found.

She couldn't prove, yet, that Donar was involved with everything she was uncovering, but she knew he was part of it. He wasn't easy to work with and didn't seem fazed that he was unapproachable. But seeing him sitting there, she couldn't help but wonder what he was like as a kid. Was he born into a legacy, a family line, that carried a disdain against Tabrass? Was his role an expectation, or did he willingly join? Maybe his cynicism and arms-length approach to people was actually heaviness from a burden he was born into. More questions she may never have the answer to, but Donar's interest in the coughs at least made more sense.

Donar, Toril, and Solanna were already at the table when Iridienne walked in. Toril was doing most of the talking as usual.

"Hey, Iridienne. We were talking about a hitch in our search. Sit down; we'll catch ya up," Toril said. Iridienne nodded gratefully as she sat down and listened to Toril recap what was happening.

Toril briefed Iridienne on Solanna's search for the recurrent ID number, and that when she went back in to review access records and try to track down a name associated with the number, every access had disappeared from the logs. All of them. Solanna swore the number she provided was accurate; she checked it repeatedly, and now it wasn't showing up at all. For her, she was notably frustrated, cheeks flushed, and eyes glassy like she was going to cry from frustration.

"Well, the ID may not be there anymore, but the fact that someone went through the trouble to delete it from every access at least confirms this is a good trail to follow, ya?" Iridienne offered.

"Exactly. And we have the number, and Solanna wrote down every experiment that had been accessed, so we have analog data at least," Toril agreed.

Solanna added, "I was able to isolate that ID down to roughly twenty people, so our search is also narrowed significantly."

"That's solid. Good work, Solanna." Toril beamed. His infatuation couldn't be more obvious. Solanna blushed in return.

With all the information she had uncovered about coughs, she wanted to approach the next topic carefully. She felt like her anxiety and suspicion were bubbling right under the surface. "Was there a new connection or information about the coughs? Or after Astor's reaction the last time, do we think it's. . .safe to broach that again?" Iridienne asked.

Toril and Solanna shook their heads, obviously unwilling to touch the topic again, especially in front of the Governor.

"No, that pretty much was dead on arrival per the last little get-together. But maybe if we did bring it up again, it'll help call his bluff. He's not going to start hanging people," Donar shot back.

"No, but he has started arresting them," Iridienne hissed through her teeth as quietly as she could. Donar was notably shaken for the first time.

The group was sobered by her remark and leaned in, eyes intense and bodies rigid.

"No one has been arrested in ages, though," Solanna quietly remarked.

"Two brothers were arrested for cheating at The Letting to cover up that one is sick. And they were caught." It was all she could do to keep from crying. The idea of them locked up in cells was unbearable.

"Your friends from Sun Shower?" Donar asked.

"Yes, Cirro and Cirrus."

A quiet, yet tactile rage was reverberating off of Donar. "I'm sorry for that, Iridienne. Truly."

And with that, despite the reeling emotions and unprecedented events of the last few days, Donar managed to shock them most of all.

"Thanks," Iridienne said quietly. "Truly."

"I'm sorry about your friends, Iridienne. But I'd keep your connection to them on the downlow," Toril said matter-of-factly. "Everyone is under suspicion. Even Epitopes."

The way Toril said that left an uneasy feeling in her stomach.

Not too long after, their group was called in to debrief the Governor on their meager findings. After their unfruitful meeting with Astor, which made him more frustrated than anything, they were dismissed to leave after Astor barked orders to find the name connected with the ID by the next time they convened. Toril and Solanna headed off soon after with their own plans, part business and part pleasure, Iridienne assumed.

Before Donar could stalk away down the hall the other direction, Iridienne said quietly to him, "Maris makes a great cup of tea."

He spun around quickly, his eyes like hot tar, burning at her. "Don't know her," he said curtly.

"Well, she knows and claims you."

"Leave her out of this," Donar sneered and lurched off before she said anything else.

Iridienne turned and let out a hybrid sigh and frustrated groan and headed back to her office to sort through the papers she was still poring over. Her mind kept wandering back to her friends, brothers to her in their own right, and hoping they were okay. She'd only ever seen the humble excuse for a prison from a distance, but it was closer to the military buildings and platforms than the Taxalis. Maybe Soleil could help her see them, or Cy. Maybe. Either way, she had to get there.

The investigative nature of their teams lately had at least taught her that on Taxalis technology, everything was monitored, including messages. She reasoned that a vague message to Soleil was less obvious than to Cyrus if someone was looking, so she sent her a question about some summary from some report and went out to the courtyard to wait.

The warmth from the outside was comforting, even though the air was dusty. Iridienne welcomed the quiet moment and tried to stay hopeful that she could get to her friends. Soleil glided out of the building, equable and deliberate.

"Hey, Soleil. Thanks for coming. Apologies if I interrupted you," Iridienne said.

"No trouble at all, ma'am." Soleil smiled back as Iridienne shot her a look because of the familiarity. Iridienne took it as Soleil's mild way of teasing.

As they exchanged normal niceties, Iridienne slid over a piece of paper with the real reason she messaged Soleil while she talked generally enough about the latest real report that was sent out regarding the countermeasures to the storm attacks. Soleil read the paper and looked up with a concerned expression, like she wanted to say something but stopped to write something quickly and answer back to the fake conversation they were having in case someone was listening.

There's a way. You'll have to act like you're trying to get information from them.

Iridienne frowned. She didn't like that, but if that's what got her in the building, fine. She gave a single, solid nod to Soleil.

"Thanks for clearing that up, Soleil."

"Of course, ma'am. To confirm, you'll want to see the Governor about that lead for the investigation, yes?" Soleil flared her eyes just slightly to signal to Iridienne.

"Oh, yes, I do. Thank you. Would now be a good time?" Iridienne was trying to sound believable.

"I'll request a meeting and escort you there." Soleil rose, gesturing towards the door.

As she and Iridienne walked towards the Governor's suite, Soleil kept her eyes steady and straight ahead but mumbled under her breath, "You'll have to ask him for permission yourself and frame it as if you're using your friendship to get information."

Iridienne swallowed and set her shoulders a bit. "Alright then."

Before long, they were at the Governor's Suite, being buzzed in to be seen. Iridienne squeezed Soleil's arm before she walked in.

"Like light, ma'am," Soleil replied. Then Iridienne was inside.

An attendee met her and said that the Governor would be with her momentarily. Iridienne waited with her hands clasped in front of her, taking in the details of the room. It was minimally decorated and meticulously clean. She couldn't help note the juxtaposition of chipped and dusty door frames of the residential sector against the white grout and shiny surfaces here.

"He'll see you now. Follow me, please."

Iridienne walked behind her down a wide hall full of glass and doors to a set of double doors guarded by a retinal scanner.

"Please." The attendee gestured to the scanner. Iridienne leaned her face in and was swathed in blue light momentarily, then the doors clicked open. She was ushered into an open office where Astor was sitting behind a large desk covered in neat stacks of papers and three separate datapads. The right side of the room was one sweeping, floor-to-ceiling window that allowed Astor to look out over the spread of Tabrass with a glimpse of the fields, too. In the corner was a simple table with the most lovely flower she had ever seen. She took in the view out of the window, but then her eyes were locked on the flower.

Astor looked up from what he was reading, folded his hands on the desk, and watched her.

"Phalaenopsis," he said. His voice startled her.

"Excuse me?"

"The flower. Phalaenopsis—a moth orchid. Exquisite, isn't it? That was passed down to me from the last governor. With the right attention and cultivation, it can live for decades. This one is over twenty years old."

"Oh. Yes, it's beautiful. I've never seen a purple like that in person—obviously."

"What can I do for you, Iridienne?"

"Yes, Governor. . ."

"Astor, please," he interrupted.

"Uh, Astor—" She needed to get her head right, lock in to why she was here, the role she was playing. "I wanted to ask permission to visit Cirro and Cirrus, the brothers who were arrested. I'm sure you know they are friends of mine, and I think I could use that relationship to see if they know anything else or are connected to the attacks."

His expression changed; he frowned but looked surprised.

"That could be arranged. Do you think there is a connection?"

"I would like to explore the possibility, for the sake of protecting all that Tabrass stands for and holds dear. I'm not above admitting maybe I didn't know them as well as I thought. I would never have expected them to cheat." Even though she was lying to help Cirro and Cirrus, she hated pretending to betray them.

"The brothers haven't offered any information, or explanation for that matter, since their arrests. But maybe a friendly face could help." His icy eyes scanned her face as he said it.

Steady. Don't make a face. Her hand gripped the arm of the chair.

"My thoughts exactly," she said instead.

"Very well, then. I'll arrange a transport for you this afternoon." He reached over for a datapad and typed for a moment, then set it aside. "Most Tabrassians are not aware of the level of genetic testing Sun Showers provide, and that is by design. Because of those samples, we have detailed workups about each citizen as well as comparative data from the environmental effects in each sampling."

Iridienne flashed back to the files: *Project Silver. Epitope Priority.* She had expected as much, they were keeping a careful hold on more than just the ecology of the region, but hearing Astor confirm it so directly was unnerving. She hoped that meant he trusted her.

"That sounds like an efficient use of resources. Has the data collection been worthwhile?"

"Obviously. We caught your friends, didn't we?"

His words felt like a slap.

Tread lightly. "Yes, of course. Thank you for letting me be a part of the solution, Gov—Astor."

His hubris was palpable as he rose slowly from his chair. "Have you considered what you want your future to look like in the Taxalis, Iridienne?" He walked around his desk, pausing to look out the window that faced Tabrass. She could hear the slow pull of his steps on the floor.

The question caught her off guard, so she tried to play her answer closest to the truth. "I hope to serve Tabrass and her citizens to the benefit of all."

"Mm," he hummed as he moved closer to the orchid, poised on the table. "I believe that is in your future. I can see us working closely in the Governing sector as you continue to acclimate to the role." He paused, not breaking his gaze. "Do you know the secret to keeping this singular specimen alive for so long?" He looked at Iridienne, eyebrows raised.

She shook her head, trying to hide her unease. Her hands were clasped in her lap, tracing the familiar terrain of scars on her palm.

"Through meticulous cultivation. Refinement. Not allowing lesser specimens to distract from the goal." He reached a hand up, just under the delicate lines of the petals, hovering. It was the same motion he made when he touched her hair.

Saliva began to pool in her mouth. She clenched her teeth. She thought she might throw up. She shuddered involuntarily as his back was turned. Sweat was forming on her hairline. *Trace the scars. Inhale. Hold. Exhale longer.* The tension in the room was disrupted by an alert on one of the Governor's datapads. He moved back to the desk to check the message.

"This needs my attention," he said abruptly. "If that's everything, your transportation to the cells will be outside the east wall of the Taxalis in two hours."

"Thank you for your time. . .Astor."

"I hope you'll come by again."

Iridienne could feel the cold tingle of anxiety still creeping over her skin. She nodded and smiled politely and let herself out. Short of running through the halls, she made her way to the bathroom and expelled the nausea sitting in her diaphragm. Her hands trembled as she wiped her mouth. She let the water run cooly over her hands, the rush from the faucet like a hush to her swirling thoughts. Pressing her wet hands to her flushed face, she steeled herself and made her way out of the building.

As she went to the east side of the Taxalis, which saw little traffic, she finally let quiet tears roll down the sides of her face as she waited to go to the cells.

CHAPTER 21

THE BILLOWING DUST AND crunching of dirt beneath tires announced the military police jeep long before they came to a stop to pick her up. Her nerves were frayed wires, sensitive and exposed. The utility vehicle was a light tan and used to haul loads as well as people. A pair of soldiers in fatigues exited the vehicle. "Ms. Voht? We're here to take you to the holding cells."

Iridienne stood up and walked to the vehicle. She nodded at them both and buckled up in the backseat. She could see the building from where they were, but she appreciated the drive, even if it was presumably more like being chaperoned. They made the short, dusty route in silence aside from the mechanical shuttering noises of the jeep, but Iridienne's thoughts kept her company.

She squirmed at the memory of the meeting in Astor's office, so instead she tried to conjure up memories of the twin brothers through the years. Even laughing about them eating too much at The Compass seemed like a different lifetime now. She couldn't shake the nervousness that mounted as they moved closer, at what she would find once she got to the prison.

Once they parked in front of the building, one of the soldiers hopped out and opened Iridienne's door.

"We'll be outside, ma'am."

While Tabrass did have these cells, it was built decades before when the region was still navigating civil unrest and uprisings, but it was rarely used in recent years, with the exception of a fight or two between citizens or someone who had too much to drink and needed to sleep it off. It was manned by one soldier, usually a newer recruit, and was considered a punitive assignment.

Iridienne walked into the dimly lit building. The air was thick and heavy with the smell of iron and dirt. The soldier's office was right inside the entrance, with two windows facing the dozen cells that had no privacy with wall-to-floor bars. She wondered briefly if Astor was watching the feed from in here too.

The tiny rectangular windows near the ceiling highlighted the floating dust in the stale air. The lighting cast long, distorted shadows through the bars, and the only sounds were the low hum of the overhead lights and the rhythmic pulse of breathing.

She looked over, and he waved her in, completely disinterested. The cells were all empty except the middle two. On the left was Cirrus; on the right was Cirro.

"Iridienne?" Cirrus stood as he spoke, his tone guardedly hopeful. "Rids! What are you doing here?" Cirrus rushed to the front of the cell. Cirro stayed seated, propped against the wall and bars, listless. He barely raised his hand in a wave but started coughing, loose and loud, sounding like it hurt deep in his chest. He finally settled back, wheezing.

"Cirrus!" Their foreheads met in the gap of the bars. "Are you okay?"

Cirrus stepped back. "I'm alright, but, Rids, Cirro is bad off. He needs to be at the medical center." He glanced back. "I don't know how much longer he has," he said quietly. The stress and worry carved deep hollows under his eyes, red with exhaustion.

"I'll see what I can do, I promise. Cirrus, the way I got here was by telling the Governor I was coming to get information from you two. Obviously, that's not why I came, but I want you to hear the truth of it from me. Maybe if I can use something to appease him, I can try and get you released or at least some medicine."

Iridienne chewed the inside of her cheek, forehead wrinkled in worry.

"Thanks, Rids. Really."

They both grew quiet for a moment. Even as long as they had known each other, nothing could have prepared them for navigating this.

Iridienne offered, "I talked to Rhomy. I think I pieced together some of what's going on. I'm so sorry, C. I knew Cirro was sick, but I didn't realize. . ." She trailed off.

"He didn't want people to worry," Cirrus said simply. "The coughs started a few months ago, but he was mostly able to cover it. It started getting worse, and we were trying to be safe, buy us some time." He walked away from where they were talking and suddenly hit the bars that adjoined the left cell. Iridienne jumped, and the soldier looked up. She waved him back, and he settled. Cirro didn't move, but his eyes stayed open, tracking their movements.

"I didn't know they tested the blood like that, you know? Why would they look that closely? I thought they only cared if the blood was immune. It seemed harmless enough." He was pacing; this was the first time he didn't have to be the strong one.

Cirro started coughing again. A spray of blood discolored his wrist and forearm.

Cirrus looked at his brother, then up at the sky. "Rids. . ." his voice cracked. He walked back over to her. They stood, one friend's fingers laced over the other's through the bars, and cried together silently for all the heartbreak they couldn't say.

Cirrus wiped the tears harshly from his cheeks and collected himself. "They weren't rough with us. We knew some of the soldiers. They seemed so. . .apologetic. . .when they came for us. 'Ro is so sick. They were gentle, at least there was that. They said we were arrested for 'fraudulent sampling,' for 'stealing from public data' which I guess means our blood. They can't tell us how long we'll be held here. Rids, I'll stay if they'll just let Cirro out. He's no danger to anyone. . ."

Iridienne rolled her forehead on the bar, fighting an onslaught of tears.

"What gave you the idea to use your own blood instead of his? The machines still had to cut his hand, right?" she asked.

"It was a last-minute decision. I figured, being twins, what was the harm? It would be the same," he said, his palms held up earnestly, like an offering. "One stupid choice. It was my idea, not his."

"It's not your fault, Cirrus. There should be treatments, some kind of hope for the coughs. Not this. *This* is a flaw in the system. A failure against the people," she said back.

He nodded solemnly. Cirro still sat quietly in the corner.

"How's Rhomy?" Cirrus asked.

"Fretting sick, you know her."

Cirrus laughed sadly. "I figured. Tell her not to worry. . ." He trailed off again. Realization came over his face. "So, you know about Mar—"

"Mhmm. The solid cup of tea?" Iridienne cut him off with a look.

"Ah, yes, the best-kept secret in Tabrass," he said.

"We better keep it that way," she whispered with a wink.

Suddenly, the door to the prison opened; even though the light was dim outside, it still felt blinding being in this darkened sadness. "Almost time to go, ma'am. We have to be back," the male soldier announced.

"Heard. Give me one more minute, and I'll be out," she replied. He nodded, and the door shut again.

She turned back to Cirrus, the blue of her eyes darkened by the room, like a storm, tears brimming. She said, "I will do everything I can to help you two, Cirrus. I swear it." Tears began to spill, burning in her throat. "Cirro, hang in there, friend. I'll be back." His head bobbed slightly as his eyelids flickered to stay open.

"I promise," she said again. "I love you two."

"Love you too, Rids. Be safe." They touched foreheads again through the bars, and Iridienne turned to leave with one final look that stayed etched in her memory of the brothers locked in cells alone side by side. Iridienne hated herself for leaving. But she couldn't help them from in there.

After the door shut, Cirrus stepped backwards until he was against the wall. He slid down until he was sitting like a mirror image of his twin through the bars, tears running down his face. Cirrus reached through and held his brother's hand. Cirro's wheezing was painfully audible.

"You want me to sing you a song, 'Ro?" Cirrus asked.

Cirro squeezed his brother's hand slightly in response. Silent tears escaped Cirrus's eyes, creating darkened trails over his cheekbones. He took a breath and began to sing a smooth and deep melody of hope; he didn't even know if he believed it, but he would for his brother, for today.

We'll touch the tops of fields
And scoop the ground in our hands
While we dream of new and healthy lands
We'll harvest the hard work
And give thanks for future plans
Where we will see the sky and dance
And tend to our new and healthy lands.

Cirrus continued singing softly, the song a salve to them both, until Cirro's eyes closed, his shaky breaths lessened, and his hand gradually went slack in his brother's grip.

CHAPTER 22

THE RIDE BACK TO the Taxalis was short and shaky.

One of the soldiers stole a couple of concerned glances back at her through the rearview mirror. Iridienne willingly slipped into dissociation as the alien-looking building grew larger in her view. She felt helpless. The vibration from her bag broke the bubble she was trying to keep herself in. She pulled out her datapad and saw a message from Cyrus. She quickly opened the messaging screen, but all the alert said was "Office."

It was private. And urgent.

She thanked the soldiers and hopped out without a look back and made her way through the building up to the level where her office was and opened the door to find Cyrus standing inside patiently waiting, hands in his pockets. She collided with him with a sob.

"Cirro is so sick. He's so sick. I have to help them, but I don't know what to do. There's no time." She was spiraling, tears dampening the fabric of his shirt, her words muffled as he stroked her hair and muttered quiet words into the top of her scalp.

Iridienne eventually calmed herself down, looking up through wet lashes at Cyrus's face.

He studied her gently for a moment, brushing her cheek with the back of his fingers, before he said, "You went to see them. How did you manage that?" She realized he didn't know where she'd been, and he must have wanted to talk to her about something else. Whatever it was, she welcomed the serendipity of his being there.

Iridienne double-checked that she had pulled the door shut. She locked it and then turned back quickly, then explained how she played the interaction with Astor, telling him she wanted permission to visit the brothers as a way to get information from them. Cyrus's jaw flexed at Astor's name.

"I don't know what I'm going to tell him. I didn't learn anything Astor would consider useful, of course, just how sick Cirro actually is, how desperate people are becoming. Cy, it feels like the fabric of the city is being pulled apart. If either side pulls much harder, it's going to rip open."

"Then maybe that's what you tell him. That guy doesn't have the slightest clue or remember what it's like to not live in his glass tower. He says he's for the people, but he's not, Rids. And the people are coming to believe it," Cyrus said intently, an apparent hint of disdain coloring his voice.

"What am I going to do? Say, 'Hey, Governor, what I found out is that you're losing control and the region is in turmoil. So, why don't you just let my friends out?'" Iridienne said, throwing her hands up.

He steadied her shoulders. "Rids, you are charming and kind, and people are drawn to that. Him included. It's not a secret that he's fond of you. Use that with him. Astor only cares about himself, so sell it to him that he would look like the hero, rich in mercy, by letting the brothers out," Cyrus said.

She considered the angle. She felt slime creeping down her neck at the idea of Astor's interest in her. Cyrus wasn't wrong though; it just might work. She would have to play it right, act like someone she wasn't.

"Okay. . .Okay, yeah. That could work." She nodded, imagining the conversation in her head and shuddering a bit from how much Astor would play into the role of savior and the manipulation it would require from her.

After a moment, Cyrus turned and said, "Rids, I have news too. I know who 0998–34XN is."

"You found a name? Who is it? How were you able to find out without looking suspicious or people asking questions?"

"I cross-referenced the environmental transfer logs against restricted genetic archives. I can't be sure that level of digging won't raise some interest, but it's worth the risk or conversations I'll have explaining my way out of it. At any rate, Rids—the ID belongs to Nyx, that lead geneticist you asked about. He apparently requested a transfer over from Environmental a couple of years ago. Think about it: he's a genius, like certifiably, and he's worked in two sectors that would be a data gold mine for building a siege like these attacks against the region. It makes perfect sense."

It sounded like Cyrus was talking underwater. She swallowed and tried to gather herself as she half-heard Cyrus asking, "What is it? What's wrong?"

Iridienne mumbled, "Of course it's him. I should have made that connection sooner. You're right. It does make total sense. But if it's him, then Donar must be connected too. . .and Raff?" She looked up. Cyrus's expression layered worry, confusion, and betrayal, each emotion sticking to the other.

She continued, "Nyx is the one I saw Donar arguing with the night of the first attack, and then they had some other weird, like, micro-interactions. I thought maybe I was being paranoid, but I saw him pick up a paper Raff left at the end of the table at a meeting a while back. . ."

"Wait, you saw what?"

Iridienne explained all the seemingly harmless or coincidental connections and interactions with Nyx and Donar, and then the incident with Raff as Cyrus paced and listened, getting more worked up as she went on.

"What's going on, Cy? Did something else happen?"

"Now that I know all of this, it's bad. Rafferty defected. He didn't show up to work, and now no one can find him. His watch and datapad are turned off. I even went by his place, and some of his stuff was missing, like he took what he needed and left. He's been acting so cagey lately, but I thought he was just. . .I don't know. . .working through some stuff, but now it's looking like he's involved in something to do with the attacks."

"Wait, he just disappeared? No one knows where he is?"

Cyrus shook his head and threw his hands up in exasperation.

Suddenly, it all clicked. "Oh, no. No, no. Okay, this is a jump, but if I uncovered this, then someone else could have too. What if 'EP,' the Exodus Protocol and Epitope Priority, is the connection, is the massive secret that the Taxalis has been functioning in all this time. What if—oh, light—what if they were planning on *only* taking the Epitopes to Iterum. They let all those people get sick and die. . .And that's what Nyx found out."

Iridienne took a deep breath. "What if they're not attacks, but retaliation?"

Cyrus blinked once as if he hadn't understood her, then went still.

Iridienne continued, "Think about it. Nyx has to have a hand in the attacks, and he's been pulling people in. It's clear Donar is invested and upset about the coughs and treatments, and he was not exactly thrilled about being in the selection this year. He resented it. And we all know that Rafferty never hid the deep wounds well from losing his parents. What if that was the connection? That's where this started, with rage and then creating a target for that anger."

They stood in the weight of what she was hypothesizing with the uneasy understanding that this could very well be the reality that affected everything they knew.

"It makes sense," Cyrus said, resigned.

"So, what do we do now?" Iridienne asked.

Cyrus sighed and looked around, recalibrating his mind back to the present. "Before we go accusing anyone of anything, we need definitive proof that 'EP' really is the linchpin. Do you still have access to the storage room? Now that we have a filter we're working with, can you try and find proof?"

Iridienne nodded. "I made sure of it. We've got failsafes. But the most pressing thing is reporting back to Astor," she added. "If it means getting them out, playing this approach is worth it."

Cyrus nodded. "And I'm going to find Rafferty. . ." And he trailed off.

"Okay, so we know what's next. We'll update each other tonight, then?"

"That's solid," Cyrus said and pulled her in and kissed her like it was the last time he would feel her hair in his fingers and smell her skin near his face. Iridienne relaxed into him while she wrapped her arms around his back. They stayed suspended in their moment until a noise in the hallway jarred them back to her office and the tasks at hand.

"Okay then," he said, rubbing her arms.

"Okay," she replied and grabbed her bag.

"I love you, Rids."

"I love you back. Good luck."

The couple left the office with a brush of their hands lingering and went their separate ways down the hall. Cyrus turned back to catch a glance of her, and she did the same, their eyes meeting a final time before rounding the corner.

CHAPTER 23

Iridienne absentmindedly fidgeted with the charm on her necklace as she navigated through the Taxalis to Level X again. Before she crested the door, she tucked the chain safely under the collar of her jumpsuit.

Once she was in the room, she went back to the stack of boxes and folders she had been through before, but now she had a plan, and the stakes were much higher than she could've predicted. In the back of her head, the image of her friends locked in cells and the uncertainty of their future sat uncontested. Coupled with that was the dread of following up with the Governor, but she forced herself to focus on the present. She had to find proof.

Iridienne wasted no time and plopped down on the floor with the boxes and began sorting through the folders and organizing what she found based on importance and possibility. She skimmed back over the documents she had looked at previously, but with new intention and fresh eyes.

Then she started on a new box, *Bioethics II*. Interestingly, these documents were less redacted than the others and more recent. She was able to piece together more and more information now, all pointing to the idea that she hoped wasn't true. In one of the papers, Iridienne's eyes settled on the words "natural selection" and "calculated costs." She threw the stack down and rubbed her hands across her face again. It was true. And based on the dates and the fewer blacked-out lines, they weren't bothering to even hide it. She kicked the ground with her heel, grunting in frustration. She wanted to take the whole box of reports and throw them around Astor's office, letting the incrimination spin to the ground like dead leaves. Instead, she reasoned, what the people of Tabrass deserved was indisputable proof, so she kept piecing together what she could find.

Iridienne sat hunched and cross-legged, poring over the patchworked documents, when suddenly the handle to the door began to turn.

Her eyes widened with fear and her throat dropped into her stomach, heartbeat accelerating as her breathing shallowed. *Did someone follow me? Who else knows about this room? What can I use. . .I'm cornered. . .*She frantically looked around for something to protect her. Then the door opened, shedding dirty light into the dim room as a tall and lean silhouette filled the doorway.

Instinctively, Iridienne stood up and held her pen like a knife, the best she could do under the circumstances, and braced herself. *Inhale. Hold. Exhale longer.*

The figure continued moving forward, unrushed and deliberate, until the light from the storage room unveiled the sinewy frame and hardened eyes of a bitter scientist who had learned how to hijackthe weather.

"Hello, Iridienne. I don't believe we've directly met, but you seem to recognize me." Nyx moved like a cat, measuring the distance between its prey.

She swallowed but said nothing.

"I, obviously, know who you are. So, now that introductions are out of the way—"

"Did you follow me?" Iridienne interrupted.

Nyx smirked. "Did you think you were the first to learn about the Taxalis's little secret?" He gestured around the room.

"That's not what I asked. Did you follow me?"

He looked at her, eyebrow raised, his black hair pulled back tightly. Even his skin seemed pulled taut over his bones. The mean smirk hadn't left his face.

"I'll admit, yes, I did follow you this time. Or rather, I suspected you'd return here before too long. You know, I've had a little lark keeping tabs on you. You seem to have a knack for details. . .or at least noticing things you shouldn't."

Iridienne's frustration outplayed her fear as she snapped, "I'm not one for riddles, Nyx. What do you want from me? Are you responsible for the storms?"

Nyx noticed the way she adjusted her grip on her pen. "I'm not going to attack you, if that's what you're worried about."

She didn't move. "You seem to be in the business of attacks. Surely someone as calculating as you can understand it's unnerving to be cornered in a storage room no one supposedly knows about."

He shrugged complacently, conceding to her observation. "That's fair. You have my word, I'm not here to hurt you."

"Then why are you here?"

"Perhaps to remind you," he murmured, eyes flicking to the folders at her feet, "that curiosity in this place is a dangerous hobby."

Iridienne adjusted the pen still squeezed in her fist. "Dangerous for who?"

He smiled thinly. "For anyone who still believes Tabrass saves its own."

Her pulse stuttered. "The letters 'EP'. . .they mean something to you."

"Do they?" he asked, feigning innocence. "You've seen them everywhere, I'm sure. Scrawled in reports. Burned into files. Maybe you even guessed what they stand for."

"Epitope Priority," she said.

"Good. You're catching up."

He took a slow step closer, his voice lowering. "Tell me, did you ever stop to wonder why *priority* is singular?"

She frowned. "Because it's a classification."

He let out a quiet laugh, humorless. "That's what they told us. But classification was just the mask. You're clever, Iridienne. Keep peeling it back."

Her throat tightened. "What are you implying?"

Nyx tilted his head, studying her like a specimen. "You think the storms are chaos. You think we want ruin. You believe there's an Exodus waiting for everyone."

He leaned in, voice almost tender. "If only faith could change reality."

"Just say what you mean," she snapped.

"I am. You just don't want to hear it."

Iridienne's voice cracked. "You're saying they're leaving people behind."

"I'm not saying anything," he replied smoothly. "You are."

She took a trembling step forward. "And you? You're just going to destroy everything?"

His expression shifted, half pity, half contempt. "You still think destruction is the opposite of control."

Her frustration flared. "You are hurting innocent people!"

Nyx's eyes flicked back to hers. "So is your Governor."

"Why tell me any of this?" she demanded. "Aren't you afraid I'll expose you?"

He smirked. "You'll try. But you won't. You still believe the system listens to reason." He tilted his head slightly, almost kind. "You already know who they'll take with them, don't you?"

The floor swam underneath her, abruptly liquid, as if the shred of hope she was naively clinging to was ripped away, and she went under the waves of grief. Iridienne wanted so badly for Nyx to be wrong. But she knew he wasn't. She hated that her assumption and findings were right and hated even more that he was the one confirming it. Even worse, tears started involuntarily brimming in her eyes. Nyx was devoid of empathy; if anything, a flicker of amusement flashed over his face as he saw Iridienne's response.

Iridienne shook her head and bitterly rubbed the tears from her eyes with her free hand. She cleared her throat. "You didn't answer my question." Nyx just stood there, waiting.

"Are you responsible for the attacks?"

Nyx shrugged again, palms open to her, smug.

"Why? What good will it do to cause chaos and destroy what little we have left? There had to be another way. A way to work together, to make it better. What you're doing is just another version of what you're accusing Tabrass of."

Nyx stood, waiting and unfazed by Iridienne's questions.

She continued, "You've proven to them that you can control the systems, disrupt the careful balance they've tried to peddle to us, and you can still prove you know what they've been planning, but the attacks. . .the attacks themselves won't solve anything."

"They won't change, Iridienne. They won't give up their power or admit to the genocide to which they've conveniently side-stepped the blame. But what we can do is make them pay," he said simply. Then he added, "They can't exactly execute the great Epitope Exodus if the weather isn't as predictable as they planned."

He added, turning the dagger a little more, "They're not trying to protect Tabrass by counteracting the storms. They're trying to buy a window of time to expedite the process." From that point, he had been standing perfectly still, feet bolted to the floor. Now, he leaned forward ever so slightly and lowered his voice. "They're not going to fly their most prized possessions into unplanned storms."

She let the tears roll freely. There was no point in reasoning with him, someone who was resolute in his hatred. She had lessened the tension on her makeshift weapon, where sorrow had settled in her bones. "Why Donar and Rafferty?"

He paused. "If you think it's just us three against the region, you're mistaken, darling." He considered her question further and answered simply, "For them, though? Because grief can be a poisonous companion, and revenge is a convenient antidote to sell."

"We all have known loss!" she spit back. "We all have lost someone. Multiple people! The innocent should not have to pay for the sins of the few! What the Taxalis has been doing is not right, but neither is attacking the citizens for the Taxalis's lies. There has to be another way!"

"They gave us no other choice. This is the way they made for themselves, except they didn't anticipate the fork in the road. We are simply shepherding down the other path." He hadn't blinked as he spoke, the intensity making her uncomfortable. She stared back anyway.

Iridienne's terror was torn between the reality of what Nyx was confirming and the realization that he really believed everything he was saying.

He laughed, a wicked, raspy noise. "There are things in motion you cannot change, Iridienne. Because they already have more blood on their hands than we ever will." He moved toward the door, done with the conversation.

"Will?"

He paused, hand on the door, voice soft as ash. "For the days to come."

He bowed sarcastically and stalked from the room, leaving Iridienne standing in a cloud of confusion and dread.

Iridienne stood rooted, the echo of his voice still in the air. *For the days to come.* That phrase again. It used to sound like hope. Now it sounded like a curse.

The door clicked closed as eerily as it opened, and she stood there stunned, feeling like she had come out of a fever dream. She quickly gathered the documents she needed to sort through and the ones that held the remnants of proof between blackened lines. She was on her way out when her datapad buzzed. She fumbled to open the message. It was a meeting request from the Governor's office.

In the lonely, forgotten hallway, Iridienne leaned her forehead against the cold wall for support, and a scream escaped through her gritted teeth.

She understood how rage could win out. She understood why Donar and Rafferty, and whoever else, chose to burn the bridges behind them. But she couldn't snuff out the embers of something else that burned in her stronger than rage.

But first and for now, she would tap into that fury. Because he knew. All along, the Governor knew exactly what choices were made, as did the leaders before him. She didn't condone what Nyx had done, but she could understand how he got there.

But there had to be another way; if paths could fork, that means there was another unmapped path in the middle.

CHAPTER 24

THE LENGTH OF TIME Iridienne had to decide how she was going to handle Astor was how long it took her to make it from Level X to the Governor's Suite.

Her surroundings blurred as she moved through the halls, her arms aching with the weight of the folders and papers in her arms. Before leaving her floor level, she made a stop at her office. Sitting the stack of documents down on her desk, she let the reality of what she was about to do settle.

She knew once those papers were out in the open, they'd be burned, denounced, destroyed, so she separated the most important documents and took pictures of them, and saved them in an encrypted folder on her datapad. She put the papers back in the folder, took the cushion off the chair in the corner, pried the fabric loose on the bottom, and stuffed the folder inside, being careful to pull the fabric back into place and replace the seat.

She messaged Soleil where she was headed and sent her the digital folder with the message: "Have a seat." She hoped Soleil would guess the riddle if the time came she needed to.

Iridienne glanced around her office a final time and shut the door. She touched the charm under her jumpsuit, prayed Cyrus was solid wherever he was, and walked the last leg to Astor's office.

Once she arrived, she scanned her eye for entry and waited to be ushered to the massive double doors she had frequented just days before. Now, though, she was seeing things in a completely different light.

To her surprise, Astor opened the doors himself and gestured her in diplomatically. She stepped inside, datapad tucked in her left arm, and smiled as she took a seat. Astor walked around his desk quietly, sitting down across from her. Forgoing the formalities, he jumped straight in, "Well, Iridienne, I'm interested to hear what news you bring from your visit to the prison."

She tried not to flinch at the callousness of his statement. She adjusted her datapad in her lap and cleared her throat. "I'd like to say, first, thank you again for allowing me to go."

Astor smiled with a false humility, nodding his head toward her, obviously appreciating the gratitude.

"Unfortunately, I didn't uncover or ascertain any connections with the Hostis group and the brothers. One is very, very ill, however." She swallowed. "And the decision to cheat in The Letting was a hasty choice made at the last minute during the ceremony. It was a brother trying to protect a brother."

A shadow fell over Astor's expression, petulant and agitated. He was expecting different information, and Iridienne had to try to salvage the conversation. "Astor, if I may, I wanted to get your approval to propose an alternative approach to this situation."

"I'm listening," he said shortly.

The sound of a gust blowing against the wall-sized window interrupted her attention briefly. She glanced outside. The wind was picking up.

She peeled her eyes back to Astor. "As I mentioned, one brother is quite sick. What if you could use their mistake as an opportunity to showcase your mercy? A way to show your care and concern for the citizens of Tabrass. It's us against the Hostis, not citizens against citizens." Her heart was thundering in her chest. She was almost sure he could see the thumping pulse in the fabric of her clothes.

Astor was boring a direct stare, tracing her face for what she assumed were signs of deception. She continued to maintain her gaze, praying it would work.

"Mercy, hm?" He finally broke the silence. She nodded, tentatively.

Outside, the clouds were deepening, and the wind was sharp.

"The dead have no need for mercy."

Iridienne sat stunned, not processing his flat statement. "I don't understand," she said slowly. Dread crept into her skin. Lightning streaked outside.

The flash broke Astor's attention briefly as he looked out the window; the sky had turned a gray-brown, pierced by flashes behind the billowing assault on the horizon. Watching the storm form from his office broke Astor's delicate mask of diplomacy. He turned. "Your friend has died, Iridienne."

Her lungs seized. The sound left her body before her mind caught up, a broken gasp swallowed by thunder. She sat with her mouth slightly agape, tears streaming freely down her face.

"And the other brother's penance will be sitting alone with the knowledge that his impulsive choice killed his brother," Astor added. Thunder growled louder as the storm encroached on the land.

She stared at him incredulously, hands gripping the arms of the chair. "Cirro died because he needed treatment for the coughs—treatment that Tabrass has needed for decades," she said, her voice direct and low with grief.

Astor laughed cruelly. "Tabrass has adapted and done the best she could in unprecedented circumstances. We are not too proud to learn from the mistakes of the past, and now have used the learning curves and adjustments to provide predictability and management where there was not before. Evolving requires sacrifice, Iridienne."

The wind was blowing hard enough now that they could both hear it whipping against the windows.

"This isn't some diatribe at Sun Shower to hear yourself talk, Astor. Did you think that vague offering would be enough? The citizens of Tabrass *have* sacrificed. The whole premise of The Letting is that it is *random*. None of us can choose if we're immune, sick, or neutral! Regardless, Tabrass has a responsibility to care for her citizens!" She paused and then pulled the trigger. "Who is the Exodus for?"

Astor was taken aback by her questions. "Excuse me?"

"Who is the Exodus for?" she said again.

"For Tabrass."

The rain had started outside, and the storm was almost to the Taxalis.

She snorted. "But only a *prioritized* group of Tabrass, right?" she said bitterly. "EP," she enunciated. "I know the Exodus Protocol was developed for another EP, the Epitope Priority. Instead of treating the sick citizens, there was a pivot. The plan is to take the Epitopes off planet and leave the rest to die." She flung the papers at his desk.

Astor's face contorted into a snarl before he recovered himself. He stood, glancing at the thick black stripes on the documents, and faced the window that framed the weather storming the Taxalis. The sparse vegetation blew violently as the raindrops flung sideways against the glass.

Gusts of wind hit the window like a battering ram, making the framing creak.

A cruel laugh escaped his polished teeth. He shoved the piles of papers back. "Timing is one of the greatest variables. Did you also discover that we've already decoded the genes behind the immunity? Five cycles ago. We can replicate it now. We kept up Sun Shower as a way to buy us some time until Iterum was ready. Isn't that unfortunate timing for your friends? The irony is, we didn't need their blood anymore." He looked at her with mocking remorse.

"So everything you peddled about unity. . .'for the benefit of all' was a lie?"

He looked at her. "Tabrass and Iterum *will* be better with genetically-sound citizens. It *is* for the benefit of all."

The tension and fury burst through Iridienne's mouth. "You know that's not how people saw it! And you know that's not how you sold it!"

"You tell the people what they want to hear," Astor said, devoid of remorse.

"Every life has value!" Iridienne shouted back.

A massive crack of light and thunder hit the Taxalis, sending the building abruptly into darkness. Iridienne clicked her datapad rapidly before it went black and flickered with the phrase, "Blood and soil mixed as one. . ." before powering down too. The massive window was the only source of light in the room. Astor's orchid shuddered slightly with the loud rumble of the storm, dramatically side-lit from the window.

If Astor was reeling, he hid it well. He quickly gathered a few things from his desk while the rain pelted the building. Someone started knocking at the door, and they could hear a muffled, "Governor!" behind the metal.

Iridienne stood there, waiting for the Governor to do something. She expected rage or even possibly violence from Astor. Then she realized, she didn't buy into the lie, so she couldn't be controlled. To him, she was already dead. From outside, the storm sirens were wailing now. As he rounded the desk, the last thing he grabbed was his orchid.

"You'll be missed on Iterum," he said finally, and without another word, he left her alone in the dark office with a picture view of the storm raging across Tabrass.

CHAPTER 25

OUT PAST THE TAXALIS building's watchful gaze, Cyrus made it to the hangars before the worst part of the storm hit. Only once did he have to hide from a small convoy making its way through the sharp rain. It was headed into Tabrass, probably to patrol damage or return to their own homes.

The wind pulled at his clothes, and the rain stung like pellet burns on his skin. Glancing towards the bruised sky, he ducked inside the side door before a massive crack of lightning rattled the metal of the building. He was looking for Rafferty and hoped he knew his friend and crewmate enough to guess this is where he might be. Raff always tinkered with scrap parts of the jets when he needed to clear his head. Inside the metal building, the storm's sounds blurred into a loud white noise punctuated intermittently with rumblings of thunder. The room was thick with the smell of rain, diesel, and wet rubber.

"Raff? Raff!" Cyrus's voice echoed back, taunting an answer.

Cyrus moved further into the hangar, looking for any sign that someone was there. As soon as the radar picked up the storm formation and the attack protocol failed, most personnel were sent home to shelter in place. The hangar was typically sparsely staffed anyway, but it looked deserted now. The hail was punching the roof as the wet rubber of his boots squeaked on the concrete floor. The lights flickered sporadically with the storm's intensity. Still no sign of life inside.

"Raff!" Cyrus said again.

The crash of something metal falling on the floor broke the relentless noise from the rain outside. Cyrus immediately perked up, at attention and moving toward the direction of the sound. Coming around the corner, he finally caught sight of Rafferty. He was sitting frozen at a workbench that was obscured by most of the contents of the hangar. Their eyes locked, and Rafferty grabbed his bag to bolt from the hangar but stopped at the tone of Cyrus's voice.

"Raff, stop! What are you doing, man? Whatever is going on, we can figure it out."

Rafferty halted. Where was he going to go, especially in this storm? At that point, it sounded like an engine, and rain had started to seep from under the doors on the concrete.

"Cyrus, don't. Get out."

"Don't what, Raff? And it's not like I can wait outside."

Rafferty made a guttural, frustrated sound, looked around agitated, and then stared at his friend, his Captain. Rafferty's eyes were full of anger and regret. Cyrus returned the stare, unflinching, daring his friend to respond.

Rafferty snarled, "I said *leave!* This doesn't involve you!" He was calculating what type of exit strategies he could use, but the only exit from the room they were in was behind Cyrus, where he came in. He made a line for the door past Cyrus, but Cyrus grabbed Raff's arm to stop him. Raff yanked his arm back. Neither wanted to fight, but the dissonance Rafferty was drowning in was threatening to spill over.

Rafferty turned, saying, "Back off, man," and pushed him.

Rage was simmering under the surface as Cyrus grabbed Raff's collar and squared up with his friend. "Raff, are you freaking serious?" The tension in his voice was rising.

Rafferty snapped. He reared back and headbutted Cyrus.

Cyrus let go briefly and stumbled back. That was it. He shook his head, wiped a hand down his face, and swung, catching Rafferty straight in the face with a hard right hook. Raff grunted, covering his eye. Before Cyrus could say anything else, Rafferty snuck a jab at Cyrus, knuckles connecting with his mouth. Cyrus staggered back with the momentum. He reached up to touch his lip, blood on his fingertips. He spit blood on the floor, and the two were a kinetic mess, throwing punches and trying to block the blows.

"Cyrus! I'm not playing," Rafferty grunted through his heavy breathing.

He lunged at Cyrus's legs, and the two friends collided, landing on the ground with a hard thud, both men jarred from the fall. The impact knocked the wind from their lungs, bones thudding against concrete, limbs tangled in the chaos. It was a fury of grips and punches when

Rafferty scrambled back up, and so did Cyrus. Elbows flailed, fists struck shoulders and ribs, grunts escaping through clenched teeth. A crescent of blood splattered on the floor. They circled each other, wiping blood and sweat from their faces. The overhead lights flickered slightly, casting sharp shadows across their battered forms as boots scuffed against the floor.

"This isn't over until you tell me what's going on!" Cyrus spit. Rafferty lunged at Cyrus again, but Cyrus knew what was coming. He dodged the grab, shoving Rafferty to the ground, which only made him more enraged. Rafferty hit the floor with a curse, palms slapping against the concrete, then surged to his feet, jaw clenched tight. He got up, anger taking over logic, and swung again at Cyrus, who dodged the hit and instead caught his friend with a hard uppercut on the chin that sent Rafferty stumbling, smashing into the worktable, sending tools clattering to the ground. A wrench spun off the edge with a heavy clang, and Rafferty sagged against the table, blinking through a haze of pain and fury. The metallic tang of blood coated his mouth.

In desperation, Raff took a running swing at Cyrus, catching his ear slightly. Cyrus reached up subconsciously to grab the side of his face. Enough was enough. He was done, and when Raff turned again, Cyrus sprang a clean punch, sending his friend to the ground close to the wall. Raff lay there and didn't move, his breathing labored.

"Raff. . ." Cyrus said. Rafferty eventually pulled himself to sit up against the wall. Cyrus stood, swaying slightly, assessing.

Rafferty hadn't moved from his place, so Cyrus eventually sat down a couple of feet over from Raff, forearms resting on his knees. He had a bloodied nose and busted lip. Rafferty's eye was already swelling, and his nose dripped blood onto his shirt. Both had countless other bruises and cuts. The two friends sat for a long time without speaking; the wailing and assault of the storm kept them company.

As they sat in the silence, the storm knocked the power out. Then the thump of a generator kicked on and washed the room red from the emergency lights, deepening the shadows and dark slicks of blood on both men in the harsh light. Long after their breathing returned to a quiet rhythm, Rafferty glanced up at the ceiling and mumbled, "This is just the beginning, Cy."

Cyrus looked over to his friend, eyebrows raised, waiting.

Rafferty leaned his head back, talking to the sky, "I thought it would feel like vindication. Like, an eye for an eye, that revenge would taste better. . .but it's just bitter. It's all poison." His voice ached with sorrow. He spit in front of him.

"Who have you been meeting with, Raff?"

Rafferty looked over at that point.

"You've been acting off, man. Cynical, secretive. I've seen you sneaking off at weird times. At first, I thought it might've been some girl, but. . ." Cyrus trailed off.

Rafferty laughed sadly. "That would've been less complicated." They sat quietly for a bit longer, the air thick with things to be said.

"The storms. . ." Rafferty finally said. "I know who and why. . .because I'm one of them." He looked up and waved a bloody-knuckled hand in the air. "This is my fault." It was Cyrus's turn to sigh and prop his head against the wall.

Then Cyrus turned and looked at his friend. "Why?" A question asked with such sincerity, it shattered Raff.

"Because, Cy. . .they knew. The Taxalis knew how to help the people who were sick. All those people died needlessly. My parents. . ." His voice faltered. "The Taxalis decided it was more. . .*advantageous*. . .that they just run away from their problems. The planet they ruined, the people they ruined. They stood by and watched person after person die and sentenced the rest of Tabrass to death with the EP." Bitterness escaped his clenched teeth as he spoke.

The hail continued to pelt the building, pocking the metal. Cyrus and Rafferty sat in silence, carrying a shared heavy load of betrayal and loss. Cyrus silently grieved for his friend. For the life that was robbed from him, and how his desire to belong was taken advantage of, again. First by the Taxalis and now by the Hostis, it seemed. "We uncovered what the Taxalis was doing, too, Raff," Cyrus finally said quietly.

Rafferty quickly turned to his friend. "You did?"

"Rids uncovered it, and we've been piecing it together. Coming up with a plan."

Rafferty shook his head and snorted. "She was always something, huh?" Cyrus made a noise in agreement. The two men sat, backs still against a wall, as Cyrus filled Rafferty in on what Iridienne had found, her conversation with Maris and Astor, and the twins' arrest, the wider story falling together.

When Rafferty heard about Cirro and Cirrus, he hit the wall next to his side with his fist. "See, the twins don't deserve this! They are another unnecessary casualty because the Taxalis didn't see value in them.

I watched my own parents cough themselves to death and the Taxalis didn't care." He paused for a moment and then added quietly, "Did you know my mom was pregnant?"

Shock struck Cyrus like another jab to the temple.

"No, I didn't know."

"Even *that* didn't matter to them. The Taxalis uses and discards the very people they say they protect!" Rafferty snarled.

"Raff, the storms won't fix the wrong done against the people. Sure, they've sent Tabrass into a panic, and people have started talking. It's punishing the Taxalis for now, but the people are the ones reaping the consequences again. Tabrass needs to know *why*. Why the storms, why the unrest? If Tabrass knew the truth, there could be unity, and we could do something about the lies."

Rafferty hung his head. "I know, *I know*. It wasn't meant to escalate like this. He just kept pressing, saying we needed a show of force. To make them pay."

"Who? Nyx?"

"I guess I shouldn't be surprised you knew. But yeah, Nyx. How did you know?"

"Paid attention and followed the crumbs," Cyrus said simply. "What Tabrass needs is hope, Raff. Not instability. That's all that's happening now."

"There is something we've been working on, Cy, but we haven't tested it fully yet. We have a formula that could theoretically heal the atmosphere. It could clear the Shroud." He paused. Bitterness fought at the back of his voice. "Did you know that the Taxalis was working on this compound forever ago? They called it 'Lux.' I don't know why they junked it, but Nyx found the files and picked the experiments back up under the radar with Iteration 2419A using a modified carrier. Based on the crunching we've done, though, it should work. He hasn't used it yet because it needs a clear dispersal window. But to disperse it, it'll take at least one pilot," he said quietly, the intensity palpable.

"What?" Cyrus said loudly. "Then why not do that instead of hijacking the weather, creating these insane storms?"

"That's the problem, Cy. I'm telling you, Nyx's sole focus is revenge. He wants them to pay for what they've done, for who we've lost."

"This will tear the region apart or ruin any chance we have at restoring peace to the people here." Cyrus's voice was tense with the reality of what he was hearing. "What if we can still use the formula?" Cyrus said cautiously. "Give the people what they need—*hope.*"

Rafferty rubbed his bruised jaw gingerly and looked away. For a moment, his silence felt like a verdict. But then something shifted, a battle of sides evident across his face despite the dirt and blood. Then, it resolved. A decision had been made.

The men stood up slowly, grunting, with the assistance of the benches and chairs closest to them.

"I'm supposed to meet with them later, soon, actually. I know where the formula is. I can get it and bring it back. We can get it in the air after the storm passes," Rafferty said.

Cyrus was stunned and a bit skeptical. "Really? What about Nyx and the rest? You think it'll work? You can get whatever it is you need to get?

"Yeah, man. I got it. I'm sure of it."

"Alright then. Meet back here? What time?"

"Let's say 16:00? That should give me enough time, and there will be less eyes on the hangars. When we get back, we'll have to combine the mixtures and retrofit one of the old Seeders, the ones we moth balled after the last planting, for release before we go." Rafferty's expression was focused, brain churning through to-dos. He was back.

"Heard, *Captain,*" Cyrus said as he grinned and stuck out his bloodied hand to shake Rafferty's. He had always seen it in his friend. Now, when their situation was hanging in the balance, it prevailed.

Rafferty shook Cyrus's hand and pulled him into a hug, thumping Cyrus's back with his fist. Both grunted a bit from the beating they both took. "Thanks, man."

"Always, my friend. By the way, your hook has gotten better," Cyrus said, pointing at his own face as they walked through the hangar. "You been sneaking in a practice with that too?"

Not expecting a joke, Rafferty let loose an honest laugh, a juxtaposed sound bouncing from the walls compared to the noises of the storm outside. "Yeah, well, I had a good coach," he said.

They made it to the door, and Cyrus cracked it open to get a glimpse of the weather. "It looks like the hail has let up at least," Cyrus said as he glanced outside. "See you back here?"

They shook hands again, looking each other in the eyes with a brief nod, and headed their separate ways into the fray.

CHAPTER 26

The Taxalis was in controlled chaos that was threatening to boil over at any moment since the power went out.

Workers were hurrying through the hallways that looked more like spotlight-lit streets from the emergency lights sparsely highlighting the walkways. There was a buzz of conversations as people rushed by. Some single workers were jogging through the halls, headed to wherever they deemed important. Iridienne, though, felt like she was walking through water, slowly and in a daze, moving at a different pace and still processing from the conversation with Astor, who, of course, was nowhere to be found.

The storm was still too bad to navigate, and she couldn't think of where else to go, so she went to her office. Not remembering fully how she even got there, she arrived at her door and slipped inside. Someone was in the room.

"Excuse me?" Iridienne said sharply, on alert.

The person had the cushion off the chair and was hunched over, but at the sound of Iridienne's voice, they popped up. It was Soleil.

"Light, Soleil! You scared the mess out of me!" She paused, taking in the situation. "I guess you got my message."

"Iridienne, I'm so glad you're okay! The storm is devastating the region. I saw before the power went out that you were pinged in the Governor's office. Even the countermeasures didn't dissipate this storm. Is everything solid?" Soleil asked, standing to her feet.

"Um. . .no, actually." The feelings of the conversation rushed back.

"You should probably sit for this, Sol." Iridienne gestured to the chair with an open hand. Soleil's eyes never left Iridienne's face as she sat and waited for Iridienne to continue. Iridienne explained what she had pieced together from all the files, the ones Soleil was now sitting on, that were tucked in the bottom of the chair. Iridienne detailed the Exodus Protocol and Epitope Priority connection, the Governor's complicity, and Nyx's terrifying visit to the storage room. Soleil was not normally particularly expressive, but her eyes were wide and worried now as she took in the story Iridienne explained.

"Oh, Rids. . .I don't. . .I don't even know what to say. I had my suspicions, but this is bigger than I ever realized."

"Soleil, you can't let the information from these files be destroyed if you can help it."

"No, of course. They are vital in proving what the Taxalis chose to do."

Iridienne was pacing the room, trying to conjure up some kind of plan or idea, when Soleil cleared her throat and said, "Iridienne, I have something to tell you." Iridienne's stomach dropped. She felt hollow and cold, like she had drained the rest of her blood into the fields.

Soleil hesitated, thumb running over the chair seam, face drawn tight. She swallowed and quietly said, "I used to know Nyx. He and I were together a long time ago. We haven't spoken in years, but it's important you know. I thought I could keep my distance from it, from him. But the truth's dragging us all in now."

"What?" Iridienne whispered. The room tilted, and she grabbed the edge of the desk for balance. "You were *together?*" she said louder. "Yeah, Soleil, that would have been something that a *friend* would mention." Iridienne was sick of secrets, sick of the feeling she could never fully trust anyone in this corrupt building.

Soleil looked visibly distraught. She was grasping at words just out of reach, trying to find a way to explain. Iridienne jumped in, "How did you see anything good in him?"

"He wasn't the way he is now. Iridienne, it was a long time ago. He was smart and innovative, and I couldn't help but be intrigued, but then he became more and more. . .obsessed. . .manic, even with anger he wouldn't name. He started working longer hours, and gradually, the things that I loved about him all but disappeared. He became secretive, critical, and suspicious, and I eventually broke things off, and he never spoke to me again."

Now, Iridienne had no words. This revelation was making her dizzy, then an idea popped into her head: "Did you know about the storage room from him?" Soleil barely nodded.

"Wait, were you using me, Soleil? Did you suspect it was him and didn't say anything? Were you manipulating me?" Iridienne's voice was growing louder, the ache of betrayal evident in her voice.

"Rids, no! I promise that wasn't it!"

"Don't call me that," Iridienne said bitterly.

Soleil sat back like she had been slapped, her eyes becoming glassy. "Iridienne, I had my suspicions about Nyx being connected to the attacks, but I didn't want to plant seeds that were unfounded, especially because I was functioning from an obvious bias. That's why I told you about the storage room. If Nyx thought the information in that room was worth protecting, I assumed you would see its worth too, but for the right reasons."

As much as she didn't want to, Iridienne did believe Soleil. While the idea alone that Soleil and Nyx were a couple was baffling enough, it was actually that Iridienne considered Soleil a friend that made this admission devastating. "You still should have told me. I believe you, Soleil, but you have to see that. . .the dynamic was important to know upfront. Not find out like this."

"Yes, you're right. I'm sorry. I'm telling you now."

Suddenly, the lights flickered back on, and the deep, whirring buzz of the power surging back to life in the building cut the tension in the room for a moment. Both women blinked in the sudden hum of fluorescent order, light casting harsh shadows on their faces. The backup generators must have kicked on.

As soon as Iridienne's datapad turned back on, she checked her storage folders. She let out a sigh of relief. Never missing a detail, Soleil asked, "News?" Her attempt at an olive branch.

"A contingency plan. I don't even know if I can trust you, Soleil. But I have no other choice. I'm sending it to you too, in case we need it. Give it a listen, but guard it with your life. For now, though, I'm going to see if the storm has let up enough to run home. Be safe, Soleil. Like light."

"Through water, ma'am."

Their farewell was uncomfortable but not torn in half completely with no hope of mending. But not today. Iridienne left the Taxalis, running home in the rain.

By the time she arrived at her apartment, she was soaked and freezing, but at least she was home. The silence pressed in, broken only by the drip from her clothes onto the floor. Her sun charm necklace was plastered against her wet skin. She peeled the black jumpsuit off, heavy with rain.

She put back on her old familiar clothes, the fabric and color and fit a reminder of easier times. Her long, wavy hair was still damp and darker as she sat down with a tea, wrapped in a blanket, and stared out the window. Not long after, she saw a silhouette of a man coming up the street, and he was heading straight for her door. It was raining hard enough that the visibility was low, but she could recognize that gait from a long way off. She hopped up and went to the door. She opened it as he was raising his hand to knock.

"Cy!"

But before she could say another word and ask about the damage on his face, he had her wrapped against him, wet hands tangled in her hair, and he kissed her like it was the first and last time. Mixed with the rain and droplets from his soaked hair, tears escaped Iridienne's closed eyes, and she felt like she might actually be safe. If just for now.

He smelled like the storm and faintly of diesel. As she pulled off his wet clothes, she uncovered the bruises that matched the ones on his face, and her expression asked the question before her voice did. Cyrus responded, "I'm fine. Everything is fine." He kissed her again, confirming his answer.

They let their bodies say what their minds could not process of the day and what they somehow knew was going to come. Wrapped in the simplicity of the simple linen sheets, they spirited away to a place that was theirs alone, a world where only the two of them lived, free from the uncertainty of what lay beyond the walls.

They lay enfolded after, listening to the rain start to dissipate, knowing there was a clock ticking away at their time.

Rids looked up slightly and touched his lip with her thumb. "So, what happened here? And here and here and here. . ." She touched the early bruises forming already, half tickling him. Goosebumps rippled on his skin.

"Well, those are from Raff. . ." Cyrus pulled her closer, her head resting on his arm, as he told her about Rafferty, the hangar, and the guarded hope of seeing light again. As he talked and unrolled the story and the plan, her eyes were distant and eyebrows creased, listening but picturing the scenes.

Then she recalled the meeting with the Governor and Soleil as Cyrus listened intently. And then about Cirro.

"Cirro was the best of us. Astor shouldn't even speak his name." Cyrus paused. "Light, I can't believe everything we uncovered was true. We've been living it and never the wiser."

"Well, if there's a formula. If it works, it'll speak for all of us. You're supposed to meet in a couple of hours? Cy, this is huge. It could change everything!"

"Nothing will ever be the same again. Not that it is now," Cyrus said, staring at the ceiling. He looked tired past the abrasions and dried cuts on his face. Iridienne kissed his shoulder gently.

Cyrus turned to look at her. "Are you ready for all of this, Rids?"

She contemplated his question for a moment. "No, but inaction is worse."

"Mmm," he agreed. They lay together until they had to get dressed for Cyrus to leave. They showered, not in a rush, as they stood under the warm rush of water, taking inventory of each curve and line. Cyrus had pulled a clean flight suit from the closet since he moved all of his clothes into her place and was dressed when Iridienne came out of the bathroom, hair wet and still in a towel. He was holding the necklace he'd given her, tilting it slightly to catch the light.

"Whatcha looking at there?" she asked, leaning against the doorframe.

Cyrus glanced up over his shoulder at her and gave a half smile before looking back at the charm.

"I hope when you see this," he touched the necklace gently, "you'll know my love for you is like the sun. Even though we can't see it, you know it's there. Even when you're not with me, I have peace knowing you're still there. I love you."

She was taken aback by the sentiment and walked to him to wrap her arms around his waist, holding him. Eventually, she looked up. "Will you put it on me?" she asked.

Cyrus smiled as she turned, pulling her wet hair out of the way. Lifting the necklace, suspended by both ends, he linked the clasp and let his fingers trail down either shoulder, kissing the crook of her neck.

Once they were both dressed and sipping the tea past the tendrils of steam, Cyrus and Iridienne peeked outside. The deepened brown-gray clouds still sat heavy in the air, but the rain was getting close to stopping. It was time to go, but they were both stalling; neither wanted to leave the other.

Iridienne pulled him in again, being careful to avoid his bruised ribs this time, her forehead pressed against his chin, and said, "I love you, Cy. You have always been the man I thought you were."

He wrapped his hand around the nape of her neck and pulled her in hard, kissing her with the surety and finality of a soldier who was leaving. When he pulled back, they paused—she gave the briefest of nods and he nodded back—words unspoken but yet said.

Then Iridienne stood holding the sun in her hands as she watched Cyrus dissolve into the dusk.

CHAPTER 27

Rafferty was already in the hangar collecting the things they would need to get the Seeder up in the air when Cyrus slipped in through one of the side doors. The rain had eased, but the wind still hissed through the open cracks of the bay doors. Following the clanking and clattering, Cyrus found Raff collecting tools and equipment with a slight limp, courtesy of their last meeting, to execute the two-man mission. Cyrus walked up side by side with Rafferty, and without skipping a beat said, "What needs done?"

Rafferty shot a quick glance through a black eye as he acknowledged Cyrus coming in. He was efficient and serious. "We need to do an external check."

Cyrus looked around at what was already finished, then he said, "It looks like you're about done with the landing gears. I'll start on the control surfaces and fuel tanks."

"Sounds solid. Then we can outfit and fill the BIP flares." Rafferty nodded. Cyrus grabbed a step stool and heavy toolbox with a wince, the weight pulling at the bruised bones in his torso, and headed to the wings for the first checkpoint.

The two crewmates fell into step with the familiar workflow of the last several years. Like second nature, they each knew their roles and what tuning and attention the aircraft needed. But this time, the weight of time and necessity propelled them forward.

The smell of jet fuel and ozone thickened as they worked, hands blackened, skin slick with sweat in the hangar air. Cyrus and Rafferty talked through the plans and potential contingencies if different scenarios were to happen. The old twin-engine aircraft originally used for weather modification flights weren't made to be agile or particularly fast, but they required less tuning and outfitting than the other faster jets. If they were going to release the mixture into the air in essentially the same manner, it made the most sense to repurpose one of the Seeders. Raff had said of the idea, "We can give these old birds a chance to do it right." Cyrus was almost sure Raff was hoping the same for himself, too.

When it was time to mix in the compounds for the formula, Rafferty explained to Cyrus that the lab tests showed the formula worked, and he triple-checked the math that multiplied the component amounts. Without any kind of large-scale actionable data, this mission was a massive gamble, but if not now, when? As soon as they hit the air, their military careers for the Taxalis were over. By stealing the components and sharing the formula mixture, Rafferty had severed ties with Nyx's group, too. No regrets and no retreats.

As they were finishing up, Rafferty turned. "We need a failsafe in case the mission isn't successful. Somewhere to hide a copy of the formula in case Nyx or someone else destroys it."

"I thought about that," Cyrus stood. "If anyone comes looking, it would be Rids."

"Mhmm. It'd be her," Rafferty agreed.

Cyrus copied down the formula from the piece of paper Rafferty had scribbled on. He paused for a minute and at the top, like a title, wrote *Fiat Lux*, and folded it neatly in half, like a little book.

Let there be light.

He went over to the work benches where his personal area was set up. Pictures of him and Iridienne were tacked up in the corner along with a few others of his squadron, as well as technical lists and papers he needed to reference more regularly. Nostalgia caught him off guard, and he cleared his throat hard before tucking the paper directly behind the picture of Iridienne and him, the day he was made Captain. It was his favorite picture. Not because of the commissioning, while the day and honor were great, but because Iridienne was radiant, her joy beaming even through the photo. She had the same one on her counter at home. Right beside the picture on a small, exposed portion of wood on the wall, he carved a tiny sun like the charm he pictured resting against her skin.

Rafferty stood watching. When Cyrus turned, he said, "If it comes to her needing to find it, she will." The two headed back to the plane for their final checks. The plane was tuned and fueled; the BIPs were filled with the reversal mixture; now it was time to confirm the plans.

"So, you'll take the lead on flying our distinguished lady here, and I'll keep an eye on the release levels and cloud formations," Rafferty said, gesturing with bloodied knuckles.

"As close to the center point of Tabrass as possible; if and when this works, the majority will be able to see it," Cyrus confirmed.

"Agreed."

Finally, the pilots started putting on their equipment, flight suits, boots, gloves, chute harnesses, and, lastly, their helmets. Without words, they bumped gloved fists and accessed an internal place which held the balance between courage and fear, and headed towards the plane.

On the way, Rafferty hit the master button, which opened up the giant main bay doors but also the smaller side entry doors on the adjacent wall. Pistons hissed and groaned as metal panels lurched upward, their movement jerky with age and dirt.

At first it was just vibration, but then the howl of an engine punched through the hangar's thin metal skin. As the doors came up, they heard the sound of tires flying down the wet road before they saw a jeep hauling towards them through the smaller doorways, mud arching up on both sides. The engine roared, headlights bouncing over the wet road. The vehicle fishtailed as it barreled toward the hangar, brakes screeching, metal frame rattling with the force of its momentum. For a split second, Cyrus and Rafferty both locked eyes with the driver, and knew they were out of time.

"It's Nyx! He must've caught on. Get it in the plane! You're the better pilot! Go!" Rafferty shouted and took off running away from the plane.

Cyrus's muscle memory took hold as he rounded the front of the plane, all the while shouting back at Rafferty, "I need you in this plane, Raff!"

"You have to leave now! They'll be here before we can take off. Go now! You can still get through the hangar doors! I'll hold them back!"

The jeep was within thirty yards of the side door, which was wide enough for two vehicles to drive through. The side entryway cut across the main runway doors. If Nyx blocked it, Cyrus was trapped. Cyrus still needed time and clearance to taxi the plane to the runway. He had to go now, shouting one final time, "Raff!"

"Go, Cy! This fails if we both stay! My honor is here. Go!"

Cyrus gave his friend one final look as he loaded in the plane, slammed the door, and put his helmet on. He had to lock in. The decision was made. He began flipping switches and punching controls as the roar of the engines neutralized any other noise in the building. The plane began rolling slowly.

Nyx's vehicle skidded sideways to a halt as the plane began to roll from the hangar. Three men, Nyx included, jumped out shouting at Rafferty. Rafferty met them head-on. Cyrus couldn't hear what was being said as he watched from the limited view in the window. Nyx grabbed Rafferty by the collar and yanked him in close, fury palpable even from Cyrus's cockpit in the plane. Then Nyx reared back and punched Rafferty as he held the other side of his flight suit lapel.

Rafferty absorbed the punch and wasted no time returning an exchange to Nyx's eye, setting the already rage-driven man over the edge. Nyx reeled back with a snarl, blood springing from the split skin beneath his brow. The other two men jumped in at that point, and Rafferty was fighting three-to-one with every bit of grit he had. Elbows cracked against ribs, fists collided with jaws, and Rafferty's boots slid on the dust-slick floor as he ducked a wild swing and rammed his shoulder into one man's gut. A knee clipped his temple, staggering him, but he surged back with a roar, catching another square in the sternum. The guilt and anger were building in Cyrus as he watched his friend sacrifice himself to buy the pilot time.

The man's head snapped to the side with the force of the strike, blood and spit arcing into the air as he stumbled. A second later, a pipe slammed into the back of Rafferty's skull, and his body crumpled. He dropped to his knees, then fully to the ground, arms instinctively curling inward as boots rained down on him. He twisted, trying to cover his head, but there were too many. The last glimpse Cyrus had of Rafferty was after he kicked one of the men in the knee hard, but then he was hit from behind, and was taking blows from all sides as he went out of Cyrus's view.

Muffled by the enclosure of his helmet, Cyrus made a guttural growl through his gritted teeth as he increased the speed of the plane down the runway, preparing for takeoff. The engines screamed beneath him, a rising whine that vibrated through the yoke and up his arms. His gloved fingers tightened around the controls. Dust and debris kicked up as adrenaline surged through his veins, pulsing in his ears louder than the roar of the turbines.

"For the Tabrass you deserved, Raff," Cyrus said aloud, and surged forward as the engines roared, ascending for the initial climb into the Shroud.

CHAPTER 28

THE ROAR AND POWER of the engines accelerating shoved Cyrus back in his seat as the plane's wheels left the ground. The cockpit and all of the lights, buttons, and gauges were a welcome puzzle he knew well. He dialed in, relying on the years of training to focus his attention past the image of his friend, bloodied on the ground. Failure was not an option. Cyrus said a final desperate prayer under his breath for his friend, for this fraught attempt at not living under a lie, and for Iridienne, that she would be safe.

The plane rumbled through the misting clouds, wisps of deeper browns and dirty white being peeled back by the nose of the plane.

Cyrus thought back to the old wooden box that his dad repaired just for him, his first airplane. He spent hours, every spare moment, dragging the slatted box around their small apartment, outside in the dirt under the open air, and even right next to the towering plants in the fields; sometimes the planes would fly over while he was out, his face tracking in a semi-circle, silently promising to himself that would be him one day. They didn't have much, but that box was his dad's way of feeding the dream of his son. Even as a child, he would dream of flying high enough to pierce through the thickened atmosphere, even just to poke a hole for the sun to shine through.

Once Cyrus became a pilot, he realized the unlikelihood of that dream, but he would still visit the idea for nostalgia's sake. Now, though, this is the closest Tabrass has ever been, and might be, to light again.

He was encapsulated in the Shroud like he had been so many times before, but he had never been inside a storm like this. Dirty browns and muddy greige were normal, but even though this formation was the offspring of revenge and genius, the deep inky gray was achingly beautiful.

Lightning flashed to the left with its shadow of thunder rolling quickly behind, snapping Cyrus back into the present.

He was close to reaching the target of thirteen thousand feet, in the thick of the atmospheric veil warring with the manufactured storm that was dissipating but still in the fight. Like he hoped his friend was down below. The harness bit into his shoulders as the plane bobbed and shuddered with turbulence. Cyrus nimbly corrected for the pockets and dips in air pressure. Then he began to level; he was at the right height for release; now he needed to keep moving forward.

Based on the GPS screen, he would be over the heart of Tabrass in minutes. The plan he and Rafferty discussed was spraying the mixture in a circular formation over Tabrass for optimal coverage, ideally two full rotations if possible. The timing of it was imperative, though. The atmosphere had to be almost clear of the latest attack. Almost. The best conditions were the parting after the Shroud and the storm's embrace.

Unexpectedly, his radio transmission started crackling in his helmet. *Who was patching in?*

"Captain Codere? Come in, Captain. You are ordered to return to the hangars and land immediately."

"This is Captain Codere. To whom do I have the pleasure?" he said sarcastically, recognizing the voice almost immediately.

"This is your Governor. Stand down, Captain. We are prepared with a response if you do not comply. That's an order."

Cyrus grimaced at the announcement. How long had he been an unwitting participant in the lie Astor had likely inherited himself and then chose to perpetuate? Cyrus believed in what Tabrass was supposed to stand for. He believed in her people. His people.

"Ah, Governor. Quite the weather we're having, hm? Sorry, sir, can't land this lovely lady yet. She's got work to do. Stay dry."

Cyrus disconnected the call. He wouldn't give the Governor the satisfaction of losing his cool, but if they ever found themselves in the same room, recompense would be different. A promise made.

Suddenly, an idea possessed Cyrus; *"I guess the Governor is good for something,"* he thought. Cyrus started rapidly punching in information to a VHF radio he fixed up and gave Iridienne a couple of years ago. He flipped to the narrowband frequency he'd tuned into her handheld, short range, but enough if she was home. He told her it might come in handy, he joked, if she just missed the sound of his voice. But now he had to hear hers. He had no idea where she was, but he could only pray that if all of this would align, she would be home.

"*Rids, come in. It's Cy.*" He waited. There wasn't much time. "*Iridienne. Pick up.*"

The sharp noise of an alarm caught his attention from another screen. A second aircraft was detected. A Taxalis interceptor locked tone behind him. Incoming.

"*Rids! Come in!*" His voice was thick with urgency.

Then a crackle came through.

"*Cy? Cy! What's going on? Where are you?*"

Cyrus half-laughed, a sigh of relief at the sound of her voice. "*Rids! Listen, there's not much time. Nyx has Raff, but Raff—he came through.*" He paused. He was trying to keep her from hearing the alarms sounding. "*I have to finish the mission, Rids. This could change everything. Tabrass will be able to see clearly, through the lies and through the clouds.*" He stopped as alarms started dinging in the cockpit again.

"*Cy, I don't—I don't understand. Where are you?*"

And what Cyrus swore was a missile flew off to the right, a flash juxtaposed against the murky color of the clouds, missing his plane—at least this time. *"They're going to shoot me down?"* he thought. *"Bring your best, then, you coward."*

"Rids, I'm in the air. We got the formula. This is our chanc—" Before he could cut the transmit, a sharp alert shrilled with a warning.

A low guttural growl came through his gritted teeth as he maneuvered through the thick clouds, dodging the attacks from behind. He was trying his best to save her from the screaming alerts coming from the interface of his plane while checking the GPS location and keeping another eye on the incoming assault from the back.

"What was that?" He could hear the tears threatening in Iridienne's voice. *"Cy, please, I don't want any of this without you. . ."*

"Hey, hey. I was made for this. My whole life, all I wanted was to fly and love the best woman I ever met. I'm—" He killed the transmit because another missile fired, this one closer. He took a sharp left, corkscrewing down to buy himself some time. *"I'm living my dream, Rids."* The plane shuddered with the centrifugal pressure. Cyrus leveled out, climbing a bit more to get back to elevation.

Iridienne clutched the receiver to her face, her body shaking with sobs that rattled her lungs as he spoke. She knew she didn't have much time. She shoved the tears from her eyes with the butt of her hand and took some deep breaths.

"You are the best pilot in Tabrass, and—" her voice cracked, *"I am so proud of you, Cy."*

He sighed, at peace. A steely calm leveled into his voice. *"Rids. Listen, babe. This is just the beginning. . .I've always thought the blue in your eyes was the last bit of sky left. Now everyone will have a chance to see what I've seen all along. Like light through water, Rids. Remember, if you need to find answers, look to the sun. Fiat lux, my love."*

He killed the radio transmission and locked into what he had to finish. All of this would not be for naught. The idea of her heart breaking would be the neutralizer to his resolve, so he refused to let his mind wander to Iridienne now. Cyrus increased the thrust to almost maximum threshold, checked his GPS and coordinates, and started to turn. This plane wasn't a fighter jet, but she would have to do.

He began the first circle formation in the air. Another missile. Whoever they found to fire at him was a terrible shot, he thought. Thankfully, he was better. Now, it was his turn. Cyrus released the first round of the six BIP flares with the Lux formula he and Rafferty prepared. He was flying as fast as the plane would allow, and it shuddered with the tension on the engines. Another flare released.

Come on. Work. Work!

Alarms started sounding. The second pilot must have fallen into proximity again.

Another flare released.

A hit to the left side jolted Cyrus's plane down hard, loud alerts sounding from the dashboard. He was hit.

"Okay, girl. We got three more flares; nothing is wasted," Cyrus said and patted the yoke. He used the pull from the downed side of the plane to his advantage and kept turning, firing the remaining three flares straight into the clouds.

Down below, once Iridienne had lost radio signal with Cyrus, she frantically ran outside in a futile hope to see something, get some sort of answer. But to her horror, she looked up to see the glimpse of two planes through the Shroud, the second one like a demon streaking through the sky, chasing its prey in the opaque hunting grounds. The flares from the first plane—Cyrus's plane—flashed, pops of blazing fire amongst the murky cover. A searing chemical reaction from the flares started to almost boil the clouds from the inside.

The dense Shroud that loomed like a permanent ceiling over Tabrass began to rupture, curling outward in thick, convulsing plumes. The engineered particles from decades of cloud seeding, intended to manipulate precipitation, were unstable when exposed to the thermal accelerant in the flares.

Within minutes, a section of the sky tore open like paper set to flame, revealing streaks of pale light. What they saw wasn't a clear day, just the first blistered seam of a sky beginning to heal. The air shimmered with residual heat, and the metallic tang of ozone hung thick over the fields.

But under it, a black trail of smoke made a smeared arc toward the earth, Cyrus's plane falling sharply downward.

Then, as Cyrus's plane disappeared from view in the distance, from a growing hole in the atmospheric veil, a ray of light burst through, bright and brilliant. Sunlight.

Underneath the miracle, a rolling cloud of smoke, dark and ugly, was emitted from Cyrus's plane on the ground.

Iridienne was deafened by the sounds of her own screams hurled at the broken sky. Reverberations ripped through her vocal cords as she stumbled to the ground, delirious with grief. The primal sounds of visceral wounds raked through her as she clawed at the dust beneath her fingers. She pressed her forehead into the dirt, the land she had loved all her life. Now, everything before this moment seemed dingy, fake. She had never felt the bitter cold of hate before, but now, for the place and the people like Astor who asked for everything and gave nothing, she grieved in rage for the Tabrass she thought she knew. And for the only man she ever loved, who was loyal to the dream that there were better days to come.

People started pouring out of their homes to look up, murmurs turning into shouts and cheers, and even more questions. Before long, the streets were filled with people; families hung from their windows and balconies to look with shielded eyes at what they said was impossible. The first hole of many in the lies of many they had been led to believe.

Some wept openly, not from grief, but from the overwhelming release of years of doubt finally justified. Others laughed in disbelief, as if they couldn't quite believe what they were seeing. The flicker of brilliant blue, only seen in pictures of the past, was peering back. Friends gripped each other's arms, pointing skyward, trying to make sense of what couldn't be denied. The air was electric with a new kind of hope—wild, untamed, and terrifying in its implications. But as quickly as the cheers came, so did the questions. And then the anger.

Finally, from her knees, Iridienne peered up as the first sunbeam seen in generations bounced light off the tears and dirt running down her face.

CHAPTER 29

Chaos was threatening right below the surface of Tabrass. The city hummed like a hive about to swarm, chants, laughter, and arguments bleeding through the streets. The citizens wanted answers. The Taxalis wanted control, not even peace, just not mutiny.

Iridienne had eventually peeled herself from the dirt and stumbled home, a disjointed ghost drowning in the waves of heartbreak. The community was electric with movement. Questions, celebrations, rallying cries, flocks of citizens staring at the blue sky. It was the perfect cover for her to slip, ignored, to her home. It didn't matter what happened anymore. Tabrass could burn to the ground for all she cared. The cost was too much.

Her brain was charred with the images of Cyrus's plane falling from the air. Did he even see that it worked? She wanted to believe that in the free fall, he saw blue. Tears rolled their path down her face again. Her pride in Cyrus mixed with selfish rage warred like scrambling dogs. *Why him? Who ordered the second plane to shoot him down? Why would they try and stop an attempt to fix what caused all of this in the first place?* Astor, of course.

As she moved numbly down the streets, her fingers pulled roughly against her scarred palms. Most of the people out on the streets didn't pay her any mind, but some stopped to look at her. A specter of herself. No one spoke to her, though. She glanced up at the gaping hole in the Shroud. It sat in the sky like a portal to a new world. Iridienne couldn't count the number of times she daydreamed about what it would be like to see the sky in person. She walked with memories as she made her way home. Now, the sky she longed to see felt like a vast emptiness; the wound in the clouds mirrored the gaping wound in her chest.

Somewhere in a quiet recess of her mind, the faintest idea threatened the fragile stability she was clinging to. Iridienne tried to shove it away, pretending she didn't see the tiniest glow of hope. She dared not utter it. . .the smallest thought that. . .maybe Cyrus survived? The idea was dangerous. A blow she would never recover from if proven false.

Tears burned in her throat as she caught sight of her front door. All she wanted to do was be inside, in her bed. Desperation began to set in. Her hand curled around the familiar knob, and she slipped in through the open door. Iridienne tossed her bag absently as she pulled her boots off while her sole focus was getting to her room.

Iridienne pulled herself into bed, still tangled and piled from the last time she was in it. . .with Cyrus. She didn't care that she was dragging the dirt and mud from her body into the sheets. Once she settled, the first deep inhale loosened the traces of his scent still embedded in the fabric. Caught off guard by the physiological flood of memories, Iridienne clung to the pillow, knuckles white, and sobbed until she screamed from exhaustion, and lay breathing heavily and throat raw. Her breathing eventually slowed as her eyes grew distant. Time escaped her. Buried in the softness of the white linens, she lay absently tracing the curves of the charm on the necklace Cyrus gave her at their wedding, her mind long lost to a flood of memories strung together like old film reels.

The fire dancing across his face at the Pit, his shoulders moving through the crowd, their first date, their wedding.

Then, as she was absently moving the charm around her fingertips, the flat black of the sun came loose. A sharp catch knifed through her chest as desperation ignited her brain. *No, no, no, no. Not this. Not this, too. Don't break.* A whimper ached in her throat. She scrambled up to get a better view of the two pieces, carefully cradling them against her chest. When she pulled her hand back from her sternum where she caught the piece, the small gold circle of the sun lay in her palm, but in the back of the charm was the tiniest bit of paper folded in half.

"*What*?" she breathed.

Iridienne wasn't registering what she was seeing. Why was there a tiny piece of paper in her necklace? She picked at the edges until the note came out. Like the smallest book, she opened the fold to reveal the words "Fiat Lux" in Cyrus's handwriting.

Fiat Lux. Let there be light.

Her clarity was clawing through the fog of heartache, trying to make sense of what it meant. That was what Cyrus said, his last words. *What did it mean? A last hope, a reminder?* She knew him better than that. He was sentimental, but he was also intentional. Everything he said and did had purpose.

Iridienne sat back, legs still wrapped in the sheets and blanket, her hair wild, head resting on the wall. Her swollen eyes ached from crying. He had to put this in here for a reason, hoping she would find it. She sat looking at the pieces of the charm, the tiny paper. *Where would he have been last besides his plane? He wouldn't have taken something important with him there.* Loss caught in her throat, and she fought against the tears. There would be a time to mourn, but she needed a clear head. She sighed roughly, pushing the pain aside, and rubbed her face with her hands. *He would have been in the hangar. That's the last place he would've been.*

She looked at the pieces again to see if she could put them back together. It didn't seem broken. Iridienne tried to pop the piece that held the note back onto the main part of the sun. It fit snugly back in place. A rogue tear escaped down her cheek; she kissed the sun and pulled herself from bed.

Numbly, she readied herself, grabbing her bag and boots, taming her hair back into a bun out of her face. Like moving through a dream she longed to wake from, she traced the path she had traveled hundreds of times before, praying she could find Rhomy to go to the hangar together.

Outside of her apartment, Tabrass was still electric with movement and talk about the sky. She kept her eyes down and moved through the streets. Rounding the corner to Rhomy's block, she saw her friend up ahead, relief flooding her body at the sight of her. Whatever kind of facade of strength Iridienne had up, it crumbled in as she covered the distance to Rhomy.

"Rids?!" Rhomy's eyes widened, and a mixture of sorrow and concern flashed on her face as she ran toward her friend.

Iridienne ran to meet Rhomy too, and they crashed in a hard embrace as Iridienne started crying into her friend's hair. Rhomy held her until the sounds lessened and waited for Iridienne to be the first to let go. The friends' eyes met; Rhomy had been crying too. For the loss of her friend and grief for her dearest friend's loss, too.

"Rhomy, I was coming to find you. Will you come with me? I have to look for something at one of the hangars."

"The hangars?" Rhomy's face showed her confusion.

"I can explain on the way there. I think. . .I hope. . .Cy left something there before. . ." She swallowed hard, all her energy pouring into keeping herself together.

"Oh, Rids. . .Okay. Let's go," Rhomy said, and the friends fell into the familiar side-by-side stride with one another on the trek to the hangars. Rhomy listened attentively as Iridienne tried to summarize the information they uncovered, detailed her final conversation with Cyrus, and all of those components she hoped would align with the missing piece at the hangar—whatever it was. When Iridienne's voice would falter and she'd stare up to collect herself, Rhomy would gently rub her hand on Iridienne's back, a quiet assurance that she was willing to bear witness to her friend's pain. Iridienne continued explaining the details, including the revelation about Rafferty, too.

"Rids, I. . .This is so much to take in. I don't even know what to say. I can't fix the past, but you're not alone in the present." Rhomy wrestled with the reality of what Iridienne was explaining.

Now, it was Iridienne's turn to encourage her friend. She squeezed Rhomy's shoulder. "I'm sorry to drag you into this, but I'm so grateful you're here. Maybe I'm grasping. . .but that's why I have to get to the hangars. . .some last hope. . ." Iridienne said as she was holding the necklace in her hand.

"Let's see what we can find," Rhomy said resolutely as the hangars came into view. Once they were closer, they had to decide which one to try first. Only one had open doors. They made their way closer, entering through the smaller side door quietly, keeping an eye out in case they weren't alone.

It was eerily quiet and especially humid in the metal building after the storm. Not far into the door, up ahead on the concrete floor, they saw partially dried dark stains on the ground. They stood staring over it, horrified.

"Cy mentioned Raff was taken by Nyx. . ." Iridienne trailed off. Then she added quietly, "Raff held them off so Cy could get out."

"That's a lot of blood." Rhomy was still staring at the darkened floor.

"If they took him, maybe that means he's still. . ."

Rhomy shot a look at Iridienne and gave a quick nod. She didn't want to talk about it anymore. Iridienne nodded back, and they moved further into the hangar. Rhomy and Iridienne looked around, unsure of where to begin or what they were even looking for. Nothing looked out of place out in the open where they were. No signs of a struggle.

Iridienne was exhausted, frustrated, and desperate to find something. Rhomy, even in her own processing, was still methodical and thorough in how she approached her search. She picked a section of the hangar and worked her way over. Iridienne was all over the place. As she was pacing, she came around the corner and saw the workroom. There, maybe something was there.

Locked into tunnel vision, she opened the door to the workroom with the long bench of stations, personal mementos tacked on the walls. She poked her head out the door, calling for her friend, "Rhomy! Come here!" Iridienne's shout echoed brashly around the metal hangar. Rhomy came running, stopping at the doorway.

"Maybe at one of the workstations?" Iridienne said briefly over her shoulder. "What are those down there?"

They went over to the tabletop that held empty cylinders, measuring tools, and a scale. Examining the items, they picked up some of the pieces; Rhomy even sniffed one to try and determine what it previously housed. "*This had to be where they mixed the formula,*" Iridienne thought. Then a familiar picture caught Iridienne's eye. She had the same one on her counter at home. She ran her hands along Cyrus's workbench, thinking of his hands resting and working in the area. She let the tears roll freely.

Rhomy stood a couple of steps behind her friend. Close for comfort, but enough space to process. Iridienne gently pulled the stool out from under the counter, so she could sit at eye level from what he would've seen.

"If it was somewhere, it would make sense that it would be here—whatever it is," she mumbled to herself.

Work orders, checklists, depot drop reports, and in the corner, their picture. Iridienne was absently drifting to thoughts of Cyrus when it registered. Everything was straight, aligned on the wall, but the picture. It was crooked slightly. Almost absent-mindedly, she gently pressed her fingers to straighten it, and as she did, the edge of a tiny carved sun emerged as if from behind a cloud. She began to turn but then stopped.

Look to the sun, his words echoed back to her.

She held her breath, moving the picture to expose the carving. "Rhomy, look!" Iridienne pointed to the tiny image on the wall. Rhomy peered around Iridienne's shoulder. "Do you see anything by it?" Iridienne's eyes roved over the papers and items on the workstation, looking for the full answer. She lifted a couple of the papers, looking behind them, and then behind the picture of her and Cyrus.

As soon as she unpinned and flipped the picture, she inhaled sharply. There, right behind their picture and right by the sun, was a piece of paper titled "Fiat Lux" and a formula he risked everything to prove that it worked.

Same handwriting. Same words.

"I knew it. I knew it!" Iridienne said, a sob catching in her voice. Rhomy squeezed her friend's arm with a sad smile. Iridienne had what she needed; Cyrus made sure of that. Tabrass was looking for direction and answers, and she had the truth.

"Okay, now what do we do with this?" Rhomy asked.

Iridienne stood for a moment, thinking. She only knew one other person who had a connection to Nyx and the formula. She sighed. "We go find Donar."

CHAPTER 30

Iridienne tucked the formula and picture in her bag as the two friends discussed how to find Donar. Rhomy didn't have the same sour taste in her mouth as Iridienne, but Iridienne hoped that deep down, Donar had some sort of moral compass left. It was the best and only shot. Short of scouring the town to find him, Iridienne decided it was a calculated risk to send him a message to smoke him out. She typed a partial first line of the formula with her apartment number and hit send, "*2419A. ap133.*"

Ignited with a new possibility, the two friends covered the distance back to Tabrass with a direct focus. A bitter grief gnawed at the back of her mind, and a sneaky vapor of guilt curled through her thoughts, questioning why she wasn't holding vigil for her love lost. Cyrus would want her to see this through. He knew the risks and knew the sacrifice, and she knew hers. Thankfully, the rushed trek back into town gave little room for Iridienne to hyperfocus on her longing or even checking for a response from Donar, even though a couple of times the jostle of her bag sent phantom vibrations of a message.

She was beginning to think Donar was a bust when her datapad vibrated and buzzed a response.

"If there's tea."

"Insufferable. Even now," she half mumbled to herself, annoyed, but the relief was palpable that he at least responded.

Iridienne and Rhomy quickened their pace, feet squelching in the mud, the humidity coating their skin with a thick sweat. The gaping hole in the clouds above wasn't closing, but the wispy edges of the Shroud were like curling tendrils, reaching into the mesmerizing cerulean as if to cinch the hole closed like a wound.

The friends stole repeated glances at the sky, captivated by the juxtaposition hovering above them. They weren't ready to verbalize it out loud, but both silently dared to think what that blue would look like stretched taut like a canvas from horizon to horizon. *What would Tabrass be then?*

Keeping their pace, Iridienne and Rhomy made it to Iridienne's door, taking their muddy boots off and placing them inside. It might have been unnecessarily dubious, but Iridienne didn't want to risk someone following them and seeing their freshly used, muddy shoes right outside the door. Once they were inside, unlike Rhomy, Iridienne didn't wait well. She set her things down on the counter and went to start the kettle, anything to keep her busy waiting for Donar.

Rhomy raised an eyebrow, almost amused. "Tea, hm?"

"That obstinate jerk said he would come if there was tea, so. . ." Iridienne threw her hands up, exasperated.

Rhomy snorted a laugh, sat back, and waited. A few minutes later, two quiet knocks sounded at the door. The two friends shot looks at each other, and Iridienne moved to the door, praying it was Donar. To her relief, there he stood, smug and surly as ever.

"Surprised to see me?" he said. *Light, he was frustrating.*

"A little, yeah, but I think we've got a shared interest." She moved the door open more and gestured for him to come in.

He nodded a thanks, but when he came in, he immediately bristled up at the sight of Rhomy. "You didn't say there was someone else here?" He shot a glance at her.

"She knows everything. No use making her leave now."

Rhomy sat unfazed, face unmoved. The scowl made its home across his brow as he stood on the threshold.

"I do have tea, though," Iridienne gibed.

Donar nodded again and held his hand out towards a chair with a questioning look.

"Please." Iridienne gestured back, coming back over with a cup of tea for him.

Donar sat quietly and blew on the hot liquid, sending the smoke flitting into the air in the room. Iridienne and Rhomy watched him. As they made space for the awkward quiet, a jarring alert from Iridienne's datapad dinged with a message. Then, Tabrass-wide speakers and screens announced the same abrupt invitation: *"Tabrassians, mandatory convening at the Sun Shower stage at 4:00 tomorrow afternoon. All must attend."* The sky's wound had stopped widening; the light above Tabrass was fragile but holding. No doubt the Taxalis was forcing one last ditch effort at maintaining control.

The three shared glances after the announcement. Then an idea popped into Iridienne's mind. Urgent, dangerous.

"Donar, I know we haven't seen eye to eye on much, but I think we ultimately want the same things. Rafferty told Cyrus about the formula. And, as you can see, it worked." Donar didn't break eye contact. She continued, "And it may have cost them both their lives." She swallowed hard, like glass raking down her neck. She looked away and cleared her throat. "We don't know where either of them is. Do you know where Nyx is?"

Donar set his cup down quietly. "No, after. . .all of that. . .he went dark, and I haven't heard from him." He paused. "He never wanted the formula to work. Some other scientists accidentally discovered the possibility of a solution during their engineering experiments to create more severe storms. He just wanted chaos. So when he found out Rafferty had stolen the formula, he was. . .something snapped."

This was the most Iridienne had ever heard Donar say, and she was shocked. "Why were you working with him?"

"He sold me revenge, and I bought it," he said simply.

The room was quiet for a bit until Rhomy spoke up, "It sounds like Astor and Nyx were two sides of the same coin."

Iridienne looked up at her friend, gentle and calm and right. She shook her head in bitter realization. "Yeah, I think so." Donar sat picking angrily at his cuticles.

"Listen, if Rhomy's read is right, I doubt Astor would support the clearing sky as much as Nyx would. I do have an idea for that, but first, Donar, you have to swear on. . .Maris. . .that you will not betray us."

A quiet rage burned behind his dark eyes, not at them, but for the years of wrongs he had endured in Tabrass. "On Maris," he agreed roughly.

"Okay, before we figure out how to disseminate the formula, I think we need to broadcast this message first. Once people hear it, I don't think we'll have trouble convincing Tabrass to try the formula in larger batches. But we need your help to figure out how to get this out first. Listen." Iridienne grabbed her datapad, clicked and swiped, and pressed play on her own failsafe. If the sky could be split open, then so could the Taxalis's lies.

Rhomy hadn't heard the actual message either, just Iridienne's summary of the interaction. She and Donar sat as representatives of both spectrums in response to the incriminating information. Rhomy was horrified. Her gentle expression wrinkled into shock and grief. Donar's rage slowly evolved into a sucking wound of wrath. His fury was kinetic. Iridienne was the only one who lived the conversation, and the reminder of the aloof callousness snuffed out the last bit of hope that there was a chance to mend what once was.

The three sat silently after the secret recording stopped. Lost to the words they heard and at a loss to say any in return.

Eventually, Iridienne said quietly, "So, will you help us? Could we broadcast this message during the gathering?"

Iridienne's question jolted Rhomy out of her daze; she jerked her head to stare at her, eyes wide with fear and questions. Iridienne gave her a sad half-smile and nodded. "When else would we do it? All of Tabrass is sitting on the precipice of falling back into familiarity that was built on the lies we've lived for generations, or the possibility of something new and honest."

Donar looked up at her. Angry tears were threatening to spill over. She gave him the dignity of not offering pity.

"Astor won't expect it, and everyone will be there. It has to be then."

They all agreed and began brainstorming how to make this happen and who they could trust. It would be suspicious if any of them were directly seen doing anything out of the ordinary, especially Iridienne. Donar suspected there would be an increased military presence to quell the inevitable unrest of the citizens demanding answers. Rhomy, Iridienne, and Donar agreed it needed to be someone unsuspecting with internal access to the Taxalis and its computer systems, an idea of how the broadcasts worked at the stage area, or possibly someone who had complex computer experience.

"And then there's the small additive of them being sympathetic to the cause. . ." Donar added sarcastically. His strong suit was never making friends, so his connections were limited. Rhomy was coming up short, too, having not been in the Taxalis herself. Iridienne had someone in mind, as much as she wished she didn't. She reasoned with herself, though, if she could connect with Donar, she could swallow her pride and ask. For Cyrus, for Tabrass.

Iridienne cleared her throat. "I know someone who could fit the bill. Last time we spoke, it didn't end on great terms, though."

Rhomy's face was a question mark, and then a knowing look replaced her expression. She shrugged and made a face, agreeing that the choice was right.

Donar was not picking up on the nuances. "Okay, then, who?" he said shortly.

"Soleil."

Donar rarely looked surprised, but his eyebrows shot up from their regular scrunched perch, and his eyes widened.

"I didn't know you two had a falling out."

"You didn't know she and Nyx were a thing back in the day? She conveniently left that out with me, too. She knew more than she let on about all of this."

"Nyx didn't exactly share about his personal life."

"She's our best shot. I'll reach out and see what she says," Iridienne conceded. Iridienne started typing out a message to Soleil and prayed for a response again. It worked with Donar; maybe it would work with Soleil.

"Ap.133 urgent." Iridienne hoped her apartment number, the succinctness of her message, and the history of their relationship would at least get Soleil here. From there, they could appeal the plan to her.

Iridienne, Donar, and Rhomy discussed other possible plans to project the message to Tabrass, but nothing seemed to fit as well as the opportunity that presented itself if Soleil agreed. If Donar could come through, Iridienne thought, so could Soleil. While they waited, Iridienne filled Donar in on what else she had discovered in the storage room and with Cyrus, and Donar gave his perspective from the inside of Nyx's ranks.

Rhomy sat quietly, eyes bouncing between the two, but after a lull came in the exchange of stories, she gently asked, "Donar, were you a real Epitope?"

For the first time Iridienne could remember, Donar smiled. It was slight, more of a turned corner of the mouth, but genuine nonetheless.

"Statistically, maybe. By Sun Shower standards, yes. Otherwise, no, I was implanted."

"Light." Iridienne was dumbfounded. "How? Wait. . .does this have to do with the ID number Solanna found?"

Donar nodded. "Mhmm."

At this point, Iridienne sat back. This was a longer game afoot than she realized. She was wordless, her brain processing the information. It made sense but was unbelievable, nonetheless.

Rhomy asked, "So, what made you defect after all this effort?"

Donar sat quietly, a faint grimace still etched as his face's default, and considered her question. He lingered on Rhomy for a moment. Not in a menacing way, but thoughtful.

"When Nyx started voicing his approval of collateral damage if it meant revenge, I realized we were no better than Astor and the ones before." He paused. "Two sides, same coin," he said, leaning his head slightly toward Rhomy in credit. He turned to Iridienne. "I know you think I'm a snarky bastard, and I am, but I do have a conscience. I am sorry for Cyrus, but more than that, I am thankful."

Taken aback by the unexpected humanness of Donar's response, tears slipped from her eyes that she wiped away with the back of her hand. "Thank you," she said quietly.

Donar nodded again, and nothing more was said. Unofficially, yet organically still, they sat as if in a moment of silence for what they all had lost.

A quick three-knock sequence rapped at the door finished their silent remembering. Iridienne got up to answer; Rhomy and Donar sat more at attention from their respective seats. Iridienne cracked open the door to see a vertical slice of Soleil's stoic face, blonde hair pulled back neatly as always. She hid whatever she was feeling well, usually, but now she looked tired and vulnerable.

"Iridienne." She straightened a little, guarded.

"Hi, Sol. Come in."

Soleil came in apprehensively, immediately surveying the room, giving acknowledgments to Donar and Rhomy, and then turned to stand at attention facing Iridienne.

"We hoped you would come. Thank you, Sol," Iridienne said. She missed her friend but still wrestled with the feelings of distrust that lingered. Soleil nodded and waited. Iridienne explained the latest to Soleil, to catch her up, and then detailed their plan to broadcast a message during the gathering, the content and explanation that would go out to the masses, but the timing had to be right. Astor calling a convening would be the perfect setup. Soleil listened intently; Iridienne could tell the wheels were turning.

"So, we need your help. We need to be able to broadcast a message, essentially hijack the screens, and play our own message. Can you do that?" The three sat waiting. Everything hinged on this answer.

Soleil considered the question, which felt like an eternity for the rest of them. But this is why they asked her to begin with. She thought through every angle.

Finally, she answered, "Yes, I know enough of the system to patch in the video remotely. I am. . .since you left, and I remained. . .They think we are out of touch. I will be expected to be in attendance with the Taxalis at the fields. She continued, explaining, "The live video feed runs through the local network that's simple enough to patch into if we prep the video ahead of time, same format, same resolution, I can slip it into the system without raising alarms."

She tapped a small screen in the corner of her datapad. "We'll route it through a hidden relay that impersonates their usual feed and inject our video into the pipeline. I'll build it so once it starts, they can't cut it off. I can trigger it remotely. From the crowd. From my datapad. Just one tap, and our video overrides theirs."

She looked up, voice calm and even as always. "We'll override the manual controls, lock the playback loop, and block any stop commands unless someone hard-kills the whole system. They'd have to shut down the entire feed operation to stop it. And by then, Tabrass won't be able to unhear what's been said."

Iridienne and Rhomy shared a look, mouths slightly ajar. Even Donar looked impressed. Soleil looked like she had just read a grocery list.

Rhomy was the first to shift forward, looking around the room for the others' reactions. Donar didn't say anything, but rubbed his forehead and turned toward Iridienne, waiting. Soleil blinked, humbly looking around at the other three. "Will that do the job?"

Iridienne sat, abruptly exhausted, and nodded at Soleil. In her fatigue and sorrow that was threatening to bubble over, there was little margin for emotional restraint.

"Soleil, I'm sorry for how things went the last time we spoke. I am grateful for your help, truly." She was crying again. For relief, for loss, for hope.

"I am grateful for a chance at penance," Soleil said quietly, the catch of tears evident in the lowered rasp of her voice. "This is for the Tabrass so many should have known." Solemn agreement bobbed across the room. The atmosphere was quiet for a moment.

"Okay, then, that's settled." Soleil cleared her throat, smoothed her pant legs, and straightened her shoulders. "The plan needs details, hm?" She was back. And they had until tomorrow to make this happen.

CHAPTER 31

They all knew their roles.

But that didn't keep the physiological effects of their anxieties from gnawing at their brains. Donar picked at a chip in the mug while Rhomy folded and refolded a napkin, pressing the edges smooth.

After debating, confirming, and analyzing potential failure points and Hail Mary options, Iridienne, Rhomy, Soleil, and Donar had a plan they agreed on before they fractioned in their respective directions. Iridienne recorded a brief addition to the video feed they were going to patch in, and Soleil and Donar both saved an encrypted copy that traced like a videoed meeting file rather than the damning accusation the video really was.

The four settled into a quick rhythm. For the few hours they planned and rolled ideas back and forth, it forced them to hone their focus on this one thing, pushing past their grief and anger. Iridienne kept the tea brewed and filled, and the group talked amongst themselves as Soleil moved files around and began readying the components to the plan.

Donar was noticeably shocked when he found out about Soleil and Nyx's romantic involvement, to Iridienne and Rhomy's amusement. Soleil smirked slightly, and Iridienne saw Donar staring at Soleil with a puzzled look here and there. Rhomy and Iridienne shared stories about the twin brothers, Cyrus, Raff, and the others, their nights around the Pit. Iridienne got quiet, and the look of far-off sadness overcame her expression, absently reaching for the gold necklace under her collar. The other three quieted down too; Rhomy put a hand on Iridienne's arm.

It was enough to bring her back from the brink of memories. "Sorry, I. . .I was thinking of, of our wedding." Iridienne's voice cracked. She got up and went to the other room. The others pretended like they didn't hear the shuddering sobs and gasps in between.

☀

Eventually, Soleil announced she had finished combining the videos and encrypting the file. Now that it was done, it was time for everyone to go their separate ways to finish the plan before meeting at the fields the next day.

Donar was the first to leave, not being one for long goodbyes. He mumbled a gruff thank you for the tea and slipped through the door to see what reconnaissance and physical proof he could gather back at the Taxalis while being like a vapor dissipating through the halls.

Before Soleil left, she stopped at the door to gather her thoughts. But before she could say anything, Iridienne grabbed her in an embrace. Soleil was shocked at first and then hugged Iridienne back sincerely. She pulled away, gave Iridienne a nod, and straightened her collar, steeling her nerves for what she was about to do. Soleil looked over at Rhomy, and Rhomy squeezed Soleil's arm with a smile. The remaining three said nothing more as Soleil walked towards the Taxalis to finish the job.

Iridienne looked down at her watch, the worn leather an unexpected comfort. *Tomorrow.*

The next day, a nauseating form of deja vu was suffocating as Iridienne and Rhomy walked the long road to the fields for the mandatory meeting Astor called for the citizens of Tabrass. It was the same path to the same fields, yet everything was different. Iridienne's throat ached with burning loss. She desperately blinked away the forming tears, eyes turned to the sky, trying to coax them back inside, fighting to silently mourn all the ones who needlessly died, unable to breathe through the lies perpetuated in the name of unity and progress. They were walking a funeral procession.

An angry, hot tear escaped down Iridienne's cheek as she and Rhomy held hands as they walked, hoping for some transference of courage and hope that this would work. *But if it did, then what?* That was a question only afforded if the video stream splicing worked. *One thing at a time. Inhale. Hold. Exhale longer.*

The path to the fields was a muddy mess. The ground still squelched after being drenched in the storms. Mud caked a perimeter of dirty clumps around most people's shoes, and the air made it hard to breathe. Whether it was the bristly electric feel of unrest or the thick humidity, sweat and demands for answers formed on people's brows as they began to congregate back at the fields in the front of the stage, waiting. Smells of mud, bodies, and wet clothes sat thick over the crowd.

The hopeful naivety that had brimmed here before, though, was replaced with suspicion, doubt, and contempt. The crowd shuffled uneasily, their grumbling becoming the white noise backdrop of the impromptu meeting. The Taxalis attendants that shuffled around seemed uncomfortable or reluctant to be there, refusing to make eye contact or engage the citizens. They busied themselves with menial tasks and readied the platform for the Governor to soon come out. Iridienne recognized a few; she felt pity for them. Pawns just moving as they're told. As they stood in the crowd, Iridienne tried to glance around for Donar or Soleil but still hadn't seen either since she and Rhomy made it to the stage front. At this point, there was nothing else she could do. *Please work. Please.*

The electric crackle of the speakers preparing to flare the sound over the heads of the crowd was partnered with the ignition of the screens. Iridienne could feel the nerves mounting, pumping fast through her veins. She didn't realize how hard she was squeezing Rhomy's hand until Rhomy reached over and put her free hand on top of Iridienne's. Iridienne quickly looked down at Rhomy who looked back with worry veiling her face.

"It'll work," she mouthed.

Iridienne gave Rhomy's hand a couple of quick squeezes before relaxing her grip a bit. She inhaled deeply, filling her lungs to capacity, and blew the air out slowly. Suddenly, Iridienne caught a faint glimpse of familiar blonde hair with the sharp center part off to the side on the platform. Soleil. They locked eyes, and Soleil offered the quickest of winks. *This just might work.*

Not much later, the familiar tune of the Tabrassian anthem sang through the speakers while Astor appeared on the screens as he walked forward to the microphone. A noticeable shift rippled through the crowd, the discontent growing slightly louder.

"He's got some nerve sauntering on that stage. . ." an angry woman said to herself.

"For better days," Iridienne whispered half to Rhomy, half to herself. Iridienne's anxiety was thick in her veins. She picked roughly at the scars on her palms and chewed the inside of her cheeks, pulling skin off with her teeth. Her eyes darted from Astor's face to the giant monitors flanking the platform. Her heart thumped like a mallet, rattling her sternum.

Astor began to open his mouth to address the crowd.

"Citizens of Tabrass—

"I come to you not with a ceremony, but as a citizen myself, addressing the brave region I care for.

"I know there are concerns. Questions. The crash. The storms. The breach in the Shroud. For many, it feels as though the ground beneath us has shifted. I understand that feeling.

"The foundation of our survival has always been truth, even when it's difficult. We cannot move forward if we silence doubt. That's why, beginning today, a full investigation is being launched, independent, transparent, and inclusive.

"The extremist faction known as Hostis, those who reject the order we've built, who sabotage our efforts from within, they are responsible for the chaos we've endured. The breach in the sky, the manipulated storm systems. They were engineered.

"But we will not be broken. We will take what was meant to destroy us and use it to rebuild, stronger, safer, more unified than ever. We will harness the technology for a better Tabrass. Regulations will increase. Every servant sector will be restructured. And those deemed sympathetic to Hostis will be. . .eliminated."

There was no applause. Just a hum of unease.

He continued, "*We will not afford disloyalty. Not now. Not ever. The future of Tabrass depends on unity, on order, on—*"

Then the screen flickered, coupled with a sharp buzz. Astor's face sat frozen mid word for half a second. Then silence. The screens went black.

On stage, Astor stood, mouth agape, shocked. Then a new voice cut in. Calm. Clear. Unmistakably not his.

"*You've heard his version. Now, hear the truth. The Taxalis has lied to us, used us. Hostis is responsible for the storms, but the Taxalis is responsible for the fallacies that built Tabrass. They knew the Shroud made us sick; they had a way to treat it, and they chose not to. Their plan was to identify the Immune. . .for the Exodus. The Epitope Priority, a secret they've kept redacted, was their plan all along.*"

Iridienne caught her breath as the crowd audibly shifted into louder questions. Next to her in the crowd of people, an older man who looked like he had worked those same adjacent fields for as long as Iridienne had been alive glanced over, recognizing her face. He stared for just a moment before his attention turned back to the screens.

Astor and the citizens alike looked around, dumbfounded, confused. Astor's face, though, carried an expression of barely-subdued panic. Astor covered the mic as he turned back to hiss a complaint to someone behind him who scurried off.

It was too late. The second part of the video began.

The audio she had recorded secretly in Astor's office the day the storm hit now echoed across the fields. A reckoning. The truth, undeniable and damning, belonged to the people.

"Tabrass and Iterum will be better with genetically sound citizens. It is for the benefit of all."

"You know that's not how people saw it! And you know that's not how you sold it!" Iridienne shouted incredulously.

"You tell the people what they want to hear," Astor said back.

The color drained from Astor's face as he realized what he was hearing. Then primal rage lit his eyes on fire as he looked wildly out into the crowd. The audio was still playing, but the seismic shock lasted only so long before the quaking of the people began. But before the collection of citizens morphed into a full frenzy, Astor found Iridienne's gaze in the group. His glare promised violence, but he couldn't reach her, and she stood unflinchingly, daring him to do something. Then she pulled her hair out of the damp bun and shook it loose.

Rage was fuming from the crowd. Screams and shouts, fists pumping towards the air. Unintelligible curses and questions churned into a bitter mixture of anger. Others stood shocked, unable to process what they had just heard. Side conversations and even denial rippled in other parts of the crowd. The bodies began shoving and pushing forward, calls for blood propelling them.

Astor began screaming at no one in particular to shut the feed off, spit spewing from his mouth, his facade crumbling. He looked feeble and futile, scrambling to maintain control, but the sand was already falling through his fingers. All the while, the conversation between Iridienne and Astor rang out over the speakers, a conviction sealed with his own words.

Shouts from the crowd shot up into the air:

"Liar! Filthy liar!"

"How much blood is on your hands?"

"What about the dead?!"

"Grab him!"

Jeers and cries continued to create a cacophony demanding retribution for their generational losses and the decades of wool pulled over their eyes, like the Shroud pulled over the sky. But also like the blue peeking through, the wool had been pulled up, and the truth couldn't be covered up this time. The crowd was pressing harder and moving closer to the stage. Shoulders and chests jarred Rhomy and Iridienne as they looked around, eyes wide.

"We need to get out of here," Iridienne said to Rhomy. Rhomy's dark eyes were worried; she agreed. As they were looking for a way out, Iridienne glanced up at the platform just as Soleil slipped down the stairs and into the crowd. Quiet and fluid as a river, she navigated the scattered people essentially unnoticed. Momentary relief rushed over Iridienne. She didn't know where Soleil would disappear to, but Iridienne trusted Soleil would make herself safe. The other Taxalis workers, however, were a mixture of responses. Some froze and cowered, some ran, some ripped Taxalis patches off of their uniforms and threw them on the ground in solidarity with the crowd that was growing closer.

Iridienne pulled Rhomy through the crowd, fighting sideways as the unrest grew, swelling forward. They were trying to keep their footing and out of the way if a riot started. They were getting sandwiched, shoved, and stuck between bodies, screams accidentally hurtling into Iridienne and Rhomy's ears as they fought to get into the fringe. The mud caused many to slip. Others' feet were stuck in the suction. As they forged forward, Iridienne saw military personnel take the stage, which caused her to pause. The sight of the fatigues was like a knife to her throat. She half imagined Cyrus up there. She shook her mind free of the longing momentarily. *But what were they doing up there?*

Up on her tiptoes, Iridienne craned to see as five military members arrested Astor before he could flee. She recognized a face in the bunch: Toril. Iridienne spared a smile for that.

Astor was shrieking and fighting his captors, his perfectly styled hair falling out of place, his face raging like a devil. What would happen to him, only time would tell, but she suspected it would be quick. As she turned away, she felt a cold grip on her arm above her elbow; she jerked her arm and spun her head around to find Donar behind her. The scowl was still evident, but a rarer emotion was now in the mixture: satisfaction.

"More military is on Nyx's tail. They should have him by day's end. They've triangulated pings close to the prison. We need to get out of here. I know a place with a good cup of tea. You remember the way?"

Iridienne gave him a quick nod and turned to push through the rest of the crowd.

CHAPTER 32

MARIS OPENED THE DOOR as Iridienne, Donar, and Rhomy approached, the same thick rope of white hair draped across her shoulder. She simply smiled, gestured them in, and shut the door quietly once everyone was inside.

"Nice to see you again, Iridienne and Rhomy," Maris greeted the two.

"You as well."

"Thank you for letting us in."

"Think nothing of it, love," Maris replied. "Donny, would you pour some tea for everyone. The kettle is ready."

Donar grimaced at the use of his nickname as Iridienne involuntarily raised an eyebrow at him and made an amused face. He turned, annoyed, and busied himself in the kitchen with the cups and tea. He brought them over on a tray with a sugar bowl and cream.

They prepared their tea while Maris evidently was the only one not feeling shaken up or awkward. They each sipped the comforting warmth from their cups; Maris broke the silence with a question, "Donar didn't explain the details, but did say at least three of you would need somewhere to stay after today. You're welcome as long as you need. So. . .I'm assuming whatever 'it' was, it worked?"

They all half-nodded and shrugged.

"Well, it's out there now. We'll see how the dust settles," Donar grumbled. The cup rattled against the saucer as Donar set it down, his thin fingers betraying more tremor than he admitted.

"Can we fill you in?" Rhomy asked, looking over at Maris.

"I've got all the time in the world." Maris settled in, sipping her tea. The three proceeded to bounce the story back and forth about how the Taxalis was brought down.

Elsewhere out past the neighborhoods and fields and the Taxalis, a convoy of jeeps drove down a muddy road to the sole prison in the region that currently housed one prisoner and one guard. The ride was mostly silent, save for the creaking metal and hum of the engines again. The jeeps jostling towards the building carried the newest prisoners, the largest number of inhabitants the jail had seen in years. They pulled to a halt at the front of the prison building and unloaded the two men, hands cuffed behind their sweat-stained backs. One radiated a quiet rage, sneering at whoever came near him. The soldiers didn't pay him much mind because the second handcuffed man was near manic, snarling profanities and empty threats as he wrestled from the jeep to the front door.

The group of seven was buzzed in the front door. Toril led the way with the prisoners, each flanked by two soldiers. He addressed the guard, "Intake for Astor Jettica and Nyx Calen." The guard openly stared. "Did I stutter, soldier? No surprise why they assigned you here," Toril said matter-of-factly. "We are also here for the release of Cirrus Blythe. *Now.*"

The guard stumbled up and came out of his booth, where he had previously been dozing. He was notified of the incoming convoy, but wasn't expecting who was being brought in. Being assigned to the prison meant being out of the loop.

He fumbled with the keyring as he came to stand at attention.

Toril stared and kicked his head off to the side with a look to hurry up. "Release first. Mr. Jettica here will then take his place." Toril glanced over his shoulder, not bothering to hide the look of disgust at the disgraced now-former governor. While this interaction happened, Cirrus sat boring a hole in Astor as he waited for the key to turn. The guard made his way to the heavy steel door, trying two wrong keys, adding to Toril's exasperation each time, before the third key slid in, turned, and clicked the lock open.

Cirrus unfolded slowly, the ache in his joints cracking as he rose. A husk of the man he was when he was first arrested with his brother. Cirrus moved through the open door silently, waiting and then watching as Astor was unceremoniously shoved into the cell as the door clanked closed.

Nyx was next. He walked without issue into the adjoining cell next to Astor's, the deep grooves between his eyebrows never faltering, succumbing to his future here.

Then, Cirrus walked toward Astor's side, close enough to grip the bars in his hands. He stared for a moment before spitting on the floor right in front of Astor's feet. "For Cirro. He was more of a man of Tabrass than you ever were." Cirrus turned and walked off and didn't flinch when Astor flew into a rage and flung himself against the metal bars behind him.

Even as the five soldiers and Cirrus loaded into the jeeps, they could hear the faint, muffled roars of a defeated man who refused to believe he had lost.

As they crunched back down the road toward the heart of Tabrass, Toril glanced at Cirrus in the passenger seat and offered, "Astor and Nyx will be held, and a tribunal will decide their sentencing." He paused. "We're also upping the manpower at the prison in case any sympathizers get any ideas."

Cirrus acknowledged Toril but said nothing. Then he caught sight of the hole in the Shroud. He had heard the guard talking about it, but the windows didn't face that direction of the sky. He sucked in an abrupt intake of air, holding his breath. Then he smiled sadly, looking down as he shook his head.

"My brother died back there, you know?"

"I heard. I am truly sorry for that, man." Though a man of direct words, Toril meant it.

Cirrus looked at him with thanks and continued, "We used to talk about what the sky would look like. Books and reels and stuff can't quite convey that kind of real-life blue, ya know?" Cirrus cleared his throat.

"I wish he could've seen it."

They drove the rest of the way in silence until they reached the outskirts of the residential sector.

"Can I take ya somewhere in particular?"

Cirrus thought for a second and replied, "I think I'll walk the rest." He got out and looked around for a moment before he slapped the roof of the jeep twice and stepped back.

Toril gave a quick two-finger salute and signaled for the other two jeeps to follow and drove away. Cirrus stood for a while longer, out in the open, staring at the sunbeams that shone down from the break in the sky, like dusty ribbons pulled tight. He imagined that they were bridges up past the Shroud to wherever they led, maybe to Iterum. Maybe somewhere else. Maybe to Cirro.

Face turned upward, he let out a sigh that was a cross between a growl and a lament, and then started making his way home.

Two days later, Astor and Nyx were found guilty of war crimes and crimes against humanity, amongst a slew of other charges and convictions. With the Governor detained, command fell, by statute, to the Provisional Tribunal, a coalition of senior military officers and civic heads. It was an old safeguard from the first uprising, meant to steady the nation when a governor could no longer be trusted to rule. Until a more concrete governance could be appointed through regional nomination, the Tribunal held both executive and judicial authority, charged to act "in service of the people and preservation of law." For the first time in decades, the Taxalis, or what was left, answered not upward, but outward.

Right after the convictions were announced, so were the sentences.

"Astor Jettica and Nyx Calen, having been duly tried and convicted of war crimes, crimes against humanity, and violations of the laws and customs of Tabrass, this court finds that your actions led to the systematic suffering, death, and dehumanization of countless innocent lives.

"Your guilt has been established beyond all reasonable doubt. The atrocities you committed were acts of cruelty, committed with intent and with full knowledge of their impact.

"In consideration of the gravity of your crimes, and in the interest of justice for the victims who can no longer speak for themselves, this tribunal hereby sentences you to death by hanging.

"May this sentence serve as a solemn reminder that humanity and justice must prevail. Sentencing is effective immediately and will be carried out tonight at the Field Gallows."

The gavel sealed the sentencing. After the convictions and sentences were read, the crowd of citizens erupted into cheers. The video feed went blank with a verbal announcement bouncing over the speakers and pinging on people's datapads that the sentencing would be carried out that evening.

After the execution was announced, Iridienne and Rhomy went back to visit Maris and Donar.

Over tea, the four sat and discussed how Nyx was found, their thoughts on the tribunal, but when mention of the gallows began, Maris's eyes went distant. They all quieted down again when Rhomy noticed Maris and put a hand on Iridienne's knee and nodded towards their host.

In a display of gentleness unseen before, Donar laid his hand on top of Maris's. At the touch, she shook her head a bit and came back to the present. She didn't apologize but gave space to the sadness that clearly was stirred at the mention of the gallows.

Then, something clicked for Iridienne, and she started to rapidly put the pieces together in her head. Her mind was spinning. Guessing Maris's age, Maris would have been in her twenties when the uprising happened some fifty years prior. She would have been about their age the last time someone was hanged at the gallows, but for vastly different reasons. Even as many decades back as the uprising, it was still a tender scar across Tabrass's history. A great loss that was now used as an uncomfortable threat. Iridienne looked over at Maris and began to see not an enigma, but yet another casualty of a system that sold counterfeit hope and paid dearly if they questioned its validity.

Gently, Iridienne asked, almost in a whisper, "Maris, could I ask you a question?"

She breathed a smile, "Yes, love," and waited. Her dark eyes were wrapped in wrinkles that each held stories of emotions embedded within. A steadfast beauty.

"You were at the gallows. . .before. . ."

"Yes, I was."

Iridienne paused and swallowed, but Maris was merciful enough to offer the answer before Iridienne had to finish the question.

"My husband was one of the ones they hanged for the uprising. He believed in a Tabrass that transparently cared for its people. And he would be proud of what you three have done."

Donar stiffened up, the familiar anger rolling across his face again, but this time mixed with deep sorrow. Iridienne sat back, stunned, so many things making sense suddenly. Rhomy touched Maris's shoulder.

Maris steadied herself and took a breath. "Donaly was my only love. After he was gone, I never remarried, but we did already have a perfect child—Donar's mother—and she was my joy until Donar here came along." Maris squeezed Donar's hand, and he gave her a half smile.

Iridienne felt like she was gently collecting together the lost and stolen pieces of Donar and Maris's story.

"You don't have to come to the gallows tonight, Maris," Iridienne said, this time barely audible.

"No, love, this time is different. Those we lost deserve it."

At that, Iridienne wept bitterly at her own lost pieces.

Later, Iridienne fidgeted with her charm as she lapsed between chasing her own thoughts and helping Rhomy tidy up the tea. Where the silence would have been awkward in another setting, in Maris's apartment, her presence, and the overlapping experiences they all shared made the quiet tinkerings of normal life feel like a gift.

"Time to be on our feet, loves. Shall we?" Maris moved towards the door. It was now getting closer to the time to make the walk past the fields, so they grabbed their belongings and began the trek to the gallows.

CHAPTER 33

The road to the fields and beyond was well worn from the traffic of the last several days. Iridienne, Rhomy, Donar, and Maris wove through the residential streets and out onto the main road to the south of Tabrass. They could hear the buzz of the crowd before the masses even came into view. Iridienne was recognized by several people on their way there, even more so once they became part of the growing gathering themselves.

She hated the attention.

More than anything, she wanted to blend in with the sea of familiar browns, tans, and neutrals and be left with her thoughts without feeling on display. She offered polite smiles, small waves, and nods to the acknowledgments, and eventually settled in amongst the throng.

Soldiers lined either side of the masses of citizens, and dozens more were up front between them and the gallows. Iridienne barely caught sight of Elio standing amongst them; his expression was steeled, resolute against the violence waiting before them. Elio's naivety was another casualty of the men who would meet death soon themselves.

The last time she was in a group like this, her name was called. That seemed like a lifetime ago instead of a few months. Then she remembered the familiar drape of an arm around her shoulder, and an involuntary groan escaped as she winced from the pain. She longed for him, dreamt of him. Softly, Maris slipped her hand into Iridienne's and gave her a knowing look. An understanding they hated to share, but the solidarity helped staunch the bleed out of grief.

"Oh my gosh. . .I thought. . .I didn't know if we'd ever see you again!" Iridienne suddenly heard Rhomy exclaim, a cry catching in her throat. It was then she saw the familiar deep skin and wide, strong hands of their friend, Cirrus, wrapping his arms around Rhomy, setting his chin amongst her dark curls. Iridienne rushed to embrace him, too. Rhomy was crying into Cirrus's shirt, but Cirrus's eyes were lost somewhere else. Iridienne knew the look.

She stopped herself. "Cirrus, I am so sorry. I tried. I tried to get you out. Please forgive me." The tears broke as she realized the guilt burrowing a hole in her stomach for the responsibility she felt for her friend.

Cirrus shook his head. "Rids, shh. None of this is on you." He pulled her in, too. They didn't care about the onlookers around them or the whispers and stares that had started from their group's reuniting. Eventually, they unfolded, faces damp from the tears. Now, Cirrus looked up and acknowledged the others, "Hi again, Maris."

"Hello, love. It's good to see you."

Then Cirrus looked at Donar and stuck out his hand. "Donar."

"Cirrus."

There wasn't much more said between the two men; there didn't need to be. Cirrus's outstretched hand wasn't just a greeting; it was a gesture steeped in quiet recognition, a truce forged not from conflict but from survival. They'd each lost much to the same broken system, and each learned how to carry absence like a second spine. And now, in this unlikely intersection, there was an understanding that ran deeper than adjacent familiarity. Iridienne and Rhomy shared a glance but said nothing. Their growing group then settled in and waited for the first public hanging in half a century.

Before too long, a string of military jeeps could be heard enclosing the space to the gallows. Five pulled up, and soldiers poured out with some other officials, all notably not wearing the Taxalis logo. And then, they pulled the handcuffed prisoners from the vehicles. Jeers, shouts, and rippling rage flared from the crowd, who demanded justice for their crimes. Nyx's disposition had not wavered; he was steeled to the man he was, unapologetic for his actions, so much so that he was willing to die for them. Astor was resigned. His polished glow of pride was dulled by stripping the facade down to the selfish man sentenced to die, where the last thing he would see would be the faces of the citizens and the fields where they bled.

A headless voice began a brief announcement and elegy for the men on the platform:

"Citizens of Tabrass, you are gathered today for a sentence not issued lightly. By order of the Provisional Tribunal: Former Governor Astor Jettica

and Geneticist Nyx Calen have been found guilty of crimes against the people. The sentence is death by public hanging.

"This platform has not been used since the uprising executions five decades ago, when our own citizens were hanged for questioning the genetic testing and demanding care for the sick. Let it be known: today's reckoning is not for vengeance but for restoration. Justice is not a spectacle; it is a signal. A signal that we do not tolerate tyranny disguised as leadership, nor do we tolerate guerrilla tactics that disregard the same citizens oppressed under that same tyranny. Justice is a signal that truth, once suppressed, will rise. And to any who might still seek control through fear or manipulation. Let this stand as your answer.

"Ready the condemned."

Astor and Nyx were positioned under the nooses dangling at their eyes. The rough ropes were then tightened around their necks. A hush fell over the crowd. The wind whispered through the crops that surrounded the gathering, the shushes and shudderings offering the only consistent sound. Once the men were readied, Toril gave a quick nod, and a soldier pulled the lever to open the floors. The metal of the lever screamed as the wood doors rattled loose. Astor and Nyx jerked downward with a heavy yank on the ropes, handcuffs clinking behind their backs as their bodies flailed and spasmed until the movements finally slowed and their eyes went blank.

Off on the edges of the crowd, Soleil stood alone, straight and collected as a statue, staring straight at Nyx. She didn't think he saw her; his eyes were fixed in the distance, somewhere far over the tops of the fields. But her eyes were on him. In her own silent way, she mourned the man he was before, the crumbling love they shared. She allowed herself to cry, a single tear for what could have been, and then watched as he fought in death the same as he fought in life. Elsewhere, Iridienne flinched as ropes pulled taut against the weight of the men's bodies. She wanted to look away, but she made herself watch. For Cirro. For Donaly. For her mother. For Cyrus.

A final announcement jolted through the speakers:

"Citizens, you are dismissed in peace. In the days ahead, leadership will transition and new structures will take form, ones built not on silence and control, but on collective truth and accountability.

"Under the Tribunal's oversight, interim governance would pass to a rotating council of field representatives, medics, and engineers, citizens

chosen for service, not status. The system wasn't built yet, but for the first time, it would be built in daylight.

"A mandatory gathering will be announced shortly to share the direction forward. Until then, return to your duties with the understanding that the air is shifting, and with it, so must we. For better days to come. Like light," it concluded.

"Through water," the crowd responded and eventually began to dissipate, unsure quite where to go, like rain evaporating before it could make it to the ground.

CHAPTER 34

THE BODIES HUNG AT the gallows for three days.

No one left flowers, not that there were any to leave, and no one visited the dead. Kids dared each other to see how close they could get to the platform before they squealed and ran. At the end of day two, some began wondering why Astor and Nyx's bodies were left up there as long as they were and when they were going to come down. Most agreed it was a warning. The final word.

The day after Astor and Nyx were cut from their nooses and then burned on a pyre erected behind the gallows, there were plans made to meet at the Pit. It would be the first time they all went back since the wedding.

Before Iridienne left to go home, change, and grab the sun tea she had made, she found herself outside in the courtyard of the Taxalis for some air, to clear her head from the morning of debates and meetings that stretched long into the day, the first real attempts to turn the Tribunal's rulings into something sustainable. The old Taxalis hierarchy was being dismantled piece by piece, replaced with provisional councils made of citizens from every sector, engineers, medics, field workers, educators. It wasn't perfect, but it felt like sunlight seeping through old cracks. For the first time, decisions weren't made behind sealed glass but around open tables where everyone could speak.

While the Taxalis building still held a concoction of feelings for her, Iridienne had never grown tired of the interior garden area. As she sat out there, the thought of Cyrus and the visceral ache for him made it suddenly hard to breathe. It was abrupt, onset. Her body felt as if it would split in two; she missed him so badly. She picked up the sun charm and pressed it to her lips. *Inhale. Hold. Exhale longer.* She repeated over and over until the panic and the pain lessened enough to catch her breath.

"We were supposed to build our life together, see the rebuilding of this place together. I miss you so bad, Cy," she said under her breath, just barely a whisper, more like a prayer. "What you started, I'll see it through."

She sat outside for a while longer, letting the faint aroma of the few flowers coax her calm again. Eventually, she went back inside to collect her things and leave for the day. Iridienne met up with Soleil, and on their way to the front doors, they saw Donar a few stretches ahead about to leave as well.

Suddenly, Iridienne called out to him. He turned with a confused look and stopped for them to walk up to him.

"Did you need something?" he asked, always direct, even now.

"Uh, yeah, actually, some of us are meeting at the Pit here in about an hour."

Donar didn't hide his impatient confusion.

"It's a fire pit out past the fields. It's a place. . .it's, um, it's special to a lot of us. It's still going to be daytime when we get out there, so it won't have the full effect, but we wanted to invite you if you're free," Iridienne said. "It'll be Soleil's first time out there, too."

Soleil nodded to Donar, confirming. His eyebrows went up slightly, surprised at the invitation as he stood considering.

"Yeah, I can come."

Iridienne smiled. "Great, meet us at the outer edge of the residential sector in an hour, and we'll go together. It's hard to find otherwise. See ya soon."

Soleil and Iridienne ducked out through the doors in front of Donar. Once they left, he was still standing there. He dragged in a deep inhale, gave the slightest of smiles, and headed out the door.

A few hours later, scattered in a circle back around the Pit, some new, some original, the collective face of the friends had shifted. A roar of a plane overhead coaxed the group's eyes in an arced salute, watching the aircraft fly from view past the blue gap in the Shroud that would continue to expand thanks to the expedited efforts voted in by the citizens. They all sat in quietly, lost to their thoughts, their losses, for the unknown of the future. Some rubbed a foot across the dirt; others fidgeted with half-full cups.

The last time they were there was for a wedding by firelight. Now, they were here to eulogize the lost by broken daylight. Iridienne thumbed the sun charm on the chain around her neck again, thinking back to the night in this same circle, she said the best yes of her life. She let the tears roll freely; the heaviness of her loss made words feel like rocks in her mouth and thoughts like vapors she couldn't catch. But her memories, those remained a painful refuge.

Torrey and Rays mumbled to each other how strange it was to be there in the daytime. Both agreed. Rhomy glanced over and nodded. It seemed fitting, somehow, to see this protected place in the light. They had seen behind Tabrass's curtain, been educated on the truth and reality. It was right to be introduced to a new side of this place, a new way to see even the places that were good that somehow remained untouched by the Taxalis.

The fire crackled, and the glow was contained mainly to the flames. Only faint shadows fought the daytime light for a contrast on their faces.

Cirrus was the first to break the silence. He cleared his throat and started softly, his voice hoarse but steady.

"For years, the Pit has been our meeting place, a ring that held nights of stories, memories, and even a wedding." He looked at Iridienne. Tears dripped from her chin as she half-smiled and placed a hand on her chest in response. He continued, "As much as I think we want to retreat to a place that feels safe, feels the same. . .we can't. But, the ones we've added deserve to be welcomed." He raised his cup to Donar and Soleil. Iridienne, Rhomy, Torrey, and Rays did the same. "And the ones we've lost deserve to be honored. Rafferty, Cyrus, and Cirro." He swallowed. "They were the best of us, a sacrifice to a system that didn't recognize the loss. But we do. We feel it. We know it. And because of that, their final gift was the reminder to fight for a life worth living. To Raff, Cy, and Cirro. Like light."

"Through water." The others raised their cups in salute.

They all sat in thoughtful silence. Rhomy was the next to speak, gentle and paced with her words. "I remember the first time we came out here. Cirro and Cirrus were so excited to bring us. They had been on one of their many. . .expeditions," she nudged Cirrus, her eyes wrinkling at the edges in response to a happier time, "and found this clearing out here, past where anyone's got a reason to come." Cirrus nudged her back, laughing softly to himself. His face was an expression of heartbreak, but he welcomed the nostalgia.

Rhomy continued, "You both set up the Pit, right? Dragged the logs over, dug the fire ring?" Cirrus nodded. Rhomy continued, "So, the six of us—Rids, Cy, Raff, Cirro, Cirrus, and me—snuck out here one night like we were on secret land. And it took *forever* to get the fire going because Raff *insisted* on making it with flint or farrow rods or something, right? You know he could be stubborn and yet convincing all at the same time." Quiet half-laughs rolled from the friends' chests as they remembered. "Anyway, we finally got it going, but we made Raff swear to either practice or just bring matches next time. And then, that was that. We always came back." Rhomy trailed off, taking a sip of her sun tea, for Raff.

Torrey and Rays then launched into one of their favorite memories, falling into the roles of tag-teaming storytellers from past parties at the Pit, igniting a stir of laughter from the group. Torrey snorted into his cup before even getting the words out. "Okay, Rays and me were assigned to Cy and Raff's squadron about the same time, and in this one training session, Cy and Raff were arguing about whether or not to let Rays here handle the landing gear calibration on this old G-model."

Rays groaned and rolled his eyes. Torrey continued, "Cy said it was Rays's turn to get some hands-on training in, but Raff said, and I quote, *He's got the flying skills of a sleep-deprived goat.*"

The group around the fire broke into laughter.

"So naturally," Torrey went on, "Ol' Cap gives the final word and says, *He's got it under control.* So, we're coming in hot from a distribution simulation, right? But a pipe had busted by the runway, so the whole thing's slicker than Raff's pick-up lines."

Rays jumped in, eyes wide. "And bam, rear gear locks late. We bounce like a skipping stone, cockpit alarms losing their minds, Cy's laughing while giving me maneuvering orders, and Raff's cussing up a storm, shouting something like, *What did I tell you about the goat?*"

Even Iridienne laughed then.

Torrey shook his head with a crooked grin. "We rolled half the strip sideways and lived to tell it."

He paused for a moment and lifted his cup. "To the best pilots I ever flew with."

Everyone raised their cups in return. The laughter softened, but the glow of the memory stayed lit long after. The friends continued to share tales and memories; Donar and Soleil sat quietly, bearing witness to the sacred sharing of stories and mourning of the three whose absences lingered in the space. Some of the conversations turned to the future, the inevitable question: would any of them join the exodus to Iterum, if not in the first wave, then maybe later? It felt too raw to think of leaving, but, like Cirrus said, it also felt too raw to stay. No one had an answer for where they'd be in the coming months, but for now, they were here.

As the quiet chuckling died down after another rousing story from Torrey and Rays, the distinguishable sound of feet on the path caught the group's attention one by one as the conversation slowed to a stall. This meeting place was one of the group's most protected secrets; no one ever came here but the ones who knew about it. They shifted uncomfortably, moving to crane their eyes down the path leading to the Pit. Torrey, Rays, Cirrus, and even Donar stood protectively. The gait slowly sounded closer, but the walking was labored, dragging.

The light emitting from the hole in the sky created harsh shadows this time of day, silhouetting the person as they came into view. Everyone froze, eyes wide. They couldn't make out a face. The man's hunched frame cradled an arm and gave generously to a limp, the left leg notably injured.

"Who is that?" Iridienne breathed out, standing slowly.

The friends shifted to get a better view, eyes locked on the outline of the man who continued faltering down the dirt path to the Pit, backlit by the escaped sunbeams from the clouds.

EPILOGUE
The Horizon Table

In the months that followed the executions, Tabrass had entered a new era, not with certainty, but with urgency.

One of the first orders of business was the election of new leadership across key sectors, including the creation of a long-overdue Public Health Division within the Taxalis. The Horizon Table, a new central council, was formed to replace the Governor-model, consisting of seats that rotated by regional representation. Tabrass wasn't sure this would be the permanent solution, but it provided equal representation. The Provisional Tribunal dissolved itself once the Horizon Table was ratified, turning power back to elected citizens, more accountability than was there before. Daily updates were posted across public boards and data channels, listing what meetings were happening, what decisions were being made, and who was seated where. Every meeting was recorded, and all governmental data was publicly accessible. Every vote was broadcast. Every proposal was archived. It wasn't flawless. Debates lasted until dawn. Decisions were made slower, but it was transparent.

The daily updates for Tabrassian citizens were Azileh's idea. Though new to the office, she had already become a recognizable force: a voice shaped by honesty, sharpened by grief, and carried by the kind of fearless empathy the people hadn't known in years. She was named First Representative of the Military Sector, but her influence stretched beyond it. Donar, now a vital force in the Environmental Division, had taken up responsibility for managing the Fiat Lux Formula. He worked closely with Azileh to coordinate the release across the region in carefully monitored stages, ensuring both safety and efficiency as they went about the painstaking work of clearing the sky. Iridienne requested a transfer to work in the Public Health Sector, where Soleil was already playing a vital part in establishing the organizational approaches and public access. There was overwhelming work ahead, but for the first time in Iridienne's life, it felt like the right work.

Tabrass continued to navigate the laborious work of rebuilding systems, relationships, and trust. As the months stretched on, the Shroud's edges thinned, its dull gray giving way to color the citizens no longer needed to imagine.

Of all the issues brought to the Horizon Table, the one met with unanimous transparency and agreement was the Exodus to Iterum. However, now, the colonization program was opened to the general public, as they had been promised. But this time it was real. Epitopes could choose to leave for the new world, but so could other citizens, too. Cirrus was one of the first to sign up.

There would be vetting tests, applications, and job prioritization, but the choice was given back to the citizens. Data confirmed the first launch would occur in nine months, one month after terraforming was fully complete. Then, the first wave of Tabrassians would enter a new world. It seemed fitting, somehow, seeing as most everything in Tabrass felt alien now, too.

During one particular meeting, tensions flared between Azileh and Donar over how rapidly the Fiat Lux Formula should be deployed in the outer zones. Azileh argued that the region had waited long enough for relief from the seeded sky. Donar countered, citing incomplete data and the risk of chemical exposure in areas with unstable infrastructure.

"You don't fix generations of decay in a single quarter," he said from across the table.

"But you don't win back trust with half-measures," she returned, unblinking.

The room went quiet, the weight of old mistakes pressing in. The broadcast continued rolling. No edits. No redactions.

Outside the old transport hub, now retrofitted with screens looping the daily government updates, a small crowd gathered, as they did to watch the latest updates. An older man of Tabrass, skin worn from decades of work in the fields, squinted at the latest proposal on agricultural reform, muttering, "Sounds good on screen, but so did the other empty promises for decades. I'll believe it when I see it."

Next to him, a young mother nodded slowly. "But at least we can see what's happening. . .live. That's harder to fake. That's something." Her toddler scooped piles of dirt in little mounds, drawing lines in the dust with his chubby finger.

A gruff voice toward the back of the group rumbled, "It's just another power dance. It's about time Tabrass governed itself." He had turned and stalked off before a few of the others turned apprehensively to look back. It wasn't the first time someone shared that sentiment, and it wouldn't be the last. The rest stood there, still flanked by a dozen others, watching changes unfold on the screens above them.

Understandable skepticism riddled the region, both with the citizens and those trying to establish a new kind of order in the Taxalis. Some were still bitterly angry. Some were cautiously optimistic. Some just wanted to forget.

Others, though, said that the first real sign of change wasn't a new law or an impending launch, but the day the man they thought was lost found his way to the Pit, limping, silent, and carrying something none of them had dared to name: hope.